PRAISE FOR *EDSEL* AND
LOREN D. ESTLEMAN'S DETROIT NOVELS

more . . .

"With a pro's practiced skill, Estleman keeps all these plates spinning through the air with no apparent effort and a hundred different voices."
—*Boston Sunday Globe*

"As usual, Estleman brilliantly re-creates a period that may now be dead but certainly isn't forgotten."
—*AP Newswire*

"Enthralling, carefully detailed, and briskly paced. . . . The vivid adventure back in time seems to end too soon. Fun trips are like that."
—*Livonia Observer* (MI)

"Exceptional crime fiction."
—*Los Angeles Times Book Review*

"EDSEL is a good story that recaptures an era and peoples it with characters who would feel right at home with Formica™ tabletops and black-and-white televisions."
—*South Bend Tribune*

"Even if the title is a dead giveaway about the book's ultimate outcome, you'll enjoy getting there—especially if you liked Detroit in the 1950s."
—*Arizona Republic*

"Well researched, brimming with snappy dialogue and filled with a cast of memorable characters."
—*Mostly Murder*

LOREN D. ESTLEMAN is the Shamus Award-winning author of dozens of mysteries, westerns, and his highly praised series of Detroit novels. A former Detroit newspaper reporter, he became a full-time writer in 1980, and lives in Whitmore Lake, Michigan.

BY LOREN D. ESTLEMAN

THE DETROIT NOVELS
Stress • Edsel • King of the Corner • Motown • Whiskey River

THE AMOS WALKER NOVELS
Sweet Women Lie • Silent Thunder • Downriver • Lady Yesterday • Every Brilliant Eye • Sugartown • The Glass Highway • The Midnight Man • Angels Eyes • Motor City Blue

THE PETER MACKLIN NOVELS
Any Man's Death • Roses Are Dead • Kill Zone

OTHER CRIME NOVELS
Peeper • Dr. Jekyll and Mrs. Holmes • Sherlock Holmes vs. Dracula • The Oklahoma Punk

WESTERN NOVELS
City of Widows • Sudden Country • Bloody Season • Gun Man • The Stranglers • This Old Bill • Mister St. John • Murdock's Law • The Wolfer • Aces & Eights • Stamping Ground • The High Rocks • The Hider

NON FICTION
The Wister Trace: Classic Novels of the American Frontier

SHORT STORY COLLECTIONS
General Murders • The Best Western Stories of Loren D. Estleman (edited by Bill Pronzini and Ed Gorman)

LOREN D. ESTLEMAN

EDSEL

THE MYSTERIOUS PRESS

Published by Warner Books

A Time Warner Company

MYSTERIOUS PRESS EDITION

Copyright © 1995 by Loren D. Estleman
All rights reserved.

Cover design and illustration by Tom Nikosey

The Mysterious Press name and logo are registered trademarks of Warner Books, Inc.

 Mysterious Press Books are published by
Warner Books, Inc.
1271 Avenue of the Americas
New York, NY 10020

 A Time Warner Company

Printed in the United States of America

Originally published in hardcover by The Mysterious Press.
First Printed in paperback: March, 1996
10 9 8 7 6 5 4 3 2 1

To my father, Leauvett C. Estleman:
February 17, 1910—February 4, 1994

America is a mistake, a giant mistake.
—Sigmund Freud

PART ONE
Of Dinosaurs and Deuces

For me, the decade of the 1940s didn't end on New Year's Eve 1949. Nothing changed except the date on my checks, and I didn't catch *that* for two days. Hat brims stayed wide, suit coats looked like inverted grocery sacks just as they had since before Pearl Harbor, cars remained bulbous and ugly with bad heaters and dashboard radios whose big dials and lightning-bolt logos would have made Buck Rogers feel at home. Truman's narrow little butt and narrower littler mind were still firmly planted in the White House and Woody Herman booked in at the Walled Lake Casino every summer. No, the fifth decade of the twentieth century ended for me fourteen months later, on a flinty-cold afternoon in February 1951, when I stood in a crowd in front of the downtown J. L. Hudson's and saw Frankie Orr's face on six television screens at the same time.

His appearance shocked me. I don't know why, but of all the people I'd met in my newspapering days, Francis Xavier Oro was the one I hadn't expected to age. I had seen him once only, in the private dining room of the old Griswold House, and what happened there that night had burned his image into the retina of my memory. For twenty years he had remained the slender, dark, wavy-haired young gangster in full evening dress enjoying a filet mignon prepared the way they used to prepare it and don't any more, streaming mahogany-colored juice and as tender as a man's grip on life. This elderly Italian sweating under the harsh lights, flaccid-cheeked, baggy-eyed, and spotted like old cheese, belonged in a vegetable patch in Sicily, propped on a hoe. Somehow he had stumbled into a carnival booth and had his picture taken

3

with his head stuck through a hole cut into a life-size blow-up of a body wearing a two-hundred-dollar suit.

The suit, so far as could be made out on a ten-inch black-and-white screen, was gray or blue, with a tiny check that flared and left its ghost on the lens when he moved, which he did often, fidgeting in a chair not designed for comfort and certainly not inclined that way as long as it faced five senators and a government counsel and, by proxy, every housewife in the Detroit broadcast area whose ironing board stood before the rabbit-eared box in the living room.

The occasion was the Detroit stop on the national road show sponsored by the Special Senate Committee to Investigate Organized Crime in Interstate Commerce and hosted by Estes Kefauver, the junior senator from Tennessee. He and his four colleagues seated behind fat microphones shaped like oversize Luden's cough drops were on their way to New York, like any good theatrical troupe working the bugs out of their routine as they grilled local colorful mafiosi in certain key cities along the circuit. The labor racket had brought them to Michigan, but with American Steelhaulers president Albert Brock off touring the factories of Europe and beyond the reach of a subpoena, they had settled for Orr, in semi-retirement now and under federal indictment for transporting women across state lines for immoral purposes.

Nothing like it could have happened in the thirties or the forties, although both epochs had offered television in at least Pleistocene form. Inviting Frankie Orr to share the same shimmering box that contained Pinky Lee, Molly Goldberg, and J. Fred Muggs was like placing incompatible species in a terrarium. We were all in for worse, but we date things according to our own calendars, and for me there was no going back from that moment.

Clearly the chairman, whose lanky bespectacled countenance and conservative tailoring would clash with the coonskin cap he would don later to run for vice-president under Adlai Stevenson, already considered himself too important to question a geriatric pimp, for he left most of the interrogation to Rudolph Halley, chief counsel for the committee. Kefauver, soon to become as recognizable to home viewers as Speedy Alka-Seltzer, could not know that in a short time he would be as forgotten as Tammany. Even then television was beginning to display a penchant for preserving the ephemeral whilst swallowing and defecating the truly significant. I have to think now to remember the name of the pilot involved in the U-2 incident, but I will take with me to the grave all the words to "Luckies Taste Better."

But huddled on that wind-scraped sidewalk with the other holdouts against a home idol, I thought the world would never put aside that earnest panel or its D'Artagnan, Halley. The attorney's jagged, pointed profile onscreen and sharp Yankee whine issuing from the megaphone speaker mounted outside the store personified the caricature of Uncle Sam, haranguing Russian bears, flying saucers, and juvenile delinquents from editorial pages across the country. A sample of his cross-examination of Orr appeared that week in the Detroit *Times:*

Q: Mr. Orr, this committee has heard testimony that you were one of the early architects of the syndicate of crime as it exists in Detroit and Toledo, is that true?

A: Of course not. I'm in the construction business.

Q: You were not in partnership with the late Salvatore Bornea, alias Sal Borneo, the head of the local Mafia during Prohibition?

A: He was my father-in-law. He was the legally elected president of the Unione Siciliana. The Mafia doesn't exist.

Q: Mr. Orr, you are frequently and popularly known as the Conductor, is that not true?

A: No one has called me that for years.

Q: May I ask where you acquired that nickname?

A: When I was young I worked for a streetcar company in New York.

Q: Was it not in fact given to you because in nineteen twenty-eight you were tried for the fatal strangling of one Vincenzo Cugglio in front of a dozen eyewitnesses on the Third Avenue elevated railway in Manhattan?

A: I was acquitted of that charge.

Q: A mistrial was declared because the jury could not agree on a verdict.

A: The prosecution didn't try me again. They knew I was innocent.

Q: After you came to Detroit were you not implicated in the murders of Jerry Buckley, the radio commentator, and Abel S. Norman, a small-time numbers racketeer, both in nineteen thirty?

A: I was asleep in bed the night Buckley got gunned. I never knew nobody named Norman.

(At this point, watching Orr's slack face, my mind's projector stuck on a frame: the gangster's fattish dining companion at the Griswold, trying to stand with a gout of blood from his severed jugular drenching his rack of lamb in ruby red, while Orr, still holding the knife, stepped back to avoid soiling his white dress shirt.)

Q: We have heard testimony to the contrary, Mr. Orr.

A: Everybody has enemies. I can't help what people say.

Q: Appearing before this committee in closed session yesterday, Leo Bustamente, your former driver and bodyguard, stated under oath that at your orders he disposed of Norman's body inside the poured concrete foundation of the Detroit-Windsor Tunnel, which was then under construction by your firm, among others.

A: I fired Mr. Bustamente for drinking on the job. I'm surprised his liver is still operating.

Q: Do you deny his accusation that he was proceeding under your instructions?

A: Leo would give up Trotsky if you promised him a bottle.

(Laughter among the spectators present in the room. Kefauver scowled and snapped his gavel at the table.)

Q: At present, you stand accused of violation of the
Mann Act for using your connections with the
American Steelhaulers Union to transport prosti-
tutes from Miami, Florida, to various commercial
establishments owned by you in the Great Lakes
area, is that not correct?

A: On the advice of my attorney, I decline to answer
that question on grounds that it may incriminate me.

Q: There is no danger of self-incrimination in answering the question, Mr. Orr. This committee is aware
that you have been indicted by a federal grand jury.

A: Why ask the question if you already know the answer?

Here, Charles W. Tobey, the green-eyeshaded Republican
senator from New Hampshire, spoke up to warn Orr that if
he refused to answer the question he would be held in contempt of Congress. Later legend held that Orr stood, informed the panel that he'd come *in* with contempt for
Congress, and stalked out. But at his youngest and most arro-
gant he was never that clever. What he did was get up and
leave. I've often marveled at just how many popular myths
grew out of an event as scrupulously watched and recorded
as those hearings. The medium's endless succession of dancing pill bottles, loquacious sea serpents, and tumbling Latins
had managed to negate the evidence of sight and sound.

One anecdote that received no play at all, and that I heard
years later, reported that Frankie Orr had selected the
checked suit and a particularly noisy floral tie on the advice
of counsel, who believed that flaring patterns damaged camera lenses and discouraged publicity of the televised kind.
Whether or not the story was true, he wasn't called back to
testify. Due process had entered a strange new phase, regulated by network skews and the station break.

2

I never saw the Conductor again, in person or on television, not counting old file photos in the newspapers and a
hastily snapped, out-of-focus shot of him in dark glasses and
a soft cap with his overcoat slung over his shoulders Edward
G. Robinson style, on his way to board a plane for Sicily at
the time of his deportation. Striding well ahead of the beefy
federal marshals in skinny ties and Stetsons, he looked more
like the Frankie Orr of old, tense-jawed and paying absolutely no attention to the reporters present. They ran it
again years later when he disappeared in Puerto Rico. Mob
lore has it he was disposed of by rival racketeers during an
attempt to regain a foothold in the United States. That may
be so, but the new slick machined de-ethnicized crime cartel
had a lot less to fear from the return of a washed-up old bootlegger than did certain officials with the Justice Department.
But then I've reached that point in life where I'm ready to
trade in my illusions on plaid pants and a white belt.

The stop in front of Hudson's was just to kill a few minutes. I was square on time for my appointment at the
Lafayette Coney Island and I wanted to be late. Not fifteen
minutes late, which is death, almost as bad as a few minutes
early, which is like wearing a necktie that lights up and says
I'M DESPERATE, and about neck-and-neck with bang on
the hour and too eager to please. Five minutes late said I didn't
need the meeting but was too polite to keep anyone waiting
long. It's more than just a silly waltz, as anyone will agree
who has found himself back on the job market on the shady
side of fifty. I had on an old corduroy sport coat with functional patches on the elbows, pressed slacks, polished

wingtips, a new white button-down Oxford, and my lucky tie with the Beef Wellington stain tucked into my waistband. My hair was cut in a flattop to make me look in tune with youth and I carried my reading glasses in an imitation alligator case clipped to my handkerchief pocket to show I wasn't ashamed of my age.

I was, though. I had been young for so long that I looked upon each fresh sign of decomposition as treachery. I applied the same conspiracy theory to 45-rpm records, automatic transmissions, diesel locomotives. and Governor Soapy Williams' undignified bow tie. Fogeyism came to me easily, another knife in the kidneys.

The other truth is I *was* desperate, and fanatically eager to please. Half my life ago I was a journalist, a promising newcomer with his own column and his thumb on the wrist of a wide-open town, confidant of thugs and mayors, political fixers and crib girls, the great unwashed reading public's direct conduit into the glistening clubs where judges touched elbows with tailgunners on beer trucks, Joe Lunchpail's engraved invitation into three-hundred-dollar suites at the Book-Cadillac, where Charlie Chaplin sat around with his suspenders down and Herbert Hoover leaned over to touch my knee and tell me how he was going to handle Al Capone once he defeated Franklin Roosevelt for his second term in the White House. I drove a new car, lived in a nice apartment in Mayor Murphy's neighborhood, dined at the Caucus Club without reservations, and had my picture in the *Literary Digest* with Ruth Chatterton on my arm above the caption: "Detroit's Connie Minor, the preferred choice of movie stars and underworld luminaries."

Then came Depression and Repeal. The upstart tabloids folded, one by one at first, then in clusters like dying cells. With them went my syndication, and eventually my job. While I was busy chasing seven-passenger sedans loaded with big men in tugged-down hats and narrow overcoats with bulges under their arms, a new generation of newshawk had sprung up without my notice, a breed that smoked and drank moderately, clubbed not at all, and spent more time gathered around the wire desk studying the reports from overseas than they did shivering on rotting piers waiting for a boat to dock from Canada without running lights. I was a dinosaur at age thirty-five. My name was associated with hip flasks, beaded skirts, and splay-legged dances to tinny jazz music, all the silly hollow detritus of an era that meant as much to what was happening in the world as a beaver hat. I was deader than Ruth Snyder. They didn't even have to throw a switch.

I'd tried freelancing, with some success. *Liberty* had bought a piece from me comparing the organization of the Nazi Party to the Purple Gang—which had spawned a lot of angry letters, the Purples being predominantly Jewish—and I had written a retrospective column that ran in the *Free Press* Sunday supplement every third week until wartime paper shortages forced it out in favor of the news from Europe. And I had published a book. You could still find it in the ten-cent bin in most used bookstores, which was immortality of a sort. After that I had followed my used-up predecessors to that elephant graveyard, the advertising business.

It's a hell of an industry, the ad game; possibly the only one you can contribute to in a state of near-coma. While *new* and *fresh* are its two most sacred words, their definitions will clear a room faster than the Red Scare. It fears innovation, celebrates mediocrity, and aims for an intellect that would store a six-month supply of foodstuffs in a bomb shelter for protection against an atomic blast that will poison the air with radiation for six hundred years. As one of a couple of dozen monkeys chained to typewriters at the firm of Slauson & Nichols on West Grand River, I had been writing for so long with my brains in my hip pocket I wasn't sure if I could still string together a sentence that didn't contain the words *smooth*, *rich*, *power*, *mild*, or *flame-broiled*.

But today I had my chance to find out. In a fit of half-hearted determination I had for the first time in years sent out my résumé to a number of new publications in the area, and I had received one call back, from the publisher of a prospective new picture magazine based in Port Huron. He would be in Detroit on Wednesday for a meeting with his backers, and would I care to meet him for lunch? I rustled some pages on my Nehi calendar with the end of a flyswatter and said it so happened I was free at (noon's for spinsters and bank clerks, two o'clock's for drunks who sleep till noon) one-thirty.

"Fine. Where would you recommend for a good old-fashioned lunch?"

More cerebratory acrobatics. The Anchor Bar was a cliché for journalists, located as it was between the *News* and the *Free Press* with the *Times* nearby, and anyway I might run into someone I knew who knew how badly I wanted a real writing job. Anywhere in Greektown was out; parking was handy and if we hit it off my would-be employer might insist upon walking me to my car. Hedge's Wigwam might give him the impression I was accustomed to cafeteria fare. Capistrano's might make him think I was putting the arm on him for an expensive meal. The Lafayette Coney Island was right in the middle and downtown, where I could leave the Studebaker with the valets at Hudson's and out of sight. His reaction when I made the suggestion was so brisk I felt an ass for wasting so much time on it.

"Fine. See you there Wednesday at one-thirty, Mr. Meaner."

Now, grasping the door handle at precisely one thirty-five, I glimpsed my reflection in the glass—and all my confidence drained out the soles of my shoes. I looked like an old Greek. In my youth I had sometimes been taken for Italian, and once or twice for American Indian, but that was forty pounds ago, and my ears and nose had not stopped growing. Put me in a cloth cap and loose sport coat and I could be any one of those short, fat grouches you saw hanging around in front of the Grecian Gardens, drinking ouzo out of bottles wrapped in brown paper bags and cursing tourists in the old tongue. I belonged in a fluorescent-lit magazine office the way a clay pot belonged with the fine silver.

Fuck it. I'd been through a machine-gun battle on the ice of Lake Erie. Who else could say that? I squared my shoulders and went in.

"Good of you to come, Mr. Meaner. I'm Seabrook Hall."

I had trusses older than Hall. He was slender, a breath over my height, and wore a sleeveless argyle pullover on top of a pink shirt and a clip-on tie shaped like a butterfly if Lockheed designed butterflies, green with square black dots. His pegtops, which didn't go with anything, were tan poplin. He had red hair, clipped short to disguise the fact it was thinning in front, and eyeglasses whose heavy square black frames made me think of scuba diving. His skin was astonishingly pale, blue-white like skim milk, and his eyes behind the thick lenses had a slightly pinkish cast. They looked weak and possibly unable to distinguish colors, which I thought might help explain his clothes. I didn't know it then, but I was seeing the ivy league look in its earliest incarnation. It would get worse, much worse. Suit coats would grow another button, lapels and neckties would wither, shoulders would disappear and the brims of hats recede until you felt raindrops on your nose before you heard them strike the crown.

His handshake was strong enough, his smile firm and white and unstudied behind a moustache that looked like cinnamon caught in cobwebs. I gave back as much, maybe too much in the grip, and then I made it worse.

"Minor."

The pinkish eyes flickered. "I'm sorry?"

"You said Meaner. It's pronounced Minor. It's an impossible name," I added.

"Nonsense. It's real. All the names around here are real: Gunsberg and Butsikitis and Skjaerlund and Washington and Brennan. Where I come from they all sound like brands of English beer. I was born in Southampton, Long Island."

"I used to know a woman from Southampton."

"What's her name? I might know the family."

"Probably not. She married a Jewish gangster here and dropped out of sight after he got shot to pieces."

"Sit down, Mr. Minor. What's good here?"

I recommended the Reuben, and of course it was bad that day. I was losing track of just how many ways a man can screw up when he's playing with scared money. Hall had tea, I had coffee. As he bobbed the bag up and down inside his cup I noticed he wore a Princeton ring on his index finger, of all places. I twisted my worn U of D ring and wondered if we were going to be able to stand each other's society.

"My partner recognized your name," he said. "He started as a copy boy for the *Times*. You left shortly after he came on."

"Friendly divorce. Mr. Hearst took a personal interest

back then and it was tough writing around all those pictures of Marion Davies."

His expression was uncomprehending. The name meant nothing to him. I was beginning to wonder how young he was.

"Anyway, your familiarity with this area is important. I'd expect you to know all the best photo opportunities."

I lifted my eyebrows, making an eager sponge of my face. I'd never heard the term before.

"Have you seen our magazine?" he asked.

"No. I didn't know you'd published."

"We sent out a trial run of six thousand copies." He lifted the flap of a tan leather briefcase with a sling handle that reminded me too much of a ladies' shoulder bag and withdrew a slick rectangle the size of a placemat, laying it on my side of the table.

The cover was glossy, saddle-stapled, and consisted entirely of a black-and-white photo of Ava Gardner, who seemed to be having difficulty keeping both straps on her shoulders. It was the tightest, largest close-up I'd ever seen. Her lips were the size of brass knuckles; you could have inserted a quarter in either one of her nostrils. The only printing, aside from the month and year and the twenty-five-cent price, was the magazine's title, *PIX!*, in letters two inches high, each one a different primary color.

"I thought it was a local publication. What's Ava Gardner got to do with the Great Lakes?"

"My partner wanted to run a picture of Tahquamenon Falls, but I vetoed it. What is journalism's first responsibility, Mr. Minor?"

"To make money."

He beamed, the proud tutor. "Natural wonders don't sell magazines."

"*The National Geographic* will be sorry to hear it." I turned the slippery pages. The first several were full-page advertisements, Dyna-Flo transmissions and halitosis and Ronald Reagan sucking on a Camel. "National accounts?"

"Actually, we lifted them out of other publications. It makes a better impression and we're hoping they'll be grateful for the free ride. The real stuff's in back."

I skipped over. Four pages cut into quarters. Milo's Auto Repair, the Elite Clothiers, a coupon for a free shampoo and set at Dixie's Beauty Academy. It looked like the back of a high school yearbook.

"We expect to publish at a loss the first two years," Hall said. "We've got enough backing for the first year. By then we should have the circulation numbers to attract the big accounts. That's why we need talent."

"There's not much text." The bulk of the magazine was devoted to pictures of boats on Lake Huron, a baton-twirling contest in Green Bay, Wisconsin, a two-page spread on the Ford River Rouge plant, a row of cigar-shaped houses under construction in Toledo. The accompanying "articles" ran no longer than a paragraph, isolated in sixteen-point Plantin in the middle of fields of white space a child could draw on.

"The written word can't hope to compete with television. At one time the human brain was thought capable of taking in only twenty-four pictures per second, the pace of the so-called motion picture. We know now that it can consume more than a hundred. Experiments are being conducted to determine how many more it can gobble up without even being aware of it. Meanwhile its capacity for taking in words has remained a stolid ten. How can Lincoln's Gettysburg Address aspire to create as strong an impression as Uncle Miltie in an evening gown?"

I lowered *Pix!*'s cover carefully, like a coffin lid. "When I was ten years old I entered a hot dog eating contest at the state fair. I swallowed eleven dogs in ten minutes. I threw up the whole batch in less than five. Taking in isn't retaining."

"All we ask is that they remember the name of the magazine from week to week. It's a killer schedule and chews up talent. How are you on deadlines, Mr. Minor?"

"I haven't missed one since nineteen twenty-eight, when Dusty Steinhauser kidnapped me and kept me playing poker behind the Polar Bear Cafe until he won back what he owed me."

"What sort of photographer are you?"

"I'm thinking of getting one of those Polaroids and save paying for developing when I take a picture of my thumb."

"That won't do. Right now our photojournalists are using Speed-graphics but we're switching to those Japanese jobs."

"What's a photojournalist?"

"The magazine business is different from most. While everyone else is specializing, we find it more feasible economically to double up. Nobody's hiring photographers and writers any more. If you want to grow with *Pix!*, you'll have to become equally proficient with a typewriter and a camera."

"In other words, two jobs, one salary."

"To be blunt."

"Thanks for lunch, Mr. Hall." I stood.

"You don't want the job?"

"I'm a good writer. That's my talent. I'm a great reporter. That's my skill. I'll never be anything more than a mediocre photographer and I'm too old for that. Good luck finding your photojournalist. I never met a good button-pusher who could write a caption to save his life."

"Frankly I'm relieved. This is a job for a young man. You older types are too cynical."

"I hope I never get so old I wind up as cynical as you."

Seabrook Hall and I didn't cross paths again, nor did I ever see another issue of *Pix!* A couple of years later, killing time in a Rexall downtown before another interview, I saw his name on the statement of ownership page of a comic book. The cover featured a gelatinous green mass with eyes and teeth devouring a half-naked woman who looked like Ava Gardner.

3

One day in 1953, given a choice of magazines in a dentist's waiting room that included *Jack 'n' Jill, Popular Science*, and a fourteen-month-old copy of *Argosy*, I picked up *House Beautiful* to look at the homes shaped like boxes of Fig Newtons with tricky siding in front and as dull as an Eisenhower speech in back, and stopped at a line in the editor's column: "You will have a greater chance to be yourself than any people in the history of civilization." That statement remained with me long after I had ceased thinking about two-toned refrigerators and the artist's conception of a living room with space for the family car. Every now and then I hauled it out like the Riddle of the Sphinx or an elaborately tangled string of Christmas bulbs and tried to make sense of it. I still do, and have come to believe that once I have I will have succeeded in figuring out that whole era. Like the time itself, the line is as simple and diabolical as the mind of a child.

Nothing about it, line or time, should have surprised me. In my youth, we had fought a war to put the world back the way it was before the war started, only to find that the fighting itself had changed it radically and forever. It began with men in paper collars waltzing with women in toe-length hems to "After the Ball" and ended with those same men tipping up hip flasks and watching women's reflections on glossy tabletops as they wriggled to "The Black Bottom" in brief skirts and no underwear. Now we had gone to war again, first with cavalry, then with rockets. If nothing much changed between FDR's snooty profile on a newsreel screen and Frankie Orr's humble face on the box in the living room, from that point forward nothing

16

stayed put. Clark Gable's cocky grin dissolved into Marlon Brando's Neanderthal pout. Buicks sprouted holes that had no function. Sing "How Much Is That Doggie in the Window" as loudly as she could, Patti Page couldn't drown out a groin-beat with roots in Africa thumping up from the South, childish and primitive, that caused an age group we didn't know existed, something called a Teen Ager, to tear apart the seats and rip the sconces off the walls of theaters where "Shake, Rattle, and Roll" pulsed beneath the credits of *The Blackboard Jungle*. The Russians, who claimed to have invented everything from air travel to the Flo-Thru tea bag, suddenly left off trading the Czar's cufflinks for coarse bread and booted a football-size sphere studded with spikes beyond our atmosphere, adding the Space Race to the Arms Race and throwing the course of all our lives into high gear. Furniture, hitherto solidly grounded to the floor, canted backward and began to float on spidery metal legs. Block-shaped, cozy corner markets stretched and flattened like everything else into air-conditioned barns lined with aisles stacked to the ceilings with fourteen more varieties of everything than anyone required. And then there was the shadow of that acacia-shaped cloud in the East, shading all our futures with sense-memories of those vaporized crowds in Nagasaki and Hiroshima. Only we didn't *really* believe it, because if General Motors thought there was anything to it they wouldn't be offering two-year financing on the Chevy Bel-Air. So we dug fallout shelters and hired Joe McCarthy to sweep commies out from under the bed and sang along to the example of Burt, the animated TV turtle:

> Duck—and cover!
> Duck—and cover!
> He did what we all must learn to do;
> You and you and you and you—
> Duck—and cover!

You will have a greater chance to be yourself than any people in the history of civilization. I still can't explain it, or why it seems more appropriate the further the time slips behind.

In the fall of 1954—I remember the year because it was Fred Hutchinson's last season managing the Tigers and I had his autograph on my scorecard from the last at-home game with the Yankees—I paused on my way to my car to fill out the roll of film in my Argus and changed my destiny. The picture happened to show a dusty yellow Caterpillar climbing a hill of rubble in the condemned section south of Jefferson where the new Civic Center was going in, against the granite pile of the Penobscot Building, whose sawhorses I had detoured around back in 1928 when it was under construction. It turned out to be the best shot on a roll of blurred images of a rookie named Kaline attempting to steal second and a number of unidentified plays snapped from behind the sunburned bald head in the seat in front of me, but I didn't think about it from the first time I saw it in the drugstore where I had the film developed until Slauson & Nichols needed one more picture to complete the brochure it was putting together for the Detroit Chamber of Commerce.

It was one of those "Dynamic Detroit" pamphlets available in racks at the airport and bookstore local interest sections, with a historical text written by a steel-haired retired lady journalist with nicotine-colored lipstick and progressive puff about the city's future provided by the flacks at Slauson, of which I was still one. The drugstore bag containing the photograph I'd taken was in the top drawer of the desk where I'd stashed it the day I picked it up, and I was moving it to get to an eraser when a lightbulb flared over my head just like in *Morty Meekle*. When I showed the picture to the art director, a narrow-shouldered grump named Fleenor with a Hitler moustache and black hair parted in the middle like Tom Dewey's, he glanced at it, skated it across the top of his desk toward me, and told me to convince him with a caption.

I was still using the old Royal I'd liberated from the offices of the old *Banner* when the sheriff was in the hall; black and silver and dinged all over from the times it had danced off its rickety stand, it had outgrown the bounds of linear order and begun to turn out copy that looked like ransom notes. My fingers had rubbed the letters clean off several of the keys and the space gear was worn to the extent that when I hit the lever I never knew whether I was triple-spacing or about to strike over the line I'd just typed, but I had a lot more things wrong with me, and in those days we didn't get a divorce just because the wife's breasts hung like onions and her feet were as cold as river stones. Besides, those new electric jobs made whirring noises when you switched them on, waiting for you to create. It was pressure I didn't need. I rolled a fresh sheet of Rexall stock into the machine and typed:

    Like a vital organ, the city is forever regenerating itself, replacing old cells with new, proud of its history but dedicated to its future.

I was glaring at this bit of non-rhyming doggerel, loathing it, when Fleenor crept up behind me on his Neoprene soles, breathing Maxwell House fumes over my shoulder as he read. Without warning he reached past my head and tore the sheet out of the platen. The racheting noise sounded like a game of Russian Roulette. I never saw the line again until the brochure came back from the printers. I didn't like it any better in Bodoni bold than I had in faded pica.

A lot of nothing happened for a while after that. The brochures were picked up by a pair of Wayne State University student volunteers in butch cuts and pink crew-neck sweaters and I forgot about them as soon as they were out of sight. Slauson & Nichols landed the Armor-Bilt Aluminum Siding account, I did some down-and-dirty research into Howard Pyle and Harold Lamb and came up with a knight-hood-in-flower theme, complete with a moat and a draw-bridge and a gleaming white aluminum-clad castle that had as much to do with the practical applications of the product as a grubby downtown construction project had to do with the regenerative properties of the human liver. It had taken me years and a couple of trips to the unemployment office to learn that advertising copy is best written sideways. One of Fleenor's drafting-board jockeys came back with a sketch of the castle surrounded by pastel balloons labeled Flamingo,

Twilit Gray, Celery, Gulf Stream Blue, Canary, and Sand Beige.

"Why would anyone want celery-colored aluminum siding?" I asked.

The artist, a beatnik complete with goatee and a paint-streaked sweatshirt with the sleeves rucked up past his elbows, moved his shoulders. "Why would anyone want aluminum siding?"

"Whatever happened to white?"

"Shows the fallout. You want to initial this or what?"

I initialed the sketch and he slouched on out, sandals slapping the soles of his bare feet like Japanese fans. I wondered how he explained flamingo-pink aluminum siding to his friends at the coffeehouse. I wondered when was the last time I had promoted something someone could use. I wondered if I should sneak out and go home and clean out my refrigerator, the last white one east of Woodward Avenue.

The telephone, a Depression-era relic of black steel with a receiver the size of an army boot, jangled. I considered waiting it out, then got up and put it out of its misery. My office mate, the owner's son-in-law, never came in before two o'clock and I spent much of my time taking messages from his legion of close cousins who all seemed to be stewardesses on layover from San Francisco.

"Doug's in a meeting."

Air stirred on the other end. "And who might Doug be?"

One of those microphone-trained voices, bounding up from the diaphragm and trundling out of the mouth like a big ball bearing; an original echo.

"A guy who's in a meeting. This is Connie Minor. What can I do for you?"

"You can come see me when you have time. My name is Israel Zed. I don't mind telling you, Mr. Minor, I've had the devil's own time tracking you down."

The name struck a dull chord, a rubber mallet bumping a bell wrapped in wool. For no clear reason I saw a flash of red-white-and-blue bunting and confetti hailing down. I said, "I've been here right along. Do you have something you need advertised?"

"In a manner of speaking. Can you meet me at the Ford

Motor Company Administrative Center Sunday morning at
eight? I apologize for the choice of days, but I'm flying to
Washington Monday and I can't work Saturday."

"On Schaeffer in Dearborn?"

"No, the new one. It's on American Road near Michigan."

I hung up.

It rang again two minutes later. I was looking for a telephone number in my desk but I went over and caught it on
one.

"Bad gag, brother," I said. "As long as you were planning
to get me out to a weedlot, you should have passed yourself
off as Joe McCarthy or Clarabelle, someone whose name I
could place. If you're out to rob me you dialed the wrong
number. I haven't had more than forty dollars in my pocket
at any one time since the Bank Holiday."

"I assure you, I'm calling from the center right now." He
didn't sound upset at having to call back.

"I grew up with this town. Dearborn dies at the end of
American. Past that point there's nothing but cows and silos.
A windmill's the closest thing to a skyscraper for a dozen
blocks."

"I didn't call you to discuss architecture, Mr. Minor. I
suggest you look me up and if you don't like what you find
out you can sleep in Sunday morning. Otherwise I look forward to meeting you at eight o'clock at the windmill." The
connection broke.

I went back to my desk and continued looking for the telephone number. After a couple of minutes of rummaging I realized I'd forgotten whose number I was looking for and
why. I stepped out the door that hadn't been closed since I'd
been working there and down the hallway to Research,
where I found Agnes DeFilippo sitting on her heels behind a
work table stacked three feet high with manila folders, rif-
fling through the debris in the bottom drawer of a file cabinet. They were nice heels, three inches high with slings
across the back. In that position, the long muscle in her right
thigh stood out like a coaxial cable beneath her A-line skirt
and I felt the beginnings of my first erection in a week. She
was fifty, looked thirty-six, tinted her hair blond, swept it up,
and shaved her eyebrows for the Peggy Lee look. We'd gone

to lunch twice and I'd been working myself up to ask her out for dinner, the next stage before bed, when she'd kiboshed the whole thing by telling me I looked just like J. Edgar Hoover. She had a husband she never talked about and a son at West Point.

She looked up at me, red-faced from the effort of separating two drawers' worth of files jammed into one drawer, and stuck out her lower lip to blow a yellow tendril out of one eye. "Get a good look?"

I held up both palms. "Sue me. I haven't seen my African *National Geographic*s in months. I need whatever we've got on a party named Israel Zed."

She punched the drawer shut and stood, two inches taller than I; but then almost everyone was, with or without heels. Her eyes closed. Behind that unlined kitten face was a mainframe computer that would have turned John Foster Dulles apple-green with envy. The files in the windowless little room were just props.

"Truman's ambassador to Palestine at the end of the war," she said without opening her eyes. "When the British started shooting Jewish emigrants he quit, mugwumped to the other side, and ran Tom Dewey's campaign in 1948. Zed and Dewey sang together in a college quartet at Michigan. Last I heard he was some kind of PR flack for Hank the Deuce at Ford's."

"What do you know about the Ford Administration Center?"

Her eyes opened. "Building or Center?"

"There are two?"

"Well, sort of. Don't you follow the news?"

"Newspapers depress me when I'm not in them. I'm still trying to figure out how to get the picture on my new Motorola from jitterbugging all over the screen."

"You ought to get out more, Connie. 'Like a vital organ, the city is forever regenerating itself . . . '"

"Go to hell, Agnes." I left.

4

I was still driving my 1946 Studebaker sedan. Weather and Michigan road salt had scoured its royal blue finish down to the red primer, turning it the listless purple of old serge; it came off like chalk on my fingers whenever I touched it. The hood tapered to a point like the nacelle of a P-38, making it stand out further against the bulbous designs of the day, and I had taken a hit on the driver's door that jammed the latch and required all my weight to force it open from inside, raising hell with my bursitis. The radio buzzed like a housefly trapped without hope and there was a leak in the vent under the dash that released a trickle of ice-cold water onto my ankle every time I took a tight corner. The whole frame chattered like a set of wind-up teeth whenever the speedometer crept above fifty. I'd made three appointments to have the front end realigned and canceled them all. I was sure any substantial investment in the car's maintenance would be followed by an immediate and complete breakdown.

Dearborn, Henry the Great's town and the birthplace of the Model T and America's discovery of the wheel, was, like most of suburban Detroit and indeed the city itself beyond its brief eruption of downtown skyscrapers, a horizontal town, four stories tall at its highest and very much in keeping with the new trend away from the vertical. It would as soon support a colossus of the type required for the administration of a company like Ford as Ike's scalp would grow hair. In spite of Agnes DeFilippo's hints to the contrary, I felt that morning like the guest of honor at a snipe hunt. Waiting for the light to change at Myrtle I caught a farmer looking at me from behind the wheel of a Dodge stake truck loaded with al-

23

falfa, nose-heavy and chin-shy under the bill of his Allis-Chalmers baseball cap, and I was sure from his expression he was in on the joke.

A block before American I changed my mind. Above the trees planted in boxes on the sidewalk, the gaunt arm of a crane was frozen in mid-reach against the sky, a steel I-beam dangling from its end. Just below it, girders arranged in a Madras pattern sketched the rudiments of an architectural leviathan. I had lost touch, all right. Time was when the slightest tremor as far away as Ypsilanti had sent electrical shock waves straight to the center of my nervous system. Now they were throwing up buildings between my morning *Free Press* and my first cup of coffee of the day.

I found a space next to a board fence with a tin sign tacked to it warning away unauthorized personnel and got out while the Studebaker's motor hiccoughed to a stop. The fence enclosed the entire block, inside which two distinct towers, one forty feet taller than the other, were assuming shape with nothing beyond them but flat farmland. Nothing was going on, it being Sunday, and an eerie quiet hung over the project like the girder from the crane, not even swaying. I felt like the last person left in an evacuated city. In a labor town, double-time for Sunday carried the clout of a master switch.

Gravel crunched behind me. I turned as a 1954 Ford Crestline Deluxe Skyliner drifted in behind my car. It was emerald green and had a clear Plexiglas insert in the front half of its hardtop, extending the view from the windshield but otherwise serving no purpose whatever except perhaps the chance to catch a tan without the strain of having to push a button and open a convertible top. Abruptly the overhead valve V-8 under the hood stopped burbling—my engine was still going through the dry heaves—the long door on the driver's side swung open on silent hinges, and my world filled up with Israel Zed.

He was built for the role, six feet and two hundred athletic-looking pounds in saddle shoes and a brown chalk-stripe double-breasted with lapels as wide as a six-lane highway. His tie, equally wide, was burgundy silk with tiny gold saxophones in a club pattern. He had a broad forehead, square cheekbones, a large clean-shaven chin, and no eyebrows.

That lack lent the appearance of perennial surprise to his eyes—bright, clear, and amber-yellow, the color of tawny port. His gray hair, thinning at the temples, was clipped close. The only thing about him remotely Jewish-looking was his nose, bold and thick and bent sharply with a dent on either side where his reading glasses rested when he wore them; that, and the black silk yarmulke on the back of his head. His thin upper lip folded down over the lower in a V like the flap of an envelope.

I wondered at first, having been tipped off by Agnes to his identity and remembering the name vaguely, why I didn't recognize him. Later I found out that the Roosevelt administration and then the Republican Party had taken pains to keep him away from events where cameras would be present. As an orthodox Jew he refused to remove the black beanie and the sight of it was considered anathema to an electorate made up largely of Lutherans, Presbyterians, Baptists, and moviegoers who thought Jeff Chandler celebrated Easter instead of Passover. And so at those times he had sat alone in a room somewhere, listening to the events on the radio and calling in his counsel over the telephone like a baseball manager ejected from the game for spitting on the umpire.

"Good morning," he said, wrapping my hand in an oddly delicate grip considering the size of his palm and the strength I sensed in it. "Sorry the place is such a mess. I hate things in progress. The problem is when they're finished there's nothing to do but start something else."

"I apologize for doubting you, Mr. Zed. I was on top of things so long I get to thinking I still am. They tell me it's the same way when you lose an arm or a leg."

"The real publicity blitz hasn't started yet. All the better for privacy. Let's go on up."

"Up?"

He leaned inside the car and retrieved a square steel case the size and shape of a woman's makeup kit with a combination dial as big as an apple. He grasped the edge of the fence gate and rattled it until it was opened from the other side by a gray-skinned Negro in a yellow hard hat and white coveralls crusted with dried mortar, who peered at the picture ID Zed showed him and pulled the gate open the rest of the way.

When we were both inside he closed and padlocked it. More heavy equipment and stacks of girders and cement blocks cluttered the raw earth inside the fence. At Zed's direction the Negro unlocked a board shed with a slanted corrugated roof and WARNING—EXPLOSIVES stenciled on the door. The big man reached inside and brought out two hard hats, one of which he handed to me. Mine was too big and I had to double over my right ear as a shim, but his fit his broad head with just enough room for the yarmulke, as if he'd had his haberdashery run it up. Somehow it made him look even bigger and wider. I, however, was sure I looked like one of the dancing toadstools in *Fantasia*. Leaving the Negro to lock up, he led the way through the building's steel superstructure to a wooden platform upon which stood a steel cage I didn't like the looks of at all.

He spotted my hesitation. "Do you have a problem with heights?"

"Not when there's a building around me."

"Believe me, if it weren't absolutely safe I wouldn't be going up with you. My people are born worriers."

He folded aside the grate and held it while I stepped in. Joining me, he closed the grate and signaled to the Negro, who started a shiny red generator the size of a school bus and entered the maze of girders to work a lever nearly as tall as he was. The elevator jerked like a drunk snoring himself awake and rose between the rails. We cleared the fence and the top of the nearest building, after which Dearborn, Dearborn Heights, and greater Detroit spread below our feet, and beyond them the quilt patchwork of pastures and crops. We left the shorter tower behind us and still we climbed, past a fat seagull blinking at us from its perch at the end of an exposed rivet, up to where the wind freshened and the sky opened around us like a parachute.

The car didn't slow down as we approached the top of the greater tower. There was nothing above it but tattered clouds and I was starting to think we would just keep on going like in a cartoon when we stopped with a clank that nearly threw me off my feet. Zed pulled open the grate and stepped onto a platform made of two-by-sixes laid across two I-beams. A pair of steel folding chairs faced each other there, with a large wooden crate between them marked UNIONBILT TOGGLES. I pried my fingers off the handrail and followed him. The entire building swayed beneath me. I made my way across the platform in a gridiron crouch and grasped the back of one of the chairs in both hands as if it were the bar of a trapeze.

"It hit me the same way the first few times," said my host. "You get used to it. You should see the Indians we hire from up North; they hop from girder to girder like parakeets, and with a bellyful of Jack Daniel's to boot. I think it has something to do with their ancestors jumping stagecoaches and covered wagons."

I didn't say anything. The wind was stiff and puffed out the back of my sport coat like a sail. My toes gripped at the platform through the soles of my shoes until they hurt. A haulaway thundered down Ford Road and I felt the vibration behind my knees. It was like being drunk, minus the sensation of well-being.

"Sit down, Mr. Minor. You'll feel better."

Without letting go of the back, I worked my way around the chair and lowered myself onto the seat. I sat there a long time before my heart stopped hammering between my ears. "Is there any special reason we couldn't do this on the ground?" I asked then.

"Just one moment." Seated opposite me on the other side of the crate, he lifted a field telephone from its top, black steel with a dial attached to the bottom of the receiver, and dialed a number. "Me, Janet. Anything? No, he needs to get Dinah Shore out of his head, she's committed to Chevrolet for at least three years. There's a new cowboy show on the board, though. CBS wants John Wayne and they'll need a sponsor who won't squawk at his fee." He listened. "Okay, tell him we'll make it a condition: No Wayne, no deal. I'll be at this number." He laid down the telephone. "Sorry. The problem with walls is you can't tell who's listening from the other side. I used to read your column when I was clerking in the legal department at Chrysler. You had a reputation for keeping secrets. It's my observation that that's a lifelong trait."

Having thus been warned, I leaned in, folding my arms on top of the crate and opening my face.

He leaned back at the same time. I wondered if he were playing with me. "We're sitting atop the main building. Twelve stories. I imagine it feels higher." Without waiting for a response he pointed at the shorter tower. "That will be the Lincoln Mercury Building, six stories, with a parking garage in between so the employees won't have to cross a dark lot at night. Hank takes care of his people, unlike his grandfather. The business has plain outgrown the old barn on Schaeffer; also there is no privacy, people barging in at all hours without taking the trouble to knock. Once they get in that habit the only way to break it is to overawe them with their surroundings."

"I'd probably just lock the door."

"That's a retreat. Hank Ford doesn't back off. Harry Bennett thought he would and now the old bully is rotting away in that ridiculous castle he built for himself on Geddes Road, writing his memoirs. Strange, isn't it, how people who have had nothing to do with writing all their lives think they'll suddenly become writers when they retire."

"You don't have to patronize me, Mr. Zed. I'm not a writer. I'm a pitchman."

He placed his steel case on top of the crate. "I wasn't born wealthy. One summer when I was putting myself through law school I worked for the Shrine Circus. One of my duties was to poke a rake under the elephant's tail and loosen its bowels before it entered the big top so it wouldn't disgrace itself in front of the audience. This is a roundabout way of saying there are worse jobs than writing advertising copy." While he was speaking he worked the combination lock, hinged back the lid, and thumbed through the accordion files inside. From one of the pockets he drew a slim paperbound pamphlet that made me blush exactly as if I'd been caught masturbating. "Community involvement is a serious interest of Mr. Ford's. He contributes heavily to the chamber of commerce and expects everyone on his staff to stay abreast of its activities. Recently this came to my attention. As a rule I don't waste much time with cheerleading publications when I can enjoy a ball game or something else less predictable.

One picture, however, caught my attention." He opened the book to a place marked with an uncirculated five-dollar bill.

"It was the only good one I ever took," I said. "No heads to cut off."

"It has irony. I was much more impressed with the caption. I won't bore you with how much trouble I went to in order to match the passage to its author. The chamber was unhelpful and your firm is reluctant to admit it's anything but a cohesive machine and that whatever issues from it could be the product of individual effort. I was forced to remind your Mr. Slauson that the Ford Motor Company is the second biggest advertiser in the Detroit market before he would put me in touch with your art director, who in turn gave me your name. Of course I recognized it immediately."

"Let me guess. You thought I was dead."

"Not an unreasonable assumption. Your decade burned up a lot of good men young, and you have kept a low profile. Your concept of Detroit as a living thing intrigued me. How did you arrive at it?"

"Are you asking me where I get my ideas?"

He closed the book and held it in front of him in both hands, like a Bible. "I am making conversation. I have to say you have a caustic attitude to bring to a job interview."

"Is that what this is?"

"I didn't bring you up here for the view. Unless I've read the blueprints wrong, we're sitting in your office. It will be next door to mine and three doors down from Mr. Ford's."

The building swayed and I gripped the seat of my chair with both hands. It was a time to say nothing and for once I did.

Zed returned "Detroit the Dynamic" to its pocket and counted down from it to another, at length producing a fold of stiff gnurled paper of the kind the illustrators used at Slauson & Nichols. He actually glanced from side to side before spreading it out on top of the crate. It was a charcoal sketch, seemingly done in haste but with a sure hand. "Nobody on Schaeffer knows this is missing," he said. "I have to put it back in the file by noon. I've learned the hard way that sometimes you have to keep secrets from your employers in their own best interest. Do you know what this is?"

"Sure. It's a spaceship. Captain Video flies one every Monday."

"Of course it's an automobile, but not like any you've ever seen. The designer was told to forget every existing car and to draw one that looked as if it were doing eighty when it was standing still."

"It sure doesn't look like a Ford."

"Actually it's a Mercury; the body, anyway. What do you think of the grille?"

"What's this, the spare tire?"

"It's a design feature we're working on. It has a few bugs. There are other things on the board: push-button electric transmission, self-adjusting brakes, seats that actually fit the human body. We're giving Cadillac a run for its money, and at an affordable price. Ten years ago it was sliced bread. Now it's luxury on a budget."

"What are you going to call this miracle?"

"That needs work too. Hank wants to name it after his father."

For the life of me I couldn't remember the name of Henry II's father, or even what he looked like, although I'd been told I had sat next to him throughout a dinner Henry Primo threw for the press at Fairlane to celebrate the Model A's first day of production.

"What do you want me to do, sell it?"

"Any hack could sell it. I want you to make it an indispensable item in every American household." His expression as he folded the sketch was entirely serious. "That caption you wrote couldn't have been written by an ad man. You don't think like one, and that's what's going to put one of these in every driveway." He returned the paper carefully to its pocket and removed another. "This isn't our standard contract. You'll note there's a clause prohibiting you from discussing the nature of your job with anyone on pain of immediate dismissal and possibly legal action, except with me and Mr. Ford. That includes Ford employees."

"The cap's on that tight?"

"It's been this way since the war. All the former OSS men not working for Dulles are in private industry. General Motors and DeSoto each have fifteen percent more employees

on the payroll than they report to Social Security. It's reasonable to assume most of them are drawing a second salary
from their competitors and reporting back from inside."

I didn't ask how he knew about that fifteen percent. "What
if someone asks me what I do?"

"Lie." He showed his teeth. "Chances are no one will.
With half again more office space there will be plenty of new
faces for the old guard to sort out. It will be three years before they get around to wondering about you. That happens
to be the standard gestation period for a new model from
drafting room to showroom."

I ran my thumb down to the compensation clause and
flicked it at what I thought was a gnat. It turned out to be another zero. "I don't have a pen."

He produced a two-tone plastic ballpoint with the Ford
logo printed on the barrel in script. I scribbled on the crate to
get the ink flowing. It matched the color of the company's
cheaper cars.

"I almost forgot your bonus." He deposited a pair of keys
on the crate. They were on a ring attached to a miniature license plate whose numbers nudged recent memory.

"The Skyliner?"

"It's yours on a year's lease. When that's up you can
choose its replacement. If you do the job as well as I expect,
Mr. Ford himself will issue you title free and clear to a top-
of-the-line model as soon as the new car enters production.
Just remove your personal effects from your old vehicle and
I'll arrange for its disposal. The company can't afford to let a
staff member be seen driving around town in a wreck. I hope
it hasn't any sentimental value," he added.

I removed the Studebaker's keys from my lucky rabbit's
foot and laid them on his side of the crate. "It never fails.
Every time I get rid of a car it's just after I filled the tank."

And so I signed my name in Ford pelican-puke green to a
pact presented by a Devil in saddle shoes and a black skullcap. I figured one day they were all going to catch up with
me.

5

I gave notice personally to Winston Slauson the next morning. The old man, a former naval reserve officer retired with the rank of rear-admiral for losing a hand at Midway, rose from behind his big gray steel desk supporting a scale model of the destroyer he'd commanded in that battle and reached across to shake my right hand with his left, keeping his stump inside the side pocket of his blazer. He affected white muttonchops after Admiral Dewey and displayed his old dress uniform in a glass case in a corner of the office, obscuring the fact that he had spent most of his career in the recruiting department and never set foot on a bridge until after Pearl Harbor. He wished me the best and said the old tub wouldn't be the same without me. I'd had to remind him who I was when I entered.

Ironically, during the two weeks I owed the firm I created the most brilliant campaign of my long stint in advertising. We'd landed the Enrico Fermi account, assuming public relations for the world's first atomic energy plant near Monroe along with the burden of turning apocalyptic paranoia into popular acceptance of nuclear power as a common household item next to Scandinavian Modern and the Frigidaire. Someone in the art department—it might have been the beatnik, although I credited him with more subtle forms of subversion—had blocked out a sketch from a photograph showing a cluster of bulbous tanks swelling like Scrooge McDuck's money bin over dozens of identical ranch houses fanning out from their base. Evidently it was intended to create a protective-umbrella effect, but even the cheery pastels zigzagging the tanks did nothing to decrease their resemblance to a hulk-

32

ing mass of alien life forms preparing to engulf and devour the community at their feet. That motif was just then entering drive-in theaters in the image of villainous carrot-men, shape-changing Martians, and creeping globular masses of intelligent bubblegum, and hardly seemed in keeping with the nuclear lobby's quest for a wholesome identity to stand beside Betty Crocker.

"Got anything better to offer?" asked Fleenor when I brought it to his attention.

"I keep thinking of something Mr. Hearst said when I worked for him at the *Times*."

"If it has anything to do with Marion Davies naked I don't want to hear it."

"It went something like 'Show me a magazine with a picture of a child, a dog, or a pretty girl on the cover and I'll show you a magazine that sells.'"

Fleenor plucked at his Hitler moustache. "Well, no photographer I ever worked with liked taking pictures of dogs or children."

The model search took a few days. Most of the girls in the portfolios sent by the two agencies we used on a regular basis looked too much like Marilyn Monroe and the rest looked like you could cut yourself on their vaginas. Then a little mom-and-pop operation in East Lansing we'd turned to during a model strike in 1952, run by a former B-picture actor and his wife, who'd represented Michigan in the 1936 Miss America pageant, came up with Hope Crane.

Hope was a nineteen-year-old drama major at MSU who'd modeled underwear for S. S. Kresge sale bills and appeared in a brief outfit on WJBK-TV in Detroit long enough to throw a pie in Soupy Sales's face and flounce off when Soupy had yet to decide whether he was a burlesque comic or the host of a children's show. A natural honey blonde, with blue eyes the size of butter pats and red chubby cheeks like Santa Claus in the Coca-Cola ads in *National Geographic*, she managed to look as if she belonged milking a happy cow on a Mecosta County farm even when she was posing in nothing but a black garter belt and stockings. It was that serendipitous combination of female innocence and sex that made you want to chuck her under the chin even as you were de-pantsing her. The agency called her in for a preliminary shoot and hired her before the prints came back from the darkroom.

We put her in capri pants, two-inch heels, and a plain white blouse with the cuffs turned back, tied a frilly apron around her waist, and posed her at an electric grill, flipping hamburger patties with one of the big tanks in the background. When I saw the proofs I thought it was the corniest thing I'd ever seen. The Admiral took one look at that toothpaste grin, fake pearl necklace, and hint of cleavage where her blouse wasn't quite buttoned up and okayed the campaign. The picture he selected went to the Associated Press the next morning with a news release written by me and that afternoon appeared in every newspaper of note between Boston and San Bernadino. By the end of the week the Atomic Burger had become a featured item on menus across the country and Hope Crane was signed to a three-picture deal with Paramount. If you're still alert at three o'clock in the morning, you might catch her bit in Martin and Lewis' last picure together during the late show. The movie bombed, her option wasn't picked up, and until I came across a two-line filler about her double mastectomy in a back section of the Detroit *News* a couple of years ago the last I'd heard of her was she'd married a trumpet player with Xavier Cugat's orchestra and settled down in Tarzana. Meanwhile that shot of her with spatula in hand and reactor at her back shows up in every 1950s collage, sandwiched between Elvis and the hula hoop. And nuke plants are as common as instant rice.

The first fever was still on when I cleaned out my desk, shook Fleenor's carplike hand, and poked my head into the Snake Pit to wave at the beatnik whose name I never caught, lying unraveled on the swaybacked sofa sighting down his body at a half-finished painting on his easel of a ballpoint pen orbiting the earth. He lifted an index finger from his chest without looking at me and I went on to Research.

"So you're really pulling out." Agnes, seated at her desk with a platoon of potted plants lined up along the edge and a sheet of peel-and-stick file labels in front of her, glared at me over the tops of her rhinestone reading glasses.

"If you only knew how long I've waited to hear you say something like that."

She stuck out her tongue. "You ought to hang around. I understand the A. Hitler Gas Oven Company is looking for a spokesmodel."

"I thought all the ban-the-bomb nuts were out of work."

"Hope Crane's tits look a little like nuclear warheads, don't you think?"

"So does Adlai Stevenson's head. Are we going to argue politics or are you going to wish me well on my new job?"

"What is it, anyway? You never said."

"I polish the dust out of the hole in the O in the Ford insignia on every car that comes off the line."

"Go to hell, Connie."

I twisted the doorknob. "Are we still on for a movie Saturday night?"

"Not if it's another cowboy picture. I'm still scraping cowpie off my heels from the last one."

"*The Robe* is playing at the Fox, if your bladder's up to it."

"Worry about yours. I don't have a prostate. Enjoy the job."

The new Skyliner and my old Studebaker had to have been made on different planets by cultures that never communicated. The big Ford held the curves like a cast-iron bathtub and the overhead V-8 thrummed like a bass fiddle whether idling or accelerating. The interior was more comfortable than my apartment. I liked the big green steering wheel, as wide as a manhole cover, with finger contours like bicycle grips and a chromium horn ring that when depressed cut loose a stereo blast that swept pedestrians and lesser machines out of its path like dead leaves. The seat, upholstered in ivory- and celery-colored vinyl, molded itself to my lower half like naked feminine thighs. When I turned on the radio, Teresa Brewer sang at me from all sides. Even the clock worked.

Its only drawback was its main selling point. That clear Plexiglas insert in the front half of the roof, while affording a spectacular view of sky and cityscape normally obscured by steel and headliner, also exposed the car's interior and occupants to the sun, in fact magnifying its rays at certain angles the way a convex lens in the hands of a cruel little boy focuses daylight into a lethal pinpoint that fries ants in their tracks. To avoid sunburn I had taken to wearing a hat for the first time in fifteen years, and the problem of finding parking in congested areas was complicated further by the need to locate a spot in the shade to keep the upholstery from fading; or worse, fusing itself to some of my favorite parts when I sat down on it without thinking. I wanted to speak to Israel Zed about it but thought I'd wait until the job was more secure.

For the first couple of weeks it felt anything but. The Ford Administration Center wouldn't be finished for two more years, and pending the availability of my plush office just down the hall from Henry's I was holding down a desk behind a flimsy partition in the Accounting Department at the aging Administration Building on Schaeffer Road. It was a horseshoe-shaped brick building, three stories high, built in swampland, and was regularly mistaken for the local high school by new deliverymen. The cubicle's only solid wall was dominated by a huge portrait of the late Henry Imperitus, whose pinched Yankee features glared down at me from above his stiff collar as if contemplating the possible presence of a smoker or imbiber of alcohol in the Holy of Holies. Although I didn't use tobacco and hadn't drunk more than a jiggerful of bourbon in a beergarden on the way home from work since the Lindbergh kidnapping, I made it a point to keep a pint of Hiram's and a carton of Chesterfields in my desk at all times. It's the quiet revolutions that keep you sane.

Beyond keeping track of Hank the Deuce's *wunderkind*, now slated for production in fall 1957, there wasn't much to do *except* revolt quietly. The first day I hung my framed copy of the last front page of the Detroit *Banner* on the partition opposite the desk, sharpened and separated my pencils according to color, used the telephone to bet the Indians against the Giants in the first game of the Series, and made a necklace out of paperclips. The second day I took down the newspaper in favor of a print my father had left me of

George Washington crossing the Delaware, sharpened the pencils again and mixed up the colors, bet my bookie double or nothing on Cleveland in Game Two, and took the necklace apart. By the end of the week I had replaced Washington with poker-playing dogs, all my pencils were two and a half inches long, the paperclips were bent beyond use, and I was considering asking Israel Zed for an advance on my first two weeks' salary to keep my kneecaps out of jeopardy when the telephone rang and it was Zed.

"How are you settling in?" he asked.

"So far it's the best job I ever had. Getting paid for doing nothing has to be the universal dream."

"Didn't you get the new sketches?"

I said I had. They'd arrived at my apartment by special messenger over the weekend, in a briefcase chained to the wrist of a bodyguard type in a black wool suit with extra room tailored into it for the holster under his arm. The wheelbase had lengthened and interior studies included a front seat like a divan and a circle of buttons marked PRNDL in the center of the steering wheel, eliminating the need for a lever to change gears. The instrument-studded dash reminded me of an automat. "I'm still not used to that grille. Whose idea was it?"

"We won't discuss details over the telephone. Did you burn the sketches as instructed?"

"Of course." I made a note to do that as soon as I got home. I was pretty sure I'd tucked them under a stack of newspapers in the bathroom.

"Good. I'm meeting Mr. Ford at Berman's Chop House in twenty minutes. Care to come along? It's high time you met the man you're working for."

"I might be late. I'll have to swing by my place and pick up a jacket and tie. They're pretty strict."

"Don't worry. You could show up naked and be seated at the best table if you're with Hank. One thing. Don't mention his grandfather in his presence. He hates the old boy for what he did to his father."

I thanked him for the advice. Hanging up, I tried once again to remember the name of the Ford who had come between the two Henrys and came up empty once again.

6

Berman's Chop House, located in Detroit's Times Square between Clifford and Grand River, was held over from an era when men snipped the ends off their cigars with silver clippers attached to platinum watch chains and women wore whalebone and kept their mouths shut; a patriarchic, oiled and pomaded barbershop of a time hewn of dark oak and polished brass, sun-ken with the *Lusitania*. The interior was a tall box that looked and smelled like a humidor, wood-paneled, leather-studded, and hung with red velvet. Most of the light in the room came secondhand off the surfaces of the crystal chandeliers and the copper plating back of the bar. The few women seated at the tables had the look of guests, as of a men's club whose Old Guard had died off sufficiently for it to declare Ladies Night. You could order anything you liked from the leather-bound menu as long as it was beef, chops, fish, or salad. If you wanted dessert, there was Carl's around the corner.

The maitre d', fortyish and appropriately effeminate, with an advancing forehead and lively violet eyes, had apparently been briefed, for he took no notice of my open-necked knit shirt and zipper jacket when I told him the party I was meeting and conducted me through a sea of business suits and striped ties to a corner booth. Israel Zed was standing there as if he'd been waiting in that position right along, large in gray worsted with a shadow stripe and the ubiquitous black cap. He took my hand and turned me toward the table. "Mr. Ford, Connie Minor."

It would be some time before I learned that one didn't "have lunch with Mr. Ford," in the usual sense of the phrase.

Intimate, one-on-one meetings with the Boy King—he was thirty-seven at the time I met him, but the youthful title would remain as long as the gaunt gray ghost of Henry the First continued to stride through the offices, showrooms, and assembly plants of the company he founded—were nonexistent, for he was inseparable from the three men who shared the booth with him that day. For a terrible moment I was paralyzed by the sudden realization that I had no idea which of the four was my new employer. Zed made no indication by look or gesture, and although I had seen Ford's face hundreds of times in newspaper photographs and in newsreels, I was at a loss to identify his remarkably ordinary features in person.

Ford solved the problem for me by lifting himself slightly and extending a large fleshy hand. That description implies more physical activity than was actually employed. I was pretty sure that despite the impression of rising, his buttocks never left the leather seat, and the proffered hand barely cleared his side of the table so that I had to reach all the way across to grasp it. His grip itself was neither weak nor strong; it wasn't there. The sensation was as of plunging my hand into a feather pillow. He was a large soft bear of a man with thick dark hair parted on one side, baby-fat cheeks, and small light eyes that never gave the impression of making contact even when they were looking right into mine. I remembered my one meeting with his grandfather, five volcanic minutes alone with the stolid Yankee energy in that lean old frame, the hard, searching glitter in those deep-set eyes, and I understood the reasoning behind the rumors of a secret adoption in the family. There in the grandson's presence I couldn't recall ever having met a man who had so little effect on me. And potentially that made him as dangerous as anyone I'd known since Frankie Orr.

Other introductions followed. I shook hands with beefy Mead Bricker, gray, bespectacled Jack Davis, Ford's allies from the days when bully-boy Harry Bennett ran the company with his army of strikebreakers and Svengali-like influence over Old Henry, and John Bugas, the former FBI bureau chief whom Ford had lured over from government service to turn Bennett's corporate spies and enable the

Crown Prince to wrest control of the company from the palsied hands of its founder. Tall and lanky when he rose to shake my hand, Bugas exhibited a rough frontier charm that might not have been all artifice, helped along by frank dark eyes slanting away from a nose like the prow of an ice-breaker and a shy smile that showed no teeth. My instincts in the presence of so much self-effacement were the exact opposite of what they might have been half my life before. In an old-style gunfight I'd have picked him as my first target.

It was a tankful of sharks, and yet as we took our seats I felt a buoyancy in the party, as if I'd walked in on some kind of celebration. That was close to the truth. The third-quarter sales figures were in and I learned from their conversation that Ford had tied Chevrolet for the first time since 1929. The company there assembled had inherited a firm whose employees were still paid in cash by Dickensian clerks in green eyeshades and sleeve garters and in eight short years had parlayed it into a world player in the same class with U.S. Steel and Standard Oil of New Jersey.

Ford emptied his glass and banged it down. As if it were a gavel, the others ceased their talk of figures and quotas and looked to the Chief, a name I would come to call him myself, and that had been conferred upon him by his brothers when they were still children. Bugas, the erstwhile G-man, detected a secondary significance to the gesture and signaled the waiter, who replaced the empty glass with another filled to the rim with amber liquid.

"Are you a drinking man, Mr. Minor?" Ford asked suddenly.

I sorted through my options. For all I knew his glass contained ginger ale, and I remembered his grandfather's stand on any substance or activity that gave pleasure to the partaker. On the other hand, although my host's condition was difficult to gauge, it was pretty clear from the way big Mead Bricker had been forced to steady himself against the partition when he stood to take my hand, and from a general ferment in the air of the booth, that this was no gathering of teetotalers. I plunged. "Scotch and water."

The mood at the table lightened perceptibly. I'd passed a

test of some kind. Ford said, "Single malt? They have an excellent selection here."

"Oh, any kind. That iodine they smuggled out of Canada scorched off most of my taste buds twenty years ago."

Bricker laughed boozily. Davis slid away from him half a foot and adjusted his glasses. "You're *that* Connie Minor," he said. "I used to read your column. At home, of course. If the old man found a copy of the *Banner* anywhere on Ford property he'd track down whoever brought it in and fire him on the spot."

My drink arrived, giving me an excuse not to comment. A quick look from Zed had informed me that even a derogatory comment about Old Henry would be a violation.

"What do you think of our E-car?" Ford asked when the waiter had left. He was looking at me.

"E-car?"

"The Edsel." Zed's tone was a murmur.

My mind clawed for the connection. Edsel. edseledseledsel Edsel *Ford*. Henry's son. Henry II's father. *Hank wants to name it after his father*. Suddenly I tasted summer squash boiled with butter. It had been one of the more palatable dishes served at Fairlane that day I'd sat next to Edsel, who had made less of an impression on me than the squash.

"It has snazzy lines," I said. "That push-button transmission alone should sell millions. The grille is interesting."

Bricker drank. "That's Jack Reith's baby. Brought it back from Paris along with one of those little Eiffel towers and a complete Apache dancer's outfit."

"I'm not worried about the grille so much as the name," Davis said. "Cars named after people don't sell. Ask Kaiser about the Henry J. Anyway, Hank's father disliked the name enough not to give it to any of his sons."

"I liked 'Andante con Motor.'" Bricker drank.

"Oh, lay off that, Mead. We got that one from Marianne Moore, the poet, " Davis told me. "She also suggested 'Utopian Turtletop.' I don't know whose idea it was to consult her to begin with. Poets can't make a living off their own racket, let alone sell cars."

Bugas had remained silent, seated erect with his forearms resting on the table as if it were his old desk at the Bureau.

His open eyes hadn't left my face since our introduction. "Maybe Connie has some ideas in that direction. He's the writer."

Four more pairs of eyes joined his, Ford's over the top of his glass.

I sampled my Scotch and set it down gently. "I'd rather not."

"Why not?" Bugas. "We're all friends here."

"Speak for yourself, John." Bricker. "Personally I hate Jack's guts and the box they came in."

"Go fuck yourself, Mead." Davis' tone was gentle.

"Nobody blames advertising when a product fails," I said. "It's too much of an abstraction. They'll say it's the grille or the hood ornament or the oddball name. The Henry J didn't fall on its face because of what it was called. The promotion was dull; also it rusted when you gave it a wet look. If the campaign sinks the car I'll take the heat, but I don't want people saying it didn't float because Constantine Minor named it after his aunt's cat. A thing like that sticks to you."

Bricker emptied his glass. "That's just chickenshit. Where'd you find this guy, Izzy?"

I decided I didn't care for the large florid production executive. You found his kind on every playground, goading the smaller boys into jumping off the top of the slide. They were never around when the ambulance came.

"There's nothing chickenshit about it. We're not paying him to take our risks." Ford put down his drink untasted; a rare event, as I was to learn. "What do *you* want out of this campaign, Connie?"

It might have been the Scotch or the surroundings, laced as they were with testosterone. It might have been the gradual realization that I wasn't going to be fed, that there was to be no food, that a lunch date with Hank the Deuce meant catching a sandwich on the way over to soak up the bill of fare unless you wanted to lose the rest of the day. Most likely it had to do with being as old as the century and too tired to answer every question as if it were part of a job interview. Whatever it was, I said what I'd been saying to the mirror over my bathroom sink since the day I met Israel Zed and accepted his offer.

"I want out."

"Out?" His eyebrows lifted, raising the top half of his face away from the heavy bottom half. "You mean out of the account?"

"Out of advertising. I'm a journalist, Mr. Ford, or I was before I backed the right horse in the wrong race. I wrote about bootleggers until no one wanted to read about them any more and every time they saw my byline they thought they were going to get another dose. At the age of thirty-three I couldn't get arrested in the newspaper business. The only writing jobs I've been able to get in twenty years are the ones you skip past to get to the stuff you bought the magazine to read. I'm sick of it and I need out, but I'm too old and mean to leave with my tail between my legs. If I can put the Edsel in a million driveways I'll have knocked it down, kicked it in the ribs, and tromped it to death. If I can't—hell." I drank. My ice cubes had begun to melt, gone as soft as my hopes of making a good impression.

"Eleven."

The other men seated in the booth looked at Ford, waiting for the other shoe. It had started to dawn on me that despite his apparent lack of presence the scion of Detroit's First Family was developing an imperial style light-years removed from the shirtsleeved, chaw-in-the-cheek approach associated with his predecessor. He spoke slowly, rotating his glass between his big meaty palms.

"One thing I brought back from Europe along with my uniform and a couple of souvenirs was a massive erection. So did everyone else I fought with over there. We're most of us fathers now, and by the end of this decade we'll have swollen the population by about thirty-five million. The eggheads I've brought into the fold tell me we'll need to sell eleven million E-cars if we're to be noticed at all in the crowd. If Connie can do that, I'll purchase the *Free Press* and present it to him personally."

"A letter of introduction will do," I said after a moment. "There's too much desk work in owning and running a paper. You have to be nice to lawyers."

Ford guffawed. His voice was light and slightly high-pitched and it drew attention from some of the other tables. I was pretty sure he was drunk. In that bracket it's sometimes hard to tell. It doesn't seem to do much for them in the way of having fun.

The outburst was over quickly. The air in the booth seemed clearer. The party relaxed. "Has Izzy been keeping you hopping?" Ford asked.

Zed answered. "I thought it best we keep Connie out of the day-to-day until we had something more concrete to show him than sketches. The less time he spends among the general population the fewer questions get asked."

"Well, we have to put him to work. I just got through cleaning out the deadwood from the old days. I didn't do it to make room for my own. How much do you know about cars, Connie?"

"If you don't put gas and oil and water in them from time to time they don't go."

"Get him into Rouge," he told Zed. "It's how I learned the business and I guess it's good enough for him too. Let him slam doors. Let him operate a welding torch if he wants. By the time he's through I want him to be able to disassemble and reassemble a new car off the line blindfolded. He can't sell a product he doesn't know anything about."

"I'll start on his clearance right away."

"Don't bother." Ford undid his lapel pin, the company emblem circled in gold, and skidded it across the table. I caught it before it could fall off the edge. "That will get you in anywhere. Take good care of it. It belonged to my grandfather. It's the only thing the old bastard ever gave me besides a bellyful of grief and it'd be a shame if you flushed it down the shitter."

7

It takes a lot of money to make a madman into an eccentric. Once that point is reached, it takes a lot of madness to make the eccentric back into a madman. Henry One had had plenty of both—money to burn and insanity by the long ton. In the beginning his friends called him Crazy Henry because the boyhood sight of a steam thresher wheezing down a country road had convinced him that man need not be dependent upon the whims of an animal with a brain the size of a walnut to get him around, and again he had been called Crazy Henry by his enemies when in the darkness following Pearl Harbor he had promised to produce a bomber a day in his Willow Run aircraft plant. Later, when his grandson unleashed his hand-picked Whiz Kids upon a crumbling auto company whose employees were paid in cash because its puritan founder had discovered that Ford paychecks were being redeemed in saloons and whorehouses, his own family had begun calling him Crazy Henry and shunted him into the shadows. There, deprived of an outlet for his fantastic dementia, he perished.

Genius or lunatic, Henry had possessed both the energy and the wherewithal to translate the megalomania of every child's egocentric wish-dream into the dizzying world-within-a-world of River Rouge.

When you stepped out of the relative quiet of the Administration Building and waded across the narrow strip of marsh behind it, you jumped a fence onto an insane farm where rubble grew like wheat and ashes flew like chaff; where stacks stood in dense rows like cornstalks and the lowing of noon whistles and diesel horns made you think of

45

crazed livestock. Somewhere in that graysward of brick and slag, 63,000 men and women slammed doors, ran forklifts, tugged levers, poured steel, raised and lowered blocks, stacked crates, sprayed paint, stoked coal, placed calls, pulled chains, pushed buttons, threaded wires, turned screws, caught rivets, twirled knobs, pounded keys, tightened nuts, swept, polished, examined, tested, discussed, scribbled, cranked, pedaled, stamped, and watched the clock; but you could wander that vast compound of whizzing belts, throbbing locomotives, belching chimneys, and gliding ships and never lay eyes upon a single living organism. I had been there before, although not as a Ford employee, and every time I went I'd felt like a character in one of those postapocalypse tales in *Amazing Stories*, abandoned in an extinct civilization whose machines mindlessly continued to perform their functions years after their last human benefactor had gone to his reward. There was a heart-sickening perpetuity about the place that convinced you of your own obsolescence.

Lord knew, I was familiar with all the numbers. Researching Rouge for "Detroit the Dynamic," I had discovered that 100 miles of railroad wound through that self-contained kingdom like some throttled-up version of a child's tabletop train layout, transporting 25,000 tons of ore per trip from the docks where great ships registered to Ford put in to Ford's own steel mills and coke ovens—manned, along with Ford's glass plant and paper mill, by the owners of the 22,000 Fords provided for in the employee parking lot; but statistics scarcely prepared the first-time visitor for either the magnitude of the complex or its realization of Henry's flagrant dream of total autonomy. Raw iron came in one end and chugged out the other molded into the shape of shiny new cars. In between was chained chaos. I had accompanied Charlie Chaplin on a tour of the place guided personally by the owner, and watched them try to communicate by sign language against the horrendous din. The result had been *Modern Times*, Chaplin's unfunny paean to industry gone stark raving nuts at the expense of humanity. This was River Rouge at its brain-numbing peak, before Antitrust rolled up its meddlesome sleeves and began hacking away at the dream, downsizing it to mortal proportions and divvying it up among the carrion birds which for decades had circled the sky over Ford Country, searching for the odd open wound or exposed bit of entrail to pluck at and thus begin the feeding frenzy. The feast would continue, joined by the heirs to the Carnegies and the Duponts and all the other natural enemies from Ford's Paleozoic period, but in that dank early winter in the middle of the middle decade of the twentieth century the vision was still largely intact, and gray in the shadow of the hatchet-faced former machinist's-apprentice whose lapel pin I now wore.

Tours of Rouge had been a fixture almost since its inception, when a harried foreman had complained to Henry that the VIP visits he had been conducting were disruptive to the workers; his response was to make the visits a regular feature, open to the public, until the workers no longer noticed them. By then, of course, the old Yankee found there was profit in spectacle, and the tours became permanent, followed by the construction of the Ford Rotunda with its exhibits delineating the history of the world beginning with Henry's backyard in Dearborn, which in turn had led to Henry Ford Museum and Greenfield Village, those twin monuments to American industrial ingenuity, complete with the first tiny Ford plant, the workshop where Thomas Edison invented the lightbulb and the gramophone, and the Wright Brothers' bicycle shop. And Dearborn became a sort of pop-up Modern Testament, the Gospel According to St. Henry, admission one dollar (children 12 and under, fifty cents). The whole thing was a seamless combination of reality and mythology constructed along the lines of Buffalo Bill's Wild West, with the object of elevating the robber barons of the Industrial Revolution to the status of authentic American heroes; which, if the truth be told, they were, possessing all the concomitant scoundrelly attributes of a Wild Bill Hickok or an Ethan Allen. There is no quality control on God's assembly line.

Entering the Rotunda the morning after my meeting with the Deuce, I transferred the magic pin from my buttonhole to a side pocket. I wanted to make my first salaried visit incognito with the rubes, who that day comprised a young couple still admiring each other's wedding band, a mixed group of grayheads wearing comfortable clothes and walking shoes, and a gaggle of pre-pubescent girls in green rompers book-ended fore and aft by nuns in black habits. I was in line wait-ing my turn inside the door when a hand touched my arm.

"Mr. Minor?"

I turned to face a thirty-year-old model in a blue blazer and pleated skirt like stewardesses wore, only without an emblem of any kind. Her hair was black, brushed behind her ears, and she had gray eyes, a color that fascinated me, com-ing as I did from a muddy-eyed race. Her lips were painted fire-engine red, not my favorite shade by a long shot but ser-viceable on her, and she had high cheekbones that gave her face an Asian cast, although her skin was pale to the point of translucence. There was about her a certain quiet confidence in the impression she was making, slightly ameliorated by a youthful self-consciousness that saved her from conceit, and I had been acquainted with her for several minutes before I realized she had a withered left arm. A skillful tailor had cut that sleeve short and full to soften the contrast, but when she gestured with it I noticed that it was at least six inches shorter than its mate, with stunted fingers and a pudgy palm like a child's. And I knew without thinking about it that she was a victim of polio, the disease that had crippled a Presi-dent and threatened to slap great gaping holes in a genera-tion.

"I'm Janet Sherman, Mr. Zed's personal secretary. He asked me to escort you on your tour of the plant."

I shook her good hand, cool and smooth, the nails painted red to match her lipstick but trimmed short like any good typist's. "How did you recognize me?"

"Mr. Zed described you."

"I won't ask how."

"Would you like to start here and look at the exhibits? This is where the regular tour begins."

"Thanks, but I've seen the first car Ford built. It doesn't look the same without Henry sitting in it."

"In that case I guess we can dispense with the ride on the miniature test track. It's thrilling but hardly edifying. Is there a particular place you want to see?"

"The whole *schmeer*."

"Everything?"

"Well, skip the test track. I rode through a machine-gun battle once and every trip since has been anticlimactic. Let's start with the hot steel."

"But that's the standard tour. You could have just gone in with everyone else."

"I was in line when you showed up. I still can. I guess you've got better things to do than hold my hand."

"No, I'm cleared for the day." A fissure appeared in her high marble brow. "We can skip the stamping plant. A lot of people find it disturbing; all that noise, after the heat of the foundry. Some of the older tourists—"

"I'm fifty-five," I said. "Not a hundred. I can take off my coat and stick my fingers in my ears. If you need a note from my doctor—"

"*Caramba!*" She gestured with both hands like Ricky Ricardo, and that's when I noticed the withered arm. "Let's go."

I accompanied her down the front steps and into the parking lot, where she unlocked the passenger's side of a new sky-blue Lincoln Capri convertible and clattered around to the driver's side on three-inch heels. On a metallic day when our breath made gray jets she wore no coat, and I felt old in my fleece-lined leather jacket. The current generation seemed impervious to the extremes of climate, going bareheaded in January and wearing pink angora in the gluey heat of August. Some kind of revolution was in the making and I couldn't shake the conviction that I was the enemy.

The plastic seat was cold and stiff and the windows began to cloud as soon as we were both shut in, but the heat came on instantly when she turned the key and switched on the blower. I was just old enough to appreciate the improvement over the black boxes of my youth, which when they finally warmed up roasted the passengers in front while compelling those behind to wrap themselves in the ubiquitous backseat blanket. As for the rest, I missed warm durable mohair, ugly as it was, and I couldn't comprehend the functions of half the instruments in the dash.

She drove well and without awkwardness, even though

shifting required extending her short left arm its entire length
to grasp the steering wheel while she worked the lever with
her right. I noticed she drove a steady ten miles over the
fifteen-miles-per-hour limit posted throughout the complex.
She hummed the whole while in a way that suggested she
was unaware she was humming. We were pulling into the lot
outside the steel mill when I finally identified the tune: "Sixteen Tons."

My memories of that hangarlike room were cast in orange.
Actually it was gray and buff brown, like every other factory
since the invention of the steam engine, a color that happened rather than being planned; but the walls and ceiling
and the forest of posts that separated them writhed in the reflected glow from the vats of molten steel, which for all the
world could have passed for tomato soup coming to a boil.
There, workers in hard hats, gauntlets, and thick denims
soaked through with sweat stirred cascades of iron pellets
shaped like rabbit droppings into the mix, skinned off the impurities when they floated to the top, and poured the steel, no
longer red now but white-hot, into molds to form ingots the
size and shape of refrigerators.

"The ingots weigh between five and sixteen tons," said
Miss Sherman, apparently still oblivious to the tune she had
been humming moments before we mounted the high catwalk. "Sixteen hours from now the steel we're looking at
will be gassed up and driven off the line."

One of the men stirring the steel glanced up at us without
stopping his labor. We were a few minutes ahead of the regular tour, alone on the catwalk, and he probably thought we
were VIPs. His face was burned a deep cherry red and carried no expression. I thought of the faces I had seen in photographs of the survivors of Hitler's death camps, of their
lack of hope or relief or any other sign that they knew they
had been rescued. Then I remembered his hourly wage was
higher than mine and I decided I was trying to get too much
out of a face I had never seen before and would probably
never see again.

On to the other end of the building and the stamping plant,
where the temperature went down and the decibel level
soared. Far below the catwalk, workers, many of them

women, fed sheets of steel into machines whose piledriver-like stampers rose between gleaming hydraulic lifters and slammed back down, punching out fenders and door panels with a noise like freight trains colliding. Miss Sherman leaned in and cupped her hands around her mouth. I smelled tuberose.

"If you're wondering how they stand the noise, most of them are married."

I gave her a look that made her blush. She leaned in again.

"I've taken the tour six times. Someone always asks and that's the standard answer."

I shouted back. "It was the standard answer in nineteen thirty-two."

We walked out of the plant, out into the quiet and natural light and clear welcome cold of the Michigan winter. "Next stop, assembly," she said, fishing her keys out of her pocket.

The Dearborn Assembly Plant was half a mile long. In honor of the sixteenth hour in the conception, gestation, and birth of the automobile, we shuffled along the catwalk, following one of the fifty-three Fairlanes rolling off the line per minute from chassis to finished automobile. Torches splattered sparks, air wrenches whimpered, doors slammed like firecrackers going off in close order. Windshield, engine block, seats, steering column, and all the rest of the fifteen thousand parts joined as smoothly as a demolished building reassembling itself when the film is run backward through the projector. Of all the hundreds of thousands of hours that came and went at Rouge, the sixteenth was the least plausible, the hardest to explain, the most like magic. At the end of the tour a red-and-white Fairlane glistening like water took on gas and burbled away, driven by an employee in white cotton coveralls with the Ford logo scripted across the back.

Miss Sherman consulted her wristwatch, a man's model with a big luminous dial. "Just short of two hours. We beat the regular tour by five minutes. You don't ask many questions."

"I used to gig frogs here before the plant was built. When the last Model T rolled off the line I covered it for the Detroit *Times*. If there's anything you want to know, all you have to do is ask."

"I don't understand. I had a ton of letters to get out, and if I know the temporaries in this town most of them will be there waiting when I get back. Why did Mr. Zed assign me to shepherd you if you know more about the place than Mr. Ford?"

"Ask him. I came here planning to go through with the suckers."

"I will. Believe me, I will. Are you hungry?"

"Are you buying?"

"Mr. Zed's buying. I draw up his expense sheets. How about Carl's Chop House?"

"Janet, you are a corporate drudge after my own heart." We left the place of miracles.

8

That Saturday night I took Agnes DeFilippo to see *Woman's World* at the Fox. Clifton Webb played the president of an automobile company who invites three prospective vice-presidents and their wives to New York City for the purpose of identifying the pick of the litter. It was one of those TechniStereoScope jobs without a mountain range or a cast of thousands to justify the wide screen, so the actresses all wore big poofy skirts and the actors spent most of their time standing around large rooms with ten feet separating them hoisting martinis to use up space. The feature was sandwiched between a Coming Attractions trailer for *The Creature from the Black Lagoon* and a Popeye cartoon from the Roosevelt administration. Afterward we reported to the snack counter at Woolworth's for hamburgers and coffee.

"I thought you had an expense account," Agnes said, wiping a patch of ketchup from the corner of her mouth. "I dressed for an expense account."

Her dress looked like crushed charcoal, with a full skirt and a tight top that left her collarbone exposed when she took off her shawl. It was a nice collarbone for fifty, including a brown mole on the left side. I had on a windowpane sport coat and a blue tie rashed all over with red fleurs-de-lis. We had been the only ones so attired in a theater full of sweatshirts and dungarees with the cuffs turned up. I wasn't sure just when people stopped dressing to go to the movies, but it seemed to have happened around the time the first FOR SALE sign went up in front of one of the old motion-picture palaces. In another generation we'd be attending them in swimsuits. If we were attending them at all; the place had been one-third empty for the early-evening show.

I blew across the top of my cup. "You're not a client. When I've made my stripes I'll buy you a house in Miami on Mr. Ford's ticket, but right now I'm the new kid in school. What did you think of the picture? Personally I'm glad Van Heflin got the job, even though in real life he'd bankrupt the company with all those ethics. If I were Clifton Webb I'd have given it to Fred MacMurray."

"I liked June Allyson's dresses."

"The hell you did. She looked like Shirley Temple with a thyroid condition. What did you really think?"

"I'm wondering why you took me to see that particular film."

"I thought you'd like to see a woman's picture for a change. You said you were sick of westerns."

"That's not a woman's picture. The men called all the shots. The women were either scheming shrews or simpering little ninnies. If that's what Hollywood thinks women want to see, it's no wonder movies are in trouble."

A pair of pimple-pocked youths in black leather and Brylcreem and their ponytailed dates were gallumphing through the record section looking for Bill Haley and the Comets, loudly. I swiveled my stool to keep them in the tail of my eye. Young people had become a threat in ways more direct than the traditional.

"Movies are in trouble because for the price of ten Saturday nights anyone can put a box in his living room that spews out Clark Gable, Sugar Ray Robinson, and Gorgeous George all week long. That's why the people who still go to them dress like bums and talk all the way through the feature. They think they're still home."

She blinked and shook her head rapidly. "For just a second there you sounded like my father. The nurses in the home don't even listen to him any more."

"I always wanted to be an old fart." I took a bite out of my hamburger and put it down. Ground meat had changed commercially since the war. It no longer had texture. They had chopped and harrowed it so fine the raw patties must have looked like unbaked oatmeal cookies.

"Well, congratulations." Her forehead broke into a stack of creases that didn't go away when it relaxed. That depressed me somehow. I was more sensitive to signs of decomposition in my contemporaries than I was in myself. "I am worried about you, you know. You treat change as some kind of contagious disease. If you thought you could avoid it by bundling up and breathing bottled oxygen, you would."

"I don't mind change when there's purpose in it. I'm not opposed to change. I just changed jobs."

"No, you changed employers. You're still a flack. Or I think you are. You still haven't said just what it is you're doing for Sonny. And don't tell me you're the one who fixes the radios so they turn off when they go under a bridge."

I felt my face wince and poured coffee into it to cover up. That popular condescending nickname for the scion of the Ford family had never bothered me before I went to work for him. I'd used it myself once or twice. I belonged to that age group that didn't run down the man who signed its paychecks, or at least I hoped I did. I wasn't even sure I could spell sycophant, let alone be one. "I'm supposed to see to it that Ford doesn't become a division of GM. Aside from that I've been told to avoid specifics."

"Ah. Another Cadillac."

This time I didn't cover up worth a damn. She grinned beatifically. "Come on, Connie. They've been wanting to crack the luxury-car market ever since the old man died. The Lincoln didn't do it; it's what you drive until you can afford a Caddy. So Junior wants to put a car in every driveway in Grosse Pointe, and he's hired you to do the grunt work. Impressive. Very impressive. So how come my delicate stomach juices are gnawing at a raw onion instead of caviar?"

"If you can find it up on the menu I'll get some to go."

Someone jostled me hard. I swiveled my stool to beg his pardon and bumped into a black-jacketed post-pubescent stinking of sweat and motor oil. I'd lost track of Young America during the conversation and now he and his companion, a hefty redhead in a two-tone Pershing High School jacket whose cream-colored leather sleeves covered all but the tips of her fingers, crowded onto the stools on either side of us. There was a vacant pair of stools at the end of the counter, but the pair had ignored them.

The boy grinned past me at his date. Pink tongue showed where his front teeth were missing. "Pass the salt."

Red skidded the grenade-shaped shaker his way, bumping up Agnes' elbow as she did so. Toothless poured salt into a tin ashtray in front of him and set down the shaker with a bang.

"Pass the ketchup."

Bumping me with his shoulder, Toothless lunged for the red plastic squirter and rolled it down the counter. Red grabbed it and squeezed half a cup of the viscous contents onto the Formica top. A drop flew off the nozzle as she jerked the container upright and landed on Agnes' sleeve. She jumped.

"Pass the pepper."

I caught the shaker on its way down to the boy.

He leaned his body against mine. I smelled beer as strongly as if from an open keg. He was sweating pure Schlitz. "Hey, Gramps, I asked for the pepper."

"Grow up, son. Get a job. Find a wife. Have kids. Grow old and die." I slid off the stool and took Agnes' elbow.

Toothless grasped my arm, squeezing the bicep. I let go of Agnes and splayed a hand against his chest. That was where I went wrong, if you discount catching the pepper shaker. It should have been his chin, and instead of my hand it should have been the stool.

I remember the first blow and the second. After that I lost count. I remember being on the floor and something hard and sharp hitting me in the side that turned out to be the pointed toe of a motorcycle boot. I remember Agnes shrieking obscenities, being surprised at how many she knew, and I had a flash of her hitting Toothless with her purse—holding it like a sap, not swinging it by its strap like an old lady—and Red grabbing her from behind and trying to claw her face with ragged nails. I have no recollection of seeing counter help or any other store personnel, although I was told later a security man broke it up with a hammerlock and his service revolver. I passed into and out of this world in the back of an ambulance in need of shock absorbers, banging and rocking over dips and breaks in the pavement, with Agnes looking down at me through tendrils of hair hanging loose in front of her face. Stutters of light from passing street lamps found most of the cracks in her makeup, which still depressed me.

Somewhere in there I dreamed a memory, of lunch at Carl's Chop House on Howard with Janet Sherman after our tour of Rouge. She spoke sketchily of her childhood and schooling in Toledo, followed by her first employment at Ford as a secretary-typist, while delicately trimming scraps of lettuce from the edge of a tuna sandwich with her fingers. Finding the sandwich too big to handle, she had stopped to cut it in half. The operation forced her to lean a way over in order to brace the fork with her short arm, an awkward maneuver that she somehow made appear graceful. She was an extraordinarily pretty woman who had obviously spent hundreds of hours practicing such activities with the object of de-emphasizing them and distracting attention from her deformity. She was intelligent as well and spoke knowledgeably of things related to the history of the company she worked for that she could only have learned secondhand. If, as I assumed, her physical imperfection explained the lack of a ring on her left hand, she had made the best of that situation with interest, abandoning the typing pool in less than two years for a position as executive secretary to Henry II's least-dispensable Whiz Kid. And I was pleased to learn that this far on the wrong side of middle age I could still be aroused by admirable attractive women. Funny what you think of when you're bleeding.

In movies and on the clothes-closet sets of television, injured characters are always awakening to the sight of some concerned-looking doctor. In real life it's more often to the slack weary face of a bored cop. Mine, looming over me in the harsh white light of the emergency room at Henry Ford Hospital, had on the same uniform that had been handed him when he'd finished training a dozen or so years before. Far from having grown into its tired folds and gathers, he had come to resemble them. His face looked as if he could turn around inside it without disturbing any of its pockets or creases. Even his eyes were set so far back behind the

bunting of their lids I couldn't find them. I might have
caught him in mid-turn.

"Mr. Meaner, I'm Officer Kozlowski. Think you're up to
telling me what happened back there at Woolworth's?"

I had to maneuver my lips out of the way of my words.
They felt so swollen I was surprised I couldn't see them. "If
you know where it happened, I guess you know what." I was
hoarse as a dust devil. If I could have tumbled off the gurney
I'd have crawled over to the cinderblock wall and licked the
condensed moisture from the mortar between the blocks.

"The store turned the puke and his little whore over to the
precinct. You going to press charges?"

"I used to know a Kozlowski in the detective bureau. Any
relation?"

"Probably. Everybody in the family's been some kind of
cop. My mother's still working Dispatch in Royal Oak.
We're holding them two for A-and-B. You want to forgive
and understand them and set them on the right path, or would
you rather we stick their butts in juvie? Personally I don't
give a shit. Either way we get to deal with 'em all over
again."

"Could you get me a drink of water?"

"We're not supposed to give you nothing. Croakers get
awful sore. So how about it, you pressing the rap? 'Cause
chances are their parents live in Grosse Pointe and when we
pull them out of whatever party they're at to take the pukes
home they'll slap a suit on you for cutting little Buster's toes
with the busted ends of your ribs. This way you get something back."

"How's Agnes?" I was ashamed of not having asked first
thing. My face was throbbing and every time I inhaled someone sank a hat pin in my side up to the head.

"She's okay. I think she broke a nail." He flipped shut his
pad, a dime-store notebook with a cardboard cover hanging
by two loops. "Tell you what, I'll talk to you later. Right
now I'm answering all the questions. You got a strange way
of being in shock."

"I used to be a reporter."

"Yeah? Well, you must've stunk at it. You ain't reported a
thing since I been here."

He left me to stare at the tube lights in a trough on the ceiling. After a long time the dark oval of an orderly's face blocked it out and the gurney started moving. In X ray a young nurse whose skin was as pale as her cap helped me off with my shirt and pants and rolled me around on a cold steel table like an egg noodle, putting torque I didn't need to my cracked ribs and then doing it all over again half an hour later when the pictures didn't turn out. When a doctor finally made his appearance, he was half my age and his face wore an expression of even less concern than Officer Kozlowski. He poked at my abdomen and rib cage, twisted my head right and left, examined my pulse, and took six stitches in my lower lip, which was as big as a couch. While a nurse who may or may not have been the Florence Nightingale who had manhandled me in X ray sponged the blood off my face, Young Dr. Kildare scowled at my vital statistics on a clipboard in his hands.

"You have three cracked ribs, Mr. Minor," he said. "We'll tape them up before you leave, but you'll have to leave the bending over and climbing stairs to someone else for a while. I'd like to hang on to you overnight for observation; however, we have no beds available. We had a little roadshow performance of *The Wild One* on Hastings earlier tonight and some of the actors have decided to honor us with their presence."

I grunted, grateful for the reprieve. A steady stream of youths swathed in bloody gauze had delayed my treatment for almost two hours. The battle seemed to have been drawn along racial lines, reminding me uncomfortably of the '46 riots. "What about Agnes?"

"The woman who came in with you? She's in the waiting room. She has a facial contusion she refused treatment for. Otherwise she seems all right." He skinned back a page. "There's one laceration I can't account for. Did the boy who attacked you have a knife?"

"Not unless you count his boots."

"It's a four-inch gash on your upper right thigh. It seems to have had an adhesive bandage on it until quite recently."

"Oh, that. I did that to myself when I dropped my portable typewriter. I shouldn't have tried to catch it."

"That would be sometime last week?"

"More like a month. I was moving from my last job."

"Are you a slow healer, Mr. Minor?"

"I'm slower at most things than I used to be." I wondered where my clothes were.

"How is your urine?"

"As compared to what?"

"Do you have to empty your bladder frequently? Several times during the night?"

"Don't you?"

"Do you have to go right now?"

"I can wait till I get out of here."

"I'm guessing you take in as much as you put out. Are you extremely thirsty at the moment?"

"I wouldn't turn down a gallon of water and a beer chaser. Does any of this have a point or are you charging me by the hour?"

"Have you ever been treated for diabetes?"

Something caught in my stomach.

"A doctor told me I was a borderline case a long time back. It kept me out of the army. I've always thought I grew out of it."

He smoothed down the pages on his clipboard. "Chances are you're no longer borderline. I'd like to get you upstairs next week for tests. If it is diabetes mellitus, we're going to have to sit down and discuss some changes in the way you live. Dramatic changes."

PART TWO
The Glass House

PART TWO
The Glass House

9

And the leaves on the trees planted in boxes along Woodward Avenue went from sooty green to brackish orange and fell, and snow fell the color of rust and was pushed into piles like slag along the curbs, and the long coma of winter in southeastern Michigan passed into soggy spring, muddy, potholed spring; and young men in dirty yellow hard hats whose ancestors paddled birch canoes up the Detroit River laid plywood and plastic between the gaunt steel ribs on American Road in Dearborn and puttied sheets of glass the size of barn doors into their frames, and a wall of glass twelve stories tall and two city blocks wide glittered in the sun rising over the Ford Administration Center. Israel Zed conducted me on a tour of offices lined with silver-papered insulation while an April rain the consistency of thirty-weight oil smeared the windows and rataplaned the uninsulated roof. Everything smelled of sawdust and glue.

"This is where you'll work. Unless you're one of those who thinks a view is distracting."

The view at the moment was of Wayne County farmland as seen through an aquarium. The fields were plowed quicksand and the scattered houses and barns looked hunkered down, their shingled roofs shining like wet asphalt. The room, doorless, naked-joisted, and floored with sheets of plywood stenciled BAY CITY LUMBER, looked as if it would hold enough hay to feed all the sodden cows on all those farms for a season. "How many do I share it with?" I asked.

"Nobody shares here. Let the Russians share. Believe me, you'll need every square inch of it. You've got about six weeks to think about what kind of carpeting you want and whether you prefer wallpaper or paneling. I'm getting mahogany myself. I considered oak, but that's too much like a synagogue. I understand you toured Rouge again yesterday. Did you see anything you hadn't the first dozen times?"

I was growing accustomed to the way Zed changed subjects in midstream. "Not quite a dozen," I said. "Nearer ten. This time I used the lapel pin and got down on the floor to talk to some foremen. Did you know they fired a worker last month for putting an empty Coke bottle in the box frame of a Fairlane to create a mysterious rattle? The foreman thinks he was paid by GM."

His envelope-flap mouth dipped down, dragging creases from its corners to the sides of his Semitic nose. "You might want to stay away from the line for a while. The workers become suspicious when people in suits start hanging around."

"I never wear a suit when I go to Rouge."

"You don't look like someone who doesn't a lot of the time. And you don't look like someone who's accustomed to coveralls. They have a sense for that kind of thing."

"I'm just trying to learn the business the way Mr. Ford said."

"Hank's different. He could cross a picket line alone during a nasty strike and the worst he'd get would be a disapproving look. Part of it's the family mystique; mostly it has to do with his firing more than a thousand of Harry Bennett's stooges as soon as he took over. If he has a fault it's his tendency to forget that everyone didn't come down from Mount Olympus with him."

"Are you saying I'm in danger?" I didn't ask the question with quite the sardonic quality I might have before the thing in Woolworth's. The tape had been off my ribs for weeks but sometimes when I turned over in my sleep I still felt the pinch.

"Some of our present employees were on the scene when Bennett's bullies kicked Walter Reuther down the steps of the Miller Road overpass in 1938," he said. "In any case it wasn't so long ago they won't think history will repeat itself. At the very least they'll be curious and ask questions you might not be able to answer convincingly. At the most—

well, we're automating as fast as we can, but it's still a physical business, maintained and driven by brute force."

"I thought we were all in the same boat."

"The same boat, yes. But there are a great many decks between steerage and the bridge." He brightened. "Would you
like to see the car you're selling?"

"You have one?"

"Kind of. Let's go back to the old building."

We took the elevator down, a proper one this time, although the shaft was still open and the fragile-looking cable
arrangement that suspended the car exposed. I would never
again ride one without picturing those slender threads. Zed's
big Lincoln Premiere was waiting, navy and chrome with tail
fins and Turbo-Drive, and we boated away on its slightly
soupy suspension. The front seat was comfortable and the interior smelled like a rich man's office, but I wouldn't have
been surprised to turn around and see a coffin stretched out
in back. Cars, like everything else in a nation that had once
prided itself upon vertical growth, had begun to flatten and
lengthen, which in turn led to lower, wider garages and
houses to match. Having devoured the rest of the world with
its military and industrial might, the whole country was
stretching itself out like a lion in the sun. It was getting so
the only place you could comfortably wear a hat was out-
doors. More and more men and women seemed to be leaving them at home. Despite the ubiquity of Eisenhower in his
sail-brimmed fedora and Ralph Kramden golf cap, we were
starting to look like a society of shoe clerks.

In the Schaeffer Road complex we walked down the corridor Henry II had stalked a decade before, poking his
large round head into offices and firing men as he went,
past Edsel's old office where his son had holed up to plan
his strategy to seize control of the company from the de-
ranged patriarch who had built it, to the design department,
a room the size of a gymnasium that always reminded me
less of the creative branch of a world-class corporation
than a kindergarten classroom, complete with blackboards
and cork walls tacked all over with colored construction
paper cut into exotic shapes and square yellow oak tables
smeared with paint and dried modeling clay. The linoleum

floor was littered with scissored scraps of paper and the air smelled of turpentine and library paste. The room contained a half-dozen young men and one woman dressed identically in dungarees with their shirttails out; the uniform of the generation coming to power. Two were seated at drawing boards with their chins in their hands. A third was sprawled on a burst green Naugahyde sofa folding an intricate paper airplane—I think it was a Supersabre—out of what looked like an inter-office memo. Two more leaned on the windowsill sipping from king-size coffee mugs and watching a nuthatch pecking at birdseed scattered on the other side of the glass, and one sat on a stool in the far corner with his hands dangling between his knees and his head tipped so far back I could see the hairs in his nostrils flutter as he snored. This was the most secret department of the tightest-lipped industry in the world outside of munitions, an industry whose sales showrooms papered their windows when the new models were in lest the daring configurations leak to the outside world before the bombast and fanfare. The door to the room stood open day and night, sheets of flimsy cloth protected the scale models from unauthorized scrutiny, and the personnel resembled zoo animals snoozing in the heat of a lazy summer afternoon. Artistic people were the same all over. A dash of talent sprinkled at random insured them for life against the rigors of responsibility.

The ranking presence, whose name I never quite caught, turned out to be the aircraft engineer on the sofa, a pudgy twenty-odd with a scattering of golden hairs on his upper lip, who when Zed addressed him launched his creation into a high looping arc ending in an oblique trajectory, and got up with most of the noises a bear must make leaving its den in the spring. We had met before, but Zed introduced us again. The feel of the young man's languid hand in mine told me he didn't remember me from the priest who baptized him. At Zed's request he closed the door to the corridor—it creaked on its disused hinges like *Shock Theater*—and led the way to the largest of the tables, where he whisked the cover off a terra-cotta clay model the size of a bedpan.

It was a top-down convertible, longer, lower, and wider

than the Lincoln Premiere, with double-yolk headlights, long indentations along the rear fenders that made me think of speed lines in a comic strip, and a prominent front bumper split to make room for the horse-collar grille. Even the embossed lettering and the vertical streaks in the upholstery were represented. It was artistic work of more than just skill and talent. In Italy during the Renaissance its creator would have had a royal dispensation and a shot at everlasting life wherever art was celebrated. Being born four hundred years late had netted him a place on the Ford payroll and the kind of immortality that lasted until the next model change.

"Citation," Zed pointed out, in his pride mistaking the real object of my admiration. "Top of the line. You'll have a steel model on your desk next week. By then you'll be out from behind the curtain, at least where your fellow employees are concerned. We're beginning motivational training the week after that. Sell them on the car they'll be selling. A little refinement of Hank's, courtesy of a chief petty officer whose duty included preparing men psychologically to win the war. The principles are the same, even if the end result in those days was somewhat messier."

"Let's hope," I said. "The grille looks even funnier in three dimensions."

"Jack Reith borrowed that little number from the army." The languorous young man spoke of his division superior with a yawn in his voice. "He served under Hap Arnold, so they let him poke around. He says the new jet fighters have a front end just like it. Keeps their engines nice and cool when they strafe commies."

"A large-mouth bass has the same front end. I wouldn't want to drive one."

The sun set in Israel Zed's big face. He thanked the young man, asked him to replace the cover, and dumped a large meaty hand onto my left shoulder, steering me out into the corridor. Walking beside me with his head down and the yarmulke showing, he looked like the rabbi-in-residence for the Green Bay Packers.

"I think you should know I went out on a limb when I suggested you for this job." His rich voice carried further when he lowered it. "Hank likes young men. You belong to Ben-

nett's generation. If this new miracle machine turns out half
as hard to sell to America as you were to Mr. Ford—well,
the point is I couldn't lose because I had faith in you. The
world's greatest sharper couldn't sell hot biscuits to Eskimos
if he doesn't believe in them. I'm starting to think—correct
me if I'm wrong—that you have doubts about this car."

"I'm fifty-five years old, Mr. Zed. I have doubts about
everything." I wanted to leave it at that; I couldn't. "You
won't be sorry you fought for me. I've already put most of
my own time into this job, on top of all the company's."

"Time isn't as important as attitude. You need to stop
thinking of this as a job. Before the war, a car was just
something you needed to get from here to there. All it took
to sell one was to beat the other guy's price. Now people
are on the move, buying houses in what we used to call the
country and shuttling to and from the city every day. Bob
Briefcase drives twenty miles to go to work. Wife Betty
drives ten miles to the supermarket and another twenty-five
picking up and delivering Cub Scouts. That means two cars
in the garage. When vacation time comes, Bob, Betty, and
the Cub Scout throw everything into the trunk and a travel
trailer and hit the open road. After two years of this they're
sick of both cars and ready for something jazzier with fins
and a dashboard loaded with dials and gauges. Money's no
problem; they can always swing another loan at the bank
and pay it off on time. It's our responsibility to have something worthy of their expectations waiting for them when
they enter the showroom. It's not so much a job as a sacred
trust."

"I never thought of it that way."

"Neither did I, until I was in too deep to back out. We're
last-century boys, you and I. When we were born, the horse
count in this country was higher than the human population.
The city was a place you went to buy oats. Today our parents wouldn't be able to understand more than one word out
of ten in a normal conversation. That's how far we've come
in just fifty years. I have a wife and two sons in Baltimore
who haven't seen me more than a few days out of the year
since I came to work for Ford. Believe me, if I'd worked
this hard on the forty-eight campaign that would be Tom

Dewey thumbing his nose at Khrushchev instead of Old Baldy."

"I heard it was his moustache."

"I tried to get him to shave it." He waved his free hand. "Another reason I chose you is you have no family. No distractions means more concentration. But you can't put it up when you go home. When you cut your finger you have to bleed Hi-Test or it's no go."

We stopped near the staircase at the end of the corridor and faced each other. Somewhere in the building someone dropped a pencil, a distinctive clatter that can't be mistaken for anything else and carries like thunder.

"Count on me."

Zed beamed. He had perfect teeth, as even as the stones at Arlington. "I was positive I could. Everyone needs some talking now and then."

We shook hands and he went downstairs. Alone in that drafty hall I felt a cold spot between my shoulder blades, as if I were being watched. The curious onlooker might have been the me that I was twenty years before.

The telephone on my desk was ringing when I entered the office.

"Hi, Connie. This is Janet Sherman."

"Hi. If you're looking for your boss he just left."

"I know. He has a one o'clock with Mr. Ford. Actually I'm calling you. I had a lunch date but he just canceled. I didn't bring mine today and I hate eating alone in restaurants. Are you free?"

"Janet, are you picking me up?"

Pause. "I'm sorry. I thought—never mind."

"Don't hang up. It was a bum joke. Where would you like to eat?"

"I was thinking Greektown. The Greasy Gardens?"

The Grecian Gardens, in the very shadow of Detroit Police Headquarters, was the most visible of all the restaurants in that brief stretch of Monroe Street left behind by the city's once-massive Greek community. It was also the payoff point for every cop on Frankie Orr's pad. My experience with those places was that with all that guaranteed traffic, the proprietors didn't lose much sleep thinking up ways to improve the service or cuisine.

"How about the Parthenon?" I asked.

"Meet you in the parking lot. Whose car?"

I said hers would be fine. The Skyliner leaked where the Plexiglas insert met the steel roof and my seats were squishy. We hung up.

Last year's Hudson Hornet, gunmetal gray with white-walls and fender skirts that made it resemble a garden slug, glided to a swaying stop alongside me while I was waiting on the pavement by the employee entrance. The driver leaned over and cranked the window on the passenger's side. Round spectacle lenses caught the light, looking like blank cutouts under the brim of his hat. "Minor?"

I said I was. He straightened, popped open the door on his side, and came around the front of the car, heels snapping on asphalt. I'm a long way from tall, but I could have looked straight down at the crown of his hat without straining. The hat, a white Panama, was broad enough to keep the drizzling rain off his suit, a tight gray three-piece with the jacket buttoned. The narrow body under the wide brim reminded me of a mushroom. It might have been stunted in the shade.

"J. W. Pierpont." He stuck out a white hand. It was a perfect miniature, right down to the fingernails. "I'm taking you to lunch."

"Sorry. I already have an appointment."

"This one won't wait."

I started to grin; officious little pricks have always affected me that way. Behind me a leather sole scraped concrete and I turned, expecting Janet. The two men standing with their backs to the entrance were easy to miss, like the Penobscot Building when you were looking for it and suddenly realized you were standing right in front of it. The one in dirty white overalls looked like Broderick Crawford. His companion, wearing a suit coat over a corduroy shirt buttoned to the neck without a tie and green work pants, looked like something that had fallen off the back of a truck. His face and hands were as black as cast iron. They dressed out around two-fifty apiece.

J. W. Pierpont withdrew his hand unshaken. "I borrowed

these fellows from Albert Brock; the steelhaulers union, you know? Just window dressing in case I ran into an argument. Actually they wouldn't step on a bug. Walter's impatient. Things can't move fast enough for him since the overpass, you know?"

"Walter?"

"Well, Reuther. He's anxious to meet you. You know? So let's skeedaddle."

10

J. W. Pierpont was the worst driver I ever rode with. He blasted aside obstacles with his horn, changed lanes without warning or reason, and had no sense of timing at all when it came to traffic signals. I lost count of the times he failed to anticipate the red and braked in the middle of an intersection, forcing the cross traffic to fishtail past the Hudson like water around a snag, enraged horns Dopplering all the way down the block. I should have known what was in store when I climbed into the passenger's side in front and noticed that all the leather panic straps hanging from the headliner were broken.

His attention to simple automobile maintenance was no improvement over his driving. All the indicators on the dash lay all the way over to the right and he had no shock absorbers. The body swayed and bounced on its springs like the Overland stage. Within a dozen blocks I had *mal de mer* and mohair under my fingernails from the fat handle inside the door. There was a blue haze in the car from an exhaust leak under the floorboards. Barring a collision, I was a goner to asphyxiation for sure.

If I didn't know just how hard it is to drive badly on purpose, I'd have suspected pernicious design. I was kept too busy hanging on to my life and my breakfast to ask where we were going.

Wherever it was, it lay to the northwest. There the wartime concrete bunkers with common walls between the apartments and businesses that occupied them thinned out and were replaced by streets of new houses with picture windows, power-clipped lawns, and shrubs shaped like bunches of broccoli, so close to the architects' visions that any one of them could be photographed and superimposed on the original sketch with nary a line out of place. Only the odd tricycle in the front yard or basketball hoop mounted over the garage door broke the uniform pattern of row upon row of long ground-hugging brick and aluminum-cased ranch-styles laid end to end like pipe. But the surgical process by which this new way of living was delivered from the old was caesarean, and anything but antiseptic. Here and there the neat lines were spoiled by mounds of raw earth with grubby yellow bulldozers crawling over them like ants, clearing lots for new foundations. Muddy runoff from the eyesores etched brown tributaries in the emerald sod next door and oozed down the gutters in front.

At length Pierpont swung into a paved driveway exactly like its neighbors on both sides and stood on his brakes to avoid rear-ending a two-year-old Chevy Bel-Air parked in front of the garage. When the Hudson stopped rocking I pried my fingers off the dash and got out. Terra firma hadn't felt so good since I rode the car ferry across the Straits of Mackinac in the middle of a November storm. That time I'd at least had confidence in the pilot.

Of course the house was a ranch-style, with steps leading up from the trough of the driveway to a brief porch of unfinished cement. A picture window the size of a neighborhood movie screen was blanked out by drapes the color of washed-out gold. I'd never seen one covered before. Generally they seemed to exist as much for the casual passerby to glean an idea of the owners' daily routines as for the owners to see out; which made sense, the view of the opposite side of the street being the same from each side.

"Who's his landlord?" I asked Pierpont. "William J. Levitt?"

"What'd you expect, the Manooghian Mansion? Walter's a working stiff." The little man squashed the bell with his thumb. The Kong twins remained behind in the car.

Between the *bing* and the *bong*, the door swung inside, framing a Negro as big as a davenport. He had on a plaid sport coat and twill trousers that stopped two inches short of his black steel-toed high-tops, exposing a pair of white athletic socks. I figured he had an aversion to mud puddles. He was completely hairless and his head reminded me of a medicine ball. It was that big, for one thing, and for another a series of perfectly vertical stitches started at the crown and came down like seams to the thick mantel of bone that hung over his eyes. I couldn't think of any object that would cause an injury like that, so I decided he had had it done according to some fashion I wasn't aware of. Miss one issue of *Esquire* and you're behind the whole season.

The socks were the tip-off. They were an integral part of the unofficial uniform worn by union employees from New York's garment district to the avocado farms of southern California. There was a rigidity about the practice that approached fanaticism. I wanted to show him my expired press union card, but I was afraid he'd eat it.

His eyes, invisible and without luster in the shadow of their bone carapace, were something you took on faith, like the presence of a big cat in the darkness of its den at the zoo. I sensed when they shifted from me to Pierpont. At that point he shuffled aside, allowing electric light to leak out onto the porch for the first time. As he moved, his coat opened briefly and I saw the checked grip of an automatic pistol with thick rubber bands wound around it to prevent it from sliding down inside his pants.

Pierpont placed a palm against my back, gently but with pressure. I walked around the Negro's big stomach and descended two steps into a sunken living room carpeted wall to wall in the same gold as the drapes in the window. Imitation wood paneling covered the walls and a lot of furniture upholstered in green with glittering gold threads stood around on thin steel legs trying to look as if it were floating eight inches above the floor. The most expensive thing in the room was a combination TV and hi-fi phonograph in a pickled wood cabinet the size of a coffin. Family pictures and a bowling trophy stood on top of it. The room was spotless, and illuminated entirely by indirect lights in the ceiling and a Christmas-tree floor lamp in a corner. All the windows were covered.

A medium-built light-haired woman with sad eyes appeared inside an arch on the other side of the room while the big guard was patting me down for weapons. She wore a blue apron over a sweater and slacks and kneaded a checked dish towel in her hands.

"It's jake, May," Pierpont said. "Walter's expecting."

She turned and left with a snap that said everything I needed to know about her opinion of the little man in the big hat. I never saw Mrs. Reuther again, and I'm told it's my loss. She was a fixture on every UAW picket line since the wedding, handing out fat ham sandwiches and pouring steaming coffee from an army of Thermoses. They say her first reaction after a shotgun charge obliterated a window in her kitchen in the spring of 1948 was to throw her arms around her severely wounded husband.

When nothing more lethal than three sticks of Beechnut gum turned up on my person, the Negro stepped away and I accompanied Pierpont around a blind corner, down another flight of steps, and into a basement room. Here a low ceiling textured like cottage cheese swallowed all sound, deadening even the sharp clatter of billiard balls colliding on blue felt.

This room was the darkest yet. Even the welled windows near the ceiling had been painted over, leaving only a yellow circle on the pool table from a Tiffany-shaded fixture suspended from a chain above it. The man in white shirtsleeves pursuing the balls with a short cue was invisible from the neck up until he leaned down for a difficult bank shot. Then the light caught a pair of slightly puffed eyes under pale brows, a nothing sort of a nose, full lips curved like a woman's, and cheeks shaped like parentheses. In a couple of years they would be full-fledged jowls, and if his metabolism went to hell as thoroughly as mine had he would be Winston Churchill by the end of the decade.

It wasn't a face you'd remember on short acquaintance, but the intentness in the eyes as he lined up the shot was familiar enough from newsreels and the papers. Ten years older than Henry Ford II, Walter Reuther, national president of the United Auto Workers and Ford's frequent adversary at negotiation talks, looked and acted five years younger. There was an electric energy in his step as he moved around the table that seemed beyond the powers of the bearlike Boy King at any age.

And he was a good pool player, skinning the three-ball past the eight on a two-cushion shot to sink it in the corner. I was just bad enough at the game to appreciate the shot, because he made it look easy. What I couldn't figure out, as he paused to chalk his cue, was the presence of a child's flesh-colored rubber ball slightly bigger than a walnut balanced on the end of the table. It looked like a hatchling belonging to one of the ivories on the felt.

The squeaking of the chalk was the loudest sound in the room. Pierpont stood in the gloom with his fingers curled at his sides, waiting for Reuther to speak, and I was aware of the silent looming attendance of the huge guard behind us in the shallow hallway at the base of the stairs. There was something imperial about that waiting quiet, but given the remoteness of that subterranean room with its painted windows in that anonymous neighborhood it was less like Versailles than St. Helena. I had heard that since the attempt at assassination this Man of the Common Worker had become more difficult to get close to than Farouk in his golden exile; so far everything seemed consistent with the rumor.

After what I would have called an inordinate amount of chalking, the player blew across the top of the cue, and I swear I heard the particles falling to the carpet. They made a faint sizzling noise, like new snow settling on green grass. Then a furnace kicked in somewhere close with a click and a rush, and the throne room atmosphere drifted away on the stench of fuel oil and surburban survival.

Reuther appeared to notice the difference, and something like annoyance rippled under his incipient bulldog features. It came out in his tone. "If your head's cold, Jerry, I can tell May to crank up the thermostat."

Pierpont swept off his Panama. "Sorry, Walter. I forget I have it on, you know?" He looked older without it. His hair, white on the sides and greasy black on top, lay flat on his scalp with alleys of pink skin showing through, and his ears stuck out like car doors. His head, as was the way with men who wore hats most of the time, looked naked and almost obscene. Looking at it I remembered the night I was driving with Agnes on Jefferson when a souped-up Model A coupe pulled alongside and a teenage boy hung his pimply bare ass out the window on the passenger's side. My reaction was the same now as then.

The pool player arranged an almost impossible combination on the table and plunked the eleven-ball in the opposite side pocket without taking more than a second to aim. Then he threaded the stick into the wall rack and came around to our side, scooping the rubber ball off the rail on the way.

"This is Minor?"

"This is him. Didn't I say I'd get him?" Pierpont's voice cracked with pride. It was a high thin pioneer twang of a sort I hadn't heard in a long time; that was dying out with his generation.

Reuther stopped in front of me. He was shorter than I'd expected, although taller than either Pierpont or myself, and slight. Union people especially photographed large. As he looked me up and down he squeezed the ball rhythmically in his right hand. "Who's paying you?"

I turned the question over like the foreign coin it was. "Ford."

"You admit it?"

"I said it."

"You don't look the part. I guess that's the idea." He squeezed the ball once, twice. "Funny, I thought Sonny was more subtle than the old man. Back in thirty-seven it took us months to spot the spies."

The word surprised me so much I laughed in his face. That was a mistake. The skin of his forehead darkened suddenly, the muscles in his jaw stood out like rivets. I thought for a second the rubber ball would explode in his fist.

He held fast. The storm receded. He spoke quietly. "I didn't ask you here to entertain you. How long have you been spying for Ford?"

"Who says I'm a spy?"

Squeeze, squeeze. What had begun as therapy for the shoulder chewed up by the shotgun blast had become a fixation. If the muscles hadn't recovered by now they never would.

He changed his tack. "Do you shoot pool?"

"I tried a few times. I was banned from the billiard room at the Press Club after I tore my third felt."

"It isn't like life. Each ball has its own number and color. You can tell them apart. When I joined labor I thought it was us and them, the suits on one side and the coveralls on the other. One of my best friends on the line at River Rouge gave Harry Bennett a list with my name on it. The only time I ever saw him in a coat and tie was at his funeral."

"Natural causes, I hope."

Squeeze, squeeze. "I learned from the experience. I have people in Personnel at Ford. The files there have you down as a public relations consultant hired by Israel Zed. I find that fetchingly vague. When you don't know what a man's duties are it's hard to tell when he's doing something he shouldn't be. I do have to wonder why a Glass House executive has been spending so much time on the floor at Rouge."

"Glass House?"

"The new building on American has more windows than the rest of Dearborn put together. May I see your hands? No, the other side. I'm not going to rap your knuckles." His eyes flicked over my palms. "What has a man with so few calluses in common with a foundry foreman? Or a quality control worker in the assembly plant? Or any of the other dozen or more people you've been pestering with questions from the docks on the river to the sixteenth hour?"

"If you talked to them you know the questions I've been asking are all about the operation, not about them or their fellow employees. What does a spy care how the doors are hung on a Fairlane?"

"What does a PR man care?" He stopped squeezing the ball. "My sources aren't all employed in factories. You were a newspaper reporter. Reporters are paid to gather information. What's Zed planning to do with the information you've been gathering at Rouge?"

"Zed wouldn't know what to do with it if I gave it to him. I'm gathering it for myself."

"Bullshit."

I let out air. For the first time since Pierpont trotted out the walking artillery at Schaeffer I wasn't afraid for my skin. It's difficult to be nervous in the presence of a man who's more nervous than you or anyone else you ever met. "If you know I was a reporter you know that was twenty years ago. I'm a pitchman. Zed hired me to pitch the E-car. All I knew about cars going in is who to take them to when they stop working. This is homework. Selling the car is the first real chance I've had to make good since I left newspapering. It helps to know what you're selling."

He rolled the ball over in his palm, pushing it with his thumb. Agnes and I had gone to see *The Caine Mutiny* at the Roxy over Christmas and I thought of Bogart's Captain Queeg and his steel ball bearings. "What's your drink? Jerry."

Pierpont scuttled behind a midget bar in the room's gloomiest corner, paneled in knotty pine to match the walls. A light came on above it, striping a row of bottles on the Formica top. He placed his hat on an unoccupied section.

"No alcohol," I said. "I'm on a special diet."

"Diabetic, right?"

I knew a sharp pang of distress. "I didn't know it showed."

"I wouldn't know what to look for if it did. I said I have sources. Club soda, Jerry. Scotch for me, neat." Reuther looked down, saw what he was doing with the ball, colored a little, and put it in his pocket; I guessed he'd seen the same movie. He was wearing loose slacks and penny loafers. In the extra light I saw that his button-down Oxford shirt was pale blue, not white. He made a lot of appearances on television, which banned white for its effect on camera lenses. The gentleman's conservative white shirt shaped up to be the next casualty of the cathode tube.

I wasn't thinking about shirts right then, however. Something in my host's new manner told me I was about to be confided in by the man who ran the most powerful labor union in the most powerful country in the world.

11

"Have you ever been shot, Minor?"

Reuther and I were both holding glasses now. J. W. Pierpont, having switched off the bar light, had returned to his original place, hat in hand. I had already decided the headpiece served the same purpose for him as the rubber ball did for his employer.

I said I hadn't.

"Westerns are bullshit. It doesn't hurt when it happens but once it starts it doesn't let up. The shoulder is one of the worst places you can get shot and live. It fucks up your leverage for months. Even sex is hell. Not that I've a right to bitch. They shot my brother Victor and he lost an eye."

"They got the men that shot you, I heard."

"They got a witness who changed his story more often than Hudson's changes its window. Now the son of a bitch he fingered is suing the union. Anyway he's a stalking horse. I've put Pierpont here on retainer to flush out the real culprits."

I took a sip to cover my smile. I'd never heard anyone use the word *culprits* out loud before. The club soda tasted like boiled water. I never knew what anyone ever saw in it without some kind of nail. "Pierpont's a detective?"

"Best in Detroit." The little man twirled his hat on the end of his fist. "Progressive Investigations, Ink. Three offices on the second floor of the Buhl Building. Eight employees: five investigators, three clerical. I'm heading this one up myself, you know?"

"How long have you been on it?"

"Three weeks."

"Three weeks, and I'm all you've come up with?"

He stuck out his jaw. It was skin over bone with three white whiskers poking out of it. "Not just you. I got leads up the ass."

"He's already come up with more than the police have in seven years," Reuther said. "Do you know the Ballista brothers?"

The question threw me. The FBI had snared Antonio and Carlo along with a dozen others in an investigation of the Detroit-Toledo Black Market during the war. The case fell apart, federal evidence-gathering practices having made no improvements since Dillinger.

"Not personally," I said. "Frankie Orr barely let Tony and Charlie Balls hold his coat when I knew that crowd. They were street soldiers: a hundred to break a leg, five hundred to do great bodily harm less than murder, on up."

"Their rates are steeper now. Do you know what a carpet joint is?"

"A roadhouse with an advertising budget."

"They've got one on Lone Pine Road, the Highwayman's Rest. They run the Oakland County pinball and jukebox concession out of it, but they're still the Ballistas and they keep their hand in whenever a heavy weight needs lifting. On top of the standard scare tactics and bribery, they stay out of prison by being identical twins. On those rare occasions when the police manage to scrape up an eyewitness who will testify against one of them, he goes free because the witness can't tell if it was Tony or Charlie he saw wrapping a pipe around somebody's skull. It's a built-in hedge against incarceration. If they had anything more than the brains God gave a turnip, they'd be running a good deal more than Frankie Orr's errands while he's taking the sun in Sicily. As it is I doubt they can even count high enough to figure their weekly take. They dump the bills out onto a table and divide them in two piles with a baseball bat."

"You think one of them pulled the trigger on you?"

"Not just on me. You're forgetting Victor." His right hand flexed in his pocket. The rubber ball had had its rest. "I'm not interested in the Ballistas, beyond what they can tell me about who picked up the tab on Victor and me. Since that's unlikely, I invited you here."

I took a large swallow of club soda, not that its lack of flavor was growing on me. It was close in that shut-up room with the furnace going and my armpits were beginning to stick. "I don't want to sound like an ungrateful guest, Mr. Reuther. If it weren't for Jerry I'd just be wasting my time having lunch with a pretty girl. I have to ask why me."

"My union colleagues are all agreed my brother and I were targeted by dissenters inside the UAW. Lord knows there are plenty of them; the very existence of a labor union depends upon a healthy population of malcontents. I smell a larger breed of rat. Union crabs didn't pull Dick Frankensteen's coat over his head and throw him down the steps of the Miller Road overpass and me after him. They didn't open fire with a machine gun on unarmed employees at Rouge."

"You think someone at Ford hired Tony and Charlie to take you out?"

He smiled for the first time. It took some of the heat out of the room. "Sonny Ford may not have inherited many of his grandfather's characteristics, but he has one thing the old man didn't have: a publicist working around the clock to keep his face clean. He can endow all the hospitals and orphanages he wants, but he can't change the fact he's a Ford. I think he or someone close to him would find any of my critics in the UAW easier to work with if I were out of the picture."

"Someone like Israel Zed."

"One of several things Zed and I have in common is an infinite capacity to hate. You know Hitler's ovens claimed the European branch of his family."

"I didn't know."

"It's not so unusual when you figure there are at least six million Jews who lost relatives the same way. Zed's special gift is his ability to focus that rage constructively—I should say destructively—and eliminate his opponents. That's another thing we have in common," he added.

"It makes sense. What doesn't is why you're telling me all this."

He took the ball out of his pocket, flipped it back and forth from one hand to the other for a minute. Finally he walked over to the pool table and placed it in the exact spot on the rail where he'd taken it from. Without letting go he scowled down at it while the light from the hanging lamp painted shadows under his jowls. Pierpont cleared his throat restlessly, a crackling sound like dry kindling. When Reuther looked up, his eyes glittered in the shade of the bony mantel of his forehead. "You need information to gather information. I thought you might find it useful."

"I haven't been in the information-gathering business in twenty years."

"It's in the blood," Pierpont put in. "You know? I mean, if you were any good at it to begin with."

Reuther said, "A lot of people think union executives spend all their time looking after the affairs of the rank-and-file. In a way we do, but only indirectly. Most of my working day goes into developing sources of information. The only real power comes from knowing more about the people you're going up against than they know about you. When your opponents can buy and sell you and the box you came in a hundred times over, it means twenty-hour days and no weekends or holidays. Sometimes the point gets lost and you forget you're here for any other reason than to muck around in someone else's shit. I canceled an appointment with a United States senator for this meeting. He's waffling on a labor bill that will enable striking employees to draw unemployment. That's how important it was I talk to you. Please tell me why you're shaking your head."

"I'm no spy. I can't even bluff at poker. It's a Greek thing. Everything I'm thinking shows. Anyway, why should I spook for the UAW? I'm not a member."

"That's what makes you ideal. Russian spies are American. And I think you'll help us out. The Ford Motor Company will survive if the E-car fails, but you won't. A lot of things can happen between the docks at Rouge and the sixteenth hour. The E-car can gum up in a slowdown on the line. The tap screw that secures the universal joint to the steering assembly can come up short one turn. An automobile has fifteen thousand parts and three ways to go wrong for each part. No one man can make a car a hit, but it takes only one to make it fail. All I need is the finger I use to dial the telephone."

Pierpont's voice crackled. "Walter don't play jacks and hopscotch. You know?"

I looked away, at one of the painted windows. I felt the way I had when the doctor at Henry Ford Hospital told me I was diabetic. The way a dog must feel when someone takes a tuck in its leash.

"What do you want to know?"

The atmosphere lifted a little. Reuther selected a stick from the rack and picked up the chalk. "Just keep your ears open for now. Jerry will be in touch."

"If I give you something good, really good," I said, "will you cut me loose?"

"I don't cut people loose." The chalk squeaked. "What would be your definition of good?"

"The name of the man who gave the order."

"Anyone can pronounce a name."

"His name, and the evidence to convict him."

Squeak, squeak. There would always be a substitute for the rubber ball. My memory of Walter Reuther is of a nervous man with his finger on a big trigger.

"Do that," he said finally, "and I'll put Eisenhower behind the wheel of the first car off the line." He sank the three and the seven in one shot. The noise was like an axe splitting hickory.

12

The rain had stopped when Pierpont and I left the house. The sun peered around a corner of the overcast like a beaten serf, drying the mud on the asphalt in crusted patches like dead skin. When the Hudson's motor cut in the detective gave the key another twist to make sure, tearing a grating howl from the starter that made my teeth ache. We started forward with a chirp, scraped the oil pan on the curb on the corner, and came within an inch of a five-year stretch for manslaughter involving a fat woman with a shopping cart in the middle of McNichols. The instructor who gave him his license must have been blind, deaf, and autistic.

"What made Reuther settle on you?" I asked when we were in thick traffic and relatively immobile. "There must be a dozen detective agencies listed in the Yellow Pages before Progressive."

"Fourteen. Only that ain't where he found me. I was with the Pinkertons when the UAW sat down at GM in Flint. Christmas thirty-six it was."

"The Pinkertons were hired as strikebreakers."

"Heads is what we broke mostly. Not that we had no monopoly. Old John L. Lewis laid into me personal with a steam wrench. Eight weeks in St. John's with a tube hooked to my pecker. Listen." He swept off his hat, baring that obscene dome, and rapped his knuckles above his right temple. The sound was like a ballpeen hammer striking a hubcap wrapped in cotton. "My old mother'd be proud. We never could afford sterling when I was a kid. You know?"

"What made you change sides?"

"Pinks cut me loose with a month's severance and no disability. A man's got to eat, you know? Plus I know how that side handles things." He slammed the Panama back on. "I should of figured an outfit that made its money smashing workers all to hell ain't going to look after its own. You might say old John L. done me a favor when he let light into my brain pan."

I glanced back over the seat, toward the two big men watching the scenery slide past. It was certainly the most interesting company I'd been in since I'd left journalism.

"I happened to be looking out the window when your ride dropped you off," Janet Sherman said. "I've been stood up for blondes and redheads, but this is the first time anyone ever threw me over for the man in *American Gothic*."

She was seated at her desk in the office outside Israel Zed's, fingers resting on the keyboard of a battleship-gray Underwood electric whose motor whirred like a tank: Sherman's tank. Her black hair was pinned back and she wore a white silk blouse with a frothy jabot at her throat, business attire, but the short left arm made her dip her shoulder to touch the keys and she looked as if she were posing for a glamor shot. She had on white-framed reading glasses with an Oriental slant that accentuated the exotic tilt of her eyes.

"Has anyone ever told you you look like Nancy Kwan?" I asked.

"Gene Tierney, more often. And you're not off the hook. I waited in the parking lot twenty minutes."

"Would you believe me if I told you I was kidnapped?"

"By who? Pa Kettle at the wheel?"

"You didn't see Gorgeous George and Strangler Lewis in the backseat?"

"If you don't want to be seen with me, please say so. I've heard all the excuses. They try to be polite, but the kindest came from Eddie Grabowski in seventh grade. He said he wasn't good enough to dance with someone whose arms didn't match."

At least you could have ice cream later without going into shock. Aloud I said, "I'm sorry. Something came up and I didn't have a chance to call and cancel. I hope you're giving rain checks."

She sat back, crooking her right arm automatically to de-emphasize the difference. "No, *I'm* sorry. I had an idea we could be friends, but I'm acting like I wanted something more. Do you like baseball? I have a friend who can get tickets to the Tigers' first home game."

"Terrific. I'll buy the hot dogs."

"Are they on your diet?"

"Probably not. But if anyone takes a picture of me eating yogurt at the corner of Michigan and Trumbull I'm through in this town."

She was laughing when I left. A troubled sort of laugh. I hoped we were going to be just friends. I was having enough trouble with Agnes, and all her limbs were the same size as their mates.

In the office, still on Schaeffer, I snapped on the cheap Bakelite radio that came with the furnishings and dialed the *News*. I hated having the radio on when I worked but it was the only way to make a call in privacy in that fishbowl. I asked the unfamiliar voice that answered for Chet Mooney. He had never heard of him, so I got the city desk, where I learned that Mooney had retired the week before. City shunted me over to Personnel, who gave me a number where he could be reached in Florida.

I didn't like Chet Mooney. He had been a *News* crime reporter during the city's most dramatic criminal period, and as far as I knew he had never stepped outside the circle of his desk in the city room, the home he had built on Lake St. Clair with his wife's inherited auto money, and a back table in the Anchor Bar where he bought drinks for more active reporters whose guards fell down after the third Scotch and whose anecdotes crept under Mooney's byline the following day. Having caught on to his method, a trio of scribes from the *Times*, *Free Press*, and *Banner* on one occasion had coached a cub from the Freep to accept Mooney's invitation and feed him an apochryphal story, planning to expose and discredit him when it appeared in the *News*. It had to do with the sanguinary death at the hands of his wife of a city councilman in the arms of a police stenographer in Room 114 of the Book-Cadillac Hotel. The plot backfired when publisher Will Scripps, who happened to have had lunch with the deceased councilman only an hour previously, saw Mooney's account in typesetting and junked it before the edition went to press; Mooney was suspended for a week, but his aw-shucks style had so captured readers who had had enough of truth in their daily diet that a flood of angry letters to the editor persuaded Scripps to reinstate him, assigning him his own opinion column; opinions not being as dependent upon the facts as was hard news. A columnist he had remained, and the city's unofficial voice, commenting avuncularly upon the passing scene with his toe twisting quaintly in the dirt until his retirement. Along the way he had published a couple of memoirs of the *Detroit Is My Beat* variety and gravel-voiced his way through a prepared script on WWJ radio every weekday from 11:00 to 11:05 A.M. for sixteen years. It's a unique feeling to turn on the radio on your way to the unemployment office and hear one of your own experiences read back to you by the man who had appropriated it.

No, I didn't like Chet Mooney; and I didn't want to call him. But he was the only acquaintance left from my newspapering days still in the business—or anyhow still close to it—and in a position to give me what I needed to keep Walter Reuther from hanging an anchor around the neck of my last chance to make something of my lot.

"This is Chet Mooney."

He sounded different from the way I remembered, even as recently as his radio spot. The shanty Irish lilt, laid on so much more thickly in recent years over that hardscrabble voice, like coal sliding down a chute, was almost entirely absent, and the voice itself was hollow and without energy, the tone of a very old man just this side of an oxygen tent. I drew no triumph from this evidence of dissipation. Mooney had been two years behind me at the University of Detroit and was too young to vote for Coolidge.

"Chet, this is Connie Minor. Do you remember me?"

The wheezing noise on his end of the line was either laughter or a tobacco hack or bad wires. "Jesus, Connie, I thought you were dead."

"No, just in advertising. I hear you cleaned out your desk."

"Yeah, well, things never were the same after the war. They cut four inches off my column to save paper and never put 'em back. When that little shit Jimmy Scripps told me I had to rotate with gardening tips from the A.P. I told him to shove it up his ass. So he gave me a gold watch and here I am watching a bunch of fat kikes browning their blubbery butts in Fort Myers."

I'd heard WWJ had employed a team of editors just to scissor the anatomical, scatological, and ethnic references out of Mooney's taped broadcasts. He recorded them at fifteen minutes and they aired for five. "It's a young world. They kicked Churchill out too. I need a favor, Chet."

"I'd like to help you out, Connie. Truth is I'm busted out. What Grace left me barely covered the bungalow. My pension checks come down Old U.S. 12 by broken bicycle."

"I'm not putting the arm on you. Not for money. I need a contact. All mine are dead or in Alcatraz."

"What kind you need?" Talk of contacts had always softened him up. He was like a semi-literate flattered to be asked to lend his one book.

"Someone who can put me in touch with one or both of the Ballistas. I understand neither of them has a phone."

"Telephones can be tapped. Those boys are primitive, not stupid. What's keeping you from just driving out to Oakland County and spending a couple of bucks on beer and the slots?"

"You know it isn't that easy."

The pause on his end was just long enough to tell me he *didn't* know. All his instincts as a journalist were summed up in his monthly bar tab.

"Lionel Banks is the guy you want," he said. "These days he makes Dick Westerkamp look like he knows what he's talking about at Channel Four and feeds things to Dave Garroway in New York. I don't know if giving him my name will do you any good, though. He used to do legwork for me at the *News*, but ever since Tee Vee discovered him he don't know me."

"Maybe he does and that's why he left."

"What?" He had been having another wheezing fit.

"Nothing. Thanks, Chet. I'll forget about that fifty you owe me."

"What fifty?"

"I guess that makes two of us. How's the fishing?"

"How the hell should I know? I get mine at the Swordfish Lounge on Oceanview."

"Some things don't change, do they?" I thanked him again and broke the connection.

The receptionist at Channel 4 had never heard of Lionel Banks, but I asked for Dick Westerkamp's line and the local anchorman's secretary gave me an Ypsilanti number.

"Hello?"

"Lionel Banks?"

"You have him."

It was a Negro drawl, shortened a little by education and, I suspected, some personal effort.

"My name is Connie Minor. I got your name from Chet Mooney. I understand you used to work with him."

"That's not true."

I hesitated. He was stonewalling. I was sorting out a new approach when he said, "Working *with* someone implies you both work. I was so busy tracking down leads and conducting interviews and writing his column for him it took me two years to find out I was the one doing all the work. If you're a friend of his I'm sorry." He stopped long enough to get angry at himself for injecting the note of subservience. "I'm sorry for *you*. He's a user."

"If that's the kind of news you're feeding Westerkamp and Garroway, I wouldn't sign any mortgages if I were you. Every newshawk in Detroit has had Chet's number since the Bank Holiday."

"Who are you?"

I repeated my name.

"Where have I heard of you?"

"If I could read minds I wouldn't be calling you for information. I used to write for the old *Banner*. Maybe you remember my byline."

"Oh sure. My daddy—I used to get up at four and go with my father to help load the papers into his delivery truck. Your column was always on the front page. I can still smell that crappy newsprint and cheap ink. Connie Minor. I thought—"

"No, just in advertising." I told him what I needed.

The line had not cleared entirely of suspicion. "That's a tall order. What's the trade?"

"Just a second." I leaned over, turned up Frankie Laine, and stuck a finger in my open ear to shut out the whoops and whip-cracks of "Mule Train." "I'm with sales and promotion at Ford. We're working up a major campaign. Someone in the press is going to get an early look inside those soaped windows at the dealership. I don't know why it shouldn't be you."

"Make that a promise and I'll see what I can do."

I said a promise was what it was.

"You want to talk to Anthony Battle. We went to school together at Mumford. The Ballistas own his contract."

"Contract?"

"I don't know if you'd call it athletic or theatrical. He'll be at the Olympia tonight at seven-thirty. He's taking on the Beast of Borodino for the World Heavyweight Wrestling Championship."

"Jesus."

"If you prefer ballet, that won't get you next to Tony and Charlie Balls."

"There's a scoop. What can a musclehead tell me I can't hear from Edward R. Murrow?"

"That's up to you. Anthony hasn't lasted as long as he has by sharing everything he hears with just anyone. But he gave me the results of the national Steelhaulers election two hours before anyone else had them. Westerkamp opened with the Albert Brock victory that night."

"What costume should I look for?"

"No costume. He isn't a gimmick man like Crybaby MacArthur or the Peruvian Giant. Anthony just wrestles. That's how you'll know him. He stands out like a pretzel in a bowl of corn flakes." He breathed. "So when does this new wonder car come out?"

"Two years."

Something, probably his hand, smothered his mouthpiece for a moment. Negroes didn't swear in white people's ears if they could help it. "I guess I ought to have asked that up front," he said then. "I'm hoping in two years I won't need the boost."

"Welcome to the club."

I hung up feeling the first honest-to-Christ rush I'd had in twenty years. It was made up of two parts excitement to three parts terror. I was in no kind of shape to trade blows with that class of citizen that makes its point with power tools. On the other hand, I was too old to spend all my time at the office listening at keyholes. If there was one lesson I retained from the dead days, it was if you wanted the straight story you had to go to the source; even if that meant sitting through a tag-team bout featuring Bobo Brazil and Percival E. Pringle.

13

Buildings, it has been said, age much more quickly than humans, and with good reason. Stand any healthy person up in the same spot for twenty-seven years, expose him to a hundred and eight seasons of blasting sun, petrifying cold, grapeshot hail, and the city's daily menu of soot and exhaust, and he will have lost more than a century. The Olympia, gaunt brick barn that it was, had occupied the same lot on Grand River since 1928, hosted thousands of hockey games, labor rallies, political shit-slinging contests, and a couple of wedding receptions, and showed every event in one scar or another. It was built on a foundation of broken molars and the skeletons of at least two bootleggers that I knew of, and the cost overrun on its construction had started one prominent local family fortune that was still trying to redeem itself through endowments and donations to charity. It was an ugly old monument to no architectural style at all, but I found its friendly, dirty face reassuring as I hiked six blocks from the nearest rational parking space toward the greasy light coming through its windows, unwashed since before Black Friday. The side streets were medieval, with dark spaces like missing teeth among the wrecks parked at the curbs. Stadiums are always found in bad neighborhoods. It's a rule of some kind.

A banner slung like a diaper across the front of the building advertised PROFESSIONALS OF WRESTLING— WORLD HEAVYWEIGHT CHAMPIONSHIP in black letters two feet high. The line waiting to purchase tickets had spilled out onto the sidewalk. I ducked down Hooker Street, waited five minutes at that entrance while a ticket-taker argued a woman in her seventies out of her lethal-looking umbrella, and bought a cheap seat in the balcony.

The arena smelled of Milk Duds, new and ancient sweat, cigarette smoke as old as the building, ammonia from the pipes that made the ice the Red Wings skated on during the season, stale urine, bad breath, Old Spice, rotten apples, Evening in Paris, sardines, Juicy Fruit, coffee, blood, sweat socks, mildew, Vicks Vapo-Rub, henna, horseshit, wet chickens, burning rags, skunk collars, scorched hair, dirty wool, mustard plasters, Polish sausages, rubber galoshes, Crackerjacks, muscatel, Band-Aids, hydrogen peroxide, piccalilli, bunion pads, Brilliantine, boiled bedpans, moldy wood, and popcorn farts. When you broke that stench down to its elements you wondered how it managed to worm its way so deep into your bloodstream, bringing you back and back and making you wish you were there whenever someone opened a neglected hamper or a toilet backed up. If they bottled and sold it as cologne, no pair of lovers would ever be separated again, provided neither of them minded risking a hockey puck in the teeth. Love's like that. Everything worthwhile is. It's no wonder newborn babies cry so loud.

The man in the wooden seat next to mine was rushing the season in a Madras shirt and canary yellow slacks with cuffs as wide as a manhole cover. He had a Dutch Masters bolted in the middle of his face, paper band and all, that was in danger of going out as soon as the saliva that had darkened two thirds of its length reached the glowing ash. This he flicked off from time to time without removing the stogie from between his teeth, showering his paunch and lap with gray flakes. One of them, still burning, scorched a hole near the crease of his slacks while I was watching. He had a big waxed-paper cup of beer in one fist and a crumpled program in the other. Neither item interested him as much as what was happening in the arena, about which he appeared to be some kind of expert, judging by the loud and profane advice he was directing to the three men in the ring.

Slanting down from just below the rafters, the double tier of seats described an inverted bottle with the arena in the narrow opening at the bottom. The management had deactivated the refrigeration system and laid a temporary floor on top of the pipes, but there were puddles on the surface where the moisture had seeped through the spaces between the boards, and fresh planks had been placed end to end from the locker-rooms to the ring, forming a bridge to prevent wet feet on the part of the featured attractions.

The ring itself was a hastily built affair, fourteen feet by ten, of blue-painted plywood nailed over what were probably two-by-fours with canvas stretched across the top and professional-looking posts, turnbuckles, and ropes erected above, equipment that likely traveled with the company. At the moment, a Cro-Magnon in fur trunks and bare feet was grappling inside the enclosure formed by the ropes with a slightly less ugly specimen in laced-up boots and a black leotard, with platinum-colored hair to his shoulders; or to where his shoulders would have been if they weren't pressed against the canvas with his head doubled under into his sternum and his legs waving in the air like the feelers of some huge disoriented insect. This position was the artifice of the caveman, who was braced on one knee with his arms curled around the blond's heavy thighs and his face planted firmly in his opponent's crotch. As I watched, the third occupant of the ring, bald and thick-waisted in blue worsted trousers and a red-and-white-striped shirt with short sleeves, knelt with his broad buttocks in the air and his ear to the canvas, placing his face on a level with the blond's, and thumped the springy surface three times with his right palm. The bell clanged and the caveman leapt to his feet, grunting loudly and pounding his chest with both fists. Half the crowd was standing at this point, hooting and throwing balled-up programs and crumpled beer cups at the figure parading around the ring.

". . . in two falls out of three," bellowed the stripe-shirted referee, hoisting the caveman's right arm with one hand, "the Missing Link!"

My neighbor spat out his cigar at last. "Attaboy, Link! Ship the faggot back to Toronto in boxes."

Most of the audience's attention was concentrated on the man in fur shorts, who had shaken off the referee's hand to promenade with his arms aloft, and away from his long-haired conquest. Having slowly uncurled onto his back, the blond turned over with an effort and crawled on hands and

knees to the nearest corner, where he hauled himself upright
with both hands on the ropes. There a rodent-faced man in a
tight black suit with a single Arabic eyebrow across both
eyes—evidently his manager—climbed up to hold the ropes
while he stepped between them. The vanquished wrestler
lowered himself to the floor and, leaning on his manager,
shambled down the aisle between erect, cursing spectators
toward the visitors' locker room. I never saw him again, in
person or on television during broadcast matches, and I assume he quit the business soon after. But I've thought about
him a great deal, usually when I hear somebody dismissing
professional wrestling as pure chicanery. There are no easy
occupations.

"... this corner, weighing in at two hundred and sixty-six
pounds, Ivan Kohloff, the Beast of Borodino!"

The Beast was a ringer for Khrushchev, down to the skinhead and broken nose, which helped to explain his reception.
The audience, on its feet again after a short calm following
the Missing Link's exit, had run out of things to throw, but
its verbal abuse was highly inventive at times, going back
three generations in the Kohloff family in search of four-
legged materfamilia. His choice of tailoring did little to
knock the edge off, from the fuzzy Cossack hat he wore to
his long scarlet coat with gold frogs and, when he removed
it, red trunks decorated with black hammers and sickles. His
black boots laced up to the knees and had glittering steel toes
filed to razor-sharp points.

"... his challenger, for the title of Heavyweight Championship of the World, weighing in at one hundred and ninety-
seven pounds, Detroit's own Anthony Battle!"

The crowd's reaction turned inside out. It struck me, as the
man I had come to see strode along the bridge of planks from
the home locker room, that if Jesus had inspired this level of
widespread adoration, we would have no Easter. Standing
and craning my neck, I could see only the top of his head
among the fans straining forward to shake his hand and pat
him on the back. Even the lump in the seat next to me had
risen in the midst of lighting a fresh cigar to shout something
unintelligible but encouraging in its tone. Detroiters sup-

ported their own as enthusiastically as Americans on the whole denounced Russia and Communism.

I got my first decent look at Battle once he was in the ring and out of his robe. He was well built, solid and chunkily muscled in contrast to the other three wrestlers I had seen that evening, who ran toward plain bulk overlaid with a barely acceptable amount of flab; much of the action during the bouts had to do with the motion of loose flesh some moments after the principal parts of the body had stopped. In street clothes this one wouldn't have attracted much notice except for the coarseness of his features. He had angry eyes and a protruding forehead that would naturally inspire a young man out with his best girl to cross the street when he approached. His skin was medium dark and his hair, cropped close to his skull, was black and tightly curled. It would break any ordinary comb.

The bout, two out of three falls, came in at about forty percent honest wrestling to sixty percent showmanship and shenanigans, nearly all of the latter belonging to the Beast of Borodino. I was Greek enough to appreciate Anthony Battle's grasp of the fundamentals of honest wrestling, and knowledgeable enough from my betting days among the cash-fisting mobs pressing in around the naked grunting brutes at Greco-Roman tournaments in what was now the lounge of the Round Bar Cafe in Hamtramck, to recognize that he would make short work of Kohloff in any genuine match.

As a main event it was anticlimactic, and would have been over much sooner had the bald Russian (if Russian he was; at one point, suffering in the grip of an expert step-over toehold applied by Battle, he cried a distinctly Polish curse) refrained from throwing illegal forearm punches and lunging off the turnbuckles and producing foreign matter from inside his trunks to throw in his adversary's face. Battle, employing tactics that would have passed inspection at the Olympics, pinned the Beast the first time within three minutes of the opening bell and after running the gauntlet of hoary old tricks from the Bad Guys' Manual was well on his way to a second (and final) fall when an exhausted Kohloff disqualified himself by deserting the ring and stalking up and down the aisles reciting Lewis Carroll backward until the clock ran out, voiding the match. In effect it was his bravest act of the evening, because a number of fans had by this time ingested enough watered-down beer to take Battle's job into their own hands. The old lady I'd seen outside, for one, fetched him a blow alongside his shaved cranium with her handbag that should have raised the salary of the ticket-taker who had had the foresight to disarm her of her stiletto-like umbrella. In any case the Beast trundled out of the arena with a purple bruise on his temple and his championship belt still firmly buckled around his waist.

When Battle started out I headed for the balcony exit. The crowd was thick at ground level and by the time I got through it and around a Canadian television crew from Channel 9 and its two tons of camera and cable, security was well entrenched in front of the entrance to the home locker-room.

"Press," I told a beer-bellied guard in a gray uniform with a Sam Browne belt, and tried to push past.

The belly blocked my path. "Let's see your credentials, Dad."

He had icy eyes and a blue chin. I snapped open my wallet, giving him a glimpse of my press card, but before I could flip it shut he grasped my wrist and tore it out of my fingers.

"This expired in January 1934. Any wrestlers you get to see retired under Roosevelt."

"What's the rumpus, Sid?"

The newcomer had twenty years on him, with white sidewalls under his uniform cap and Wyatt Earp handlebars.

"Just a kid trying to duck under the tent, Captain. This one's in his second childhood." He showed him the card.

The older guard read it and squinted at me. His eyes were pale behind the underbrush of his brows. "Connie?"

Warm relief crept up from my bladder. I couldn't place him, but his tone was friendly. I nodded.

"Fred Scheffler. I was a sergeant with the old Prohibition Squad. You and me investigated a couple of dozen blind pigs, I guess."

I remembered. "We were pretty dedicated. Most of the incriminating evidence turned out to be in the bottom of all the bottles. I didn't recognize you behind the whiskers."

"It's okay, Sid." The blue-chinned guard moved a shoulder and edged off. "That crooked son of a bitch Kozlowski busted me out for drinking on the job," Scheffler said. "I figure a penny on every beer I bought wound up in his pocket."

"I ran into a relative of his recently."

"I hope it was in your car. What you doing here? I thought you'd be retired by now."

"That's the nicest thing anyone's said about me in a long time. Usually I'm dead. I'm not with newspapers any more, just doing someone a favor. Trying to get in to see Anthony Battle."

"Shit, why'n't you say so? Follow me."

He shouldered his way through the press of bodies, toward the nearest exit and away from the corridor leading to the locker room. He was a lean old cob with long legs and I had to scramble to avoid losing him in the crowd closing in behind him. We came out into the chill air on Grand River and I followed him around the corner to an unmarked fire door with another guard standing in front of it, who at a signal from Scheffler rapped and spoke to the guard who opened it from inside. Two seconds later we were in the mildewy-smelling locker room.

"Did Battle leave yet?" Scheffler asked the guard inside.

"Which one's he?"

The captain slapped my shoulder. "You're on your own. They generally bug out as quick as they can, to avoid the loonies. If he's in here you'll find him."

"Thanks, Fred."

Left alone, I surveyed my desert island. A mist of steam and shower spray dampened the air, puddles stood on the tile floor teeming with God only knew how many varieties of microscopic life. A number of athletes in sundry stages of undress stood in front of open lockers and sat on the wooden benches pulling on socks and fastening buttons. One, as large as the Fisher Building, with a helmet of tight golden curls and tattoos spread all over his shoulders and upper arms like blue ivy, straddled the aisle leading to the showers in just his jockstrap, curling a rusty eighty-pound dumbbell in one hand; on the upswing both his biceps and his immense penis swelled as if pumped full of air by a bellows. I tore my eyes from his crotch and spotted Anthony Battle emerging stark naked from the shower.

The weightlifter blocked my path. Before I could call out, my quarry had vanished on the other side of the bank of lockers to my left. I hustled that way, banging my shin on a bench. The pain came slowly, like the reverberation of a big bell. I was limping by the time I reached him.

"Mr. Battle?"

He swung open a locker with his surname stenciled on a strip of masking tape on the door and threw his towel in it. When he moved, each of the muscles involved demonstrated its function. I thought of a stamping machine I had seen at Henry Ford Museum, a working exhibit with part of its outer skin cut away to show the various moving parts in action. He was six inches taller than I, with large hands and broad meaty feet. I tried to ignore other parts. There is no greater feeling of exposure than to find oneself fully dressed in a room full of naked members.

"Who are you?" He turned toward me, squaring off. His eyes were as hostile as any I'd seen. Even the juvenile thug's had been dreamy and impersonal all the time he was beating me up.

"My name is Minor. Fred Scheffler got me in here. He's—"

"I know Fred. He a friend of yours?"

I couldn't tell if he thought that was a good thing or not. I leaped. "Yes."

After a second he nodded. "Fred's okay." He turned away and stepped into a pair of white boxer shorts. "You see the bout?"

"Tough break. You out-wrestled the Russki six ways from Tuesday."

"Son of a bitch missed his cue. I was running out of things to do instead of pin him."

"You don't want to be champ?"

"Not my turn. What you want?"

I exhaled. "I need to meet with one of your bosses. I thought you could arrange an introduction."

"What, the World Wrestling Guild? Spend a nickel." He put on a white Oxford shirt with a button-down collar. It had a twenty-two-inch neck.

"No, the Ballistas."

"Don't know them."

"Lionel Banks says they own your contract."

"You know Lionel?"

"Just slightly. He said—"

"Who are you?" He was facing me again.

"I told you, Connie Minor. I'm with Ford."

"Henry Ford the Second?"

"That's the one."

"What, you work on the line?"

"No, I'm an executive."

"You know Henry Ford?"

I was starting to get it. "Pretty well. We have lunch. About the Ballistas."

"Not here." He tucked his shirt inside a pair of Lee jeans. "You hungry?"

"We're ten minutes from Carl's Chop House. I'll drive. We can come back for your car if you have one."

"I got a better place in mind. They don't take reservations and you don't got to rent no jacket and tie."

"Just say where."

"My dump. The food's so good I married the cook."

14

"I wasn't always no wrestler," Battle said. "Oh, I wrestled some at Mumford, that's where I picked up the moves. Coach told me I'd've been All-State if they let me on the mat with white kids. I trained to box. Joe Louis, he my main man. Then I got squashed flat by some kid from Chicago in my first round at Golden Gloves."

The apartment was on Crystal Street, a neighborhood I hadn't visited in twenty-five years. I had followed the wrestler's 1950 Chevy there from the Olympia in the Skyliner. The scabbed-over building he lived in might have been the same one I'd entered the last time. The railroad flat whose kitchen we were sitting in, with all the rooms opening off one another in a straight line like a cattle chute, might have been the same apartment; I'd only been there once, and that time I was carrying fifty thousand dollars in a beat-up suitcase to ransom a gangster, so I hadn't paid close attention to details. The kitchen was comfortably shabby, with chickens on the yellow wallpaper turning brown as it neared the old pump-up gas stove and bare floorboards showing through holes the size of my head in the stained linoleum, and womb-warm in the spring cold. I felt as if I could sit at that rickety wooden table forever, with Ginny Battle's thick beef stew and crumbly cornbread warm in the pit of my stomach and a jelly glass full of her husband's homemade wine in front of me.

Mrs. Battle was no prom queen, thick-set and flat-featured with gray in her coiled hair, but she smiled easily, and after the first awkward moments of shyness and confusion over the unexpected presence of a stranger in her house, had greeted me openly and sat me down at a steaming plate the moment my Mackinaw was off and hanging on the peg. I couldn't tell if all this hospitality came naturally or if she had spent years working to offset her husband's prepossessing appearance and native distrust. Whichever was the case, within minutes I felt more at home than I had anywhere in years.

"It was Mr. Carlo offered me a contract," Battle went on, topping off our glasses from the jug he'd produced from under the sink. "I was carrying a hod then, where the High-wayman's Rest was going in on Lone Pine. Friday nights we had pick-up fights in the gravel pit down the road; it was betting on myself paid back this loan I took out to get me to the Gloves."

He shook his head. What with all the top-offs I'd lost track of how many glasses either of us had drunk, but the movement was wobbly. "Let me tell you, them bricklayers and rough carpenters can't fight for shit. I stepped inside them windmills and chopped 'em up like kindling. Mr. Carlo, he come by one night and seen me. Axed me afterwards if I ever thought about the ring. I told him what happened when I got in with real boxers. He says, 'That's 'cause you got no speed. All you need for the rings I got in mind is strength, and you got plenty of that.'

"Grass Lake was my first match, this little pole barn way out in the middle of a field. I never seen no professional wrestling matches, so I done with the guy what I done in school, step-overs and half-nelsons, pinned him in about six minutes. Crowd didn't know what the fuck I was doing, kept yelling for airplane spins. Mr. Tony—you know Mr. Tony? He Mr. Carlo's brother—Mr. Tony right away wants to dress me up in a leopard skin and stick a spear in my hand, bill me as King of the Zulus. *King Solomon's Mines*, that's his favorite picture. Mr. Carlo he says no, no gimmicks. So here I am, and let me tell you, it beats carrying a hod."

I said, "I hope it pays better."

"We're remodeling the kitchen next month. Already got me one of them two-tone Kelvinators ordered. Take a hinge at the fambly room."

I'd been careful with the wine because of my blood sugar, but it whacked me in the forehead with a baseball bat when I got up and I had to grip the back of my chair until the vertigo cleared. The next room was paneled in tan plastic with a wood grain printed on it. The carpet was wall-to-wall gold shag and there was more of that floating furniture that had begun to take over American living rooms, a table lamp with a revolving shade that simulated a forest fire when it was switched on, and a Philco television set with an exposed picture tube sticking up from the chassis like a one-eyed beast rising from a swamp in something starring John Agar. I gripped the door frame against another dizzy spell.

"Straight out of *House and Garden*," said Battle, standing behind me. "This here's just the start. Gonna rip that chicken shit off the kitchen walls and paint it Harvest Yellow. Formica everywhere. I growed up in a place with a kitchen just like we got now, but *he* sure as hell ain't. What you doing up, Champ?"

The newcomer was a boy, very dark, who had wandered in from the next room down digging a fist in one eye. He had on blue pajamas with feet and a red Superman insignia on the chest. He was about two years old.

"Charlie, you bad child." Ginny Battle pushed past us and picked him up, putting him over her shoulder.

"I heard Unkie."

The wrestler strode forward and rubbed the boy's head, a little too hard. Charlie's face screwed up. "There, there, Champ. Joe Louis he don't cry. My brother's kid," he said to me as Ginny carried the wailing child out of the room. "He in jail and nobody done know where the mother is."

"Good-looking kid. Can we go back into the kitchen?"

I began to feel stable again as soon as the family room was behind me. I hoped he wouldn't invite me back when the kitchen had been done over; the place didn't have a fire escape. But seeing him smile when his nephew had toddled into the room had been worth a little spinning. It had been like a sudden bloom in the desert.

The smile was gone by the time we were seated again at the table. "No job never meant nothing to me, not even this one, till that boy come along. That's how come I'm talking to you."

"I was under the impression I came here to talk to you."

"How bad you want to see Mr. Tony and Mr. Carlo?" He lifted the jug.

I put my palm over my glass. I had put in two years' penal servitude at the Detroit *Times*, running steadily more dotty errands for William Randolph Hearst, for agreeing to something with a full glass in front of me.

"I'm just doing someone a favor," I said. "It's not even part of my job. I've eaten your wife's cornbread and I've grinned at your brother's son, but if the cops nabbed me for driving under the influence of your homemade burgundy tonight I wouldn't be able to get my*self* out of jail, let alone that boy's father."

"Marcus got ninety-nine years in Jackson for slitting a man's throat for writing down the wrong number when he took his dollar. It weren't the first man he kilt and if all it took to spring him was I raise one finger I go straight to Mr. Carlo's tailor and axe him to sew 'em all together tight. It ain't him I want out. It's me. You know Stuart Leadbeater?"

I felt dizzy again. So many names had been buzzing through my head lately I was about to give up swatting them. It must have shown on my face, because Battle went on without waiting for an answer.

"He a lawyer with the city. I don't know what he does there, but he had something on with that crime committee that come through here a few years back. I guess that's how come he knows so much about Mr. Tony and Mr. Carlo and the people that works for them. Anyway he's running for county prosecutor or somesuch."

I nodded. I recognized the name now vaguely.

"He come here to my home last month. All dressed up he was, and polite. Brung a stuffed turtle for little Charlie. Said he knows me through Mr. Carlo, which could be, I seen men dressed up like him come and go back of the Highwayman's. I axe him to sit down and drink some of my wine, but he says no thanks, he just come to axe me a question. I say, what question? He says does I think a Communist should have the right to raise a child in the U.S. of A.? I say no sir, I doesn't. He says then what does I think I'm doing raising my nephew?"

"You're a Communist?"

"That's what I say. I say, I'm a Communist? He says according to the policy of the House, uh . . . "

"The House Un-American Activities Committee?" It was the first time I'd pronounced the phrase without smiling. The first time I'd heard it I'd wondered out loud if there were a corresponding Un-Russian Activities Committee in the USSR.

"Yeah, them. He says according to their policy, any citizen aware of treasonous activity who fails to report that activity to the proper authorities is himself guilty of treason." He closed his eyes as he picked through the thicket of words; a boy reciting the state capitals by rote.

"What treasonous activity?"

"That's what I say. I say, what treasonous activity? That's when I find out the World Wrestling Guild is under congressional investigation as a suspected front for the American Communist Party." It was a larger crop of syllables than he was accustomed to harvesting and it had him sweating worse than the bout he had fought that evening.

"What good are professional wrestlers to the Communists?"

"I didn't think to axe that one, but he tells me anyway. Mr. Stuart Leadbeater, he likes to talk. You know when wrestlers get on the TV and start calling each other names, saying how they's fixing to tie each other in knots and things at the Olympia Saturday night at seven-thirty? Mr. Stuart Leadbeater he says they're talking in code."

"Code."

"You know, like Orphan Annie on the radio, relaying military information and such. That's when they ain't corrupting the folks watching at home, feeding them all that pinko shit instead of just telling 'em when and where Dick da Bruiser's fixing to twist off Haystack Calhoun's head and stuff it up his ass."

"He thinks that?"

"Shit, who know what a lawyer's thinking? All's I know is if I don't start paying attention to who's running down the U.S. of A. in the locker-room and taking down their names and giving 'em to Mr. Stuart Leadbeater he going to put *my* name on a list and give it to the newspapers and TV. Little Charlie, he can't read but he likes to look at pictures in the paper. One day he turns a page and sees mine with a hammer and sickle next to it."

"Stop worrying about it. The press isn't any better now than it was when I left it, but they're not stupid enough to mouthpiece some city shyster with his name on a ballot."

"That's what you say. I tell Mr. Carlo about it, he puts his arm around my shoulders and says if it looks like that's going to happen he's going to have to let me go on account of the way it would look."

I shook my head, slowly to keep down the sloshing. "A gangster with public relations worries. I never thought I'd live that long."

"I don't know what them are. Mr. Carlo he says commies means feds and he don't want no trouble with feds. Feds got Frankie Orr kicked out of the country. Handle it, he says. I don't care how, just handle it. I can't fight no lawyer, mister. I didn't even finish high school." The hostility was gone from his eyes. Now they belonged to a diseased bull that had no concept of what was happening to it.

"I finished college and I can't fight a lawyer any better than you. I'm no fixer."

"You're tight with Henry Ford the Second. That's what you said. Whose town is this here if it ain't Henry Ford the Second's?"

"I was putting on some at Olympia," I said. "I was invited to lunch with him once. I didn't even eat. For that matter, neither did he. I'm just one more Indian in a great big tribe. If I asked him to fix a lawyer for a professional wrestler I know he wouldn't even bother to laugh me out of his office. He'd just push a button and someone else would come in and do it for him. I'm sorry, Battle. I want to talk to your bosses, but not bad enough to promise something I can't even dream of delivering."

He said nothing. There was nothing on his face; not hurt, not anger. A child should have that much empty space to draw pictures on.

"If it means anything, I think Leadbeater is all blow. Wrestling is big right now and he's looking for a little reflected light. Chances are he's made the same pitch to every wrestler on the circuit. If you don't tumble he'll just draw a line through your name and go on to the next."

"You believe that?"

I thought about it. I shook my head again and to hell with the liquid splashing around inside. "No. When they get that political germ they're like bull terriers. They aren't trained to let go to begin with."

He nodded then, and went on nodding as if he'd forgotten to stop. He wasn't the lug he let on. If they gave out diplomas for knowing about men and evil there would be sheepskin all over the streets of Blacktown. "What you want with Mr. Tony and Mr. Carlo?"

"The same thing Stuart Leadbeater wanted with you. I just want to ask them one question."

There was a long silence. Finally he said, "I don't guess I get to hear it."

"It won't mean anything to anyone who doesn't have the answer I want."

"You got a number I can call?"

I fished a Ford Motor Company business card out of my wallet and wrote my home number on the back of it. "Anytime after six." I held it out. When he didn't take it I laid it on a dry spot on the table. I was standing now, but he wasn't looking up at me. He wasn't looking at anything there in the room.

"I call you," he said. "It might be a while. I don't talk to them that often."

"You heard me when I said I can't help you."

"Maybe I had to talk about it. Maybe that's worth more than shit."

"Maybe not."

He stopped nodding.

"I'll make some calls," I said. "I used to know some people. It probably won't come to anything, but the more people know what Leadbeater's up to, the better that might be for you."

He didn't say thanks. I was glad for that. I thanked him for the meal and asked him to say good-bye to Mrs. Battle and took my Mackinaw off the peg. The hallway outside the apartment smelled of old meals and human waste. The eternal cycle.

15

The saying went that you could set your seasonal calendar
by the changes in Michigan's climate. When the wind lashed
your face like a willow branch when you turned a corner, it
was the first of March. When you awoke in a puddle of
grease with your eyes gummed shut, July had come.
Snowflakes the size of silver dollars outside the window
meant you had three weeks' shopping before Christmas. And
when the sopping fog that drifted north from the marshland
bordering the Ford River Rouge plant burned off before you
left the house, it was time to take your straw hat and striped
blazer out of storage. On just such a morning, I rode an upholstered elevator with a chrome steel frame from the echo-
ing ground floor of the Ford Administration Center to the
twelfth floor. My companions, if you're the kind that bothers
to note details, were Israel Zed, Henry Ford II, and four of
the gray-suited young men who had helped exhume the company that had put the world on wheels from the La Brea
Tarpits of its founder's own making.

The elevator sighed to a stop without the aid of an operator—I knew instinctively that I would miss that fixed barometer and the early warning it provided of the changes in
corporate pressure that awaited the end of the ride—the
doors glissed open, and we stepped out into a space the size
of an airport waiting room, whose carpeted floor, cork-lined
walls, and acoustical ceiling sponged up all sound. Crossing
toward the central desk was like walking in a dream, an eerie
sensation that had me listening for the noise of my own
breathing, which lately I noticed had become labored, as if
I'd climbed all twelve flights. The armed guards who rose

from behind the desk at Ford's entrance were an imposing trio, but they were subtly dwarfed by the full-length portraits that covered one wall, slightly larger than life, with the Deuce placed strategically between his father and grandfather. The presence of that Trinity did more than anything to cloak the reception area in the atmosphere of a cathedral. Without having seen the rest of the place I knew there would be no barging into offices without knocking or friendly settling of office differences around the water coolers. If there were water coolers; more and more executive offices were being equipped with their own bathrooms, eliminating both the need to go out into the hall and the opportunity for human contact outside the confines of a formal meeting. A good deal more than just half a century separated those antiseptic surroundings from the sun-flooded little office where Crazy Henry had bellowed instructions to his foremen over the din of production going on outside his open door.

The tour began with Mr. Ford's office, a room nearly as large as the reception area, with oak paneling already plastered over with framed community service certificates, the requisite photographs of Henry, Edsel, and Henry II, and a sepia-toned print in an old-fashioned frame of the 1908 Model T, its stout little body resting on spindly wheels with axles no bigger around than a woman's wrist. The floor was cloaked in tweed and the entire back wall, behind a modern sweeping walnut desk with a bare top, was glass, dazzlingly spotless. Any time he wanted to, the Chief could rotate his high-backed, squishy leather chair and gaze out at the great sprawling factory complex and the scant few blocks that lay between him and the little one-story brick building where empire had sprouted like a healthy houseplant continually in need of re-potting. I wondered if he would ever bother. A button under the desktop conjured a bar from behind a hydraulically operated panel stocked with bottles and cut-glass decanters labeled Scotch, Bourbon, Gin, and Rye—a feature that would have prostrated the abstemious first Henry in an apoplectic seizure.

From there we went to the place where Robert McNamara, Whiz Kid extraordinaire and Ford's new president, would direct the company's fortunes, a room slightly less big with brushed-aluminum panels on the walls but the same Cinerama view of Dearborn and beyond; former G-man Jack Bugas' intelligence headquarters, home of the eye that never slept and the heart of the central nervous system whose slightest tremor at the farthest extent of its reach would instantly be noted by the brain behind that beveled face and jiblike nose; Israel Zed's chamber, smaller yet but larger still than most apartments, a rabbinical cell complete with a prayer shawl folded atop a junior conference table, a mezuzah mounted over the door, and an inestimably ancient menorah, silver-encrusted and trembling on the rim of bad taste, its nine half-burned candles having dripped elaborately into its lips and whorls, standing on a credenza in front of the window. It was an odd thing to encounter this far past Hannukah, tantamount to finding a sprig of mistletoe still in place in May. The room already smelled pungently of incense, melted wax, and the rapid decay of books bound in tattered black fabric and bearing titles in Hebrew on their spines, crammed pitilessly into built-in shelves intended for style manuals and industry awards. Ford's gray eminence wore his Judaism like no one since Moses.

My office was last and smallest, but I had a window and a plant, items which I had been made to understand were conferred upon rising executives piecemeal, as designated symbols of rank. The desk was kidney-shaped, not my favorite configuration in youth, still less given the current status of my internal organs, but spacious, and I had a miniature bar that didn't travel and a wall safe behind a framed print of the original architect's conception of the Center, done in the same anemic pastels that illustrated girlie magazines. Compared to the others the office was a cloakroom, but I had shared one half that size with a political cartoonist in the Parker Block during the *Banner*'s salad days. The walk to the nearest bar hadn't been much longer then, and it had involved three flights of stairs and downtown traffic. Life's like that. If I had ever smoked, I would have quit the day before R. J. Reynolds decided to distribute cigarettes free of charge.

When the brass finished its duty call and retired, Zed stayed behind. Placing a finger to his lips like Major Hoople sneaking home past curfew, he closed and locked the door to the hall and spun the dial on the safe.

"There's a doohickey on the inside of the door where you can compose any combination you want," he said. "I suggest you do so soon if you believe a safe should be safe. Right now all the ones on this floor are set at 9-21-45. An important date."

"V-E Day?" I had always been fuzzy on details of history I had lived through.

"A footnote. I refer to the day the old man resigned and Hank took over the company. They say John Bugas and Harry Bennett actually pulled pistols on each other that day. Pistols!"

He reached inside the safe with both hands and brought out a plain wooden case with a hinged lid, slightly longer than a cigar box and several inches deeper. This he carried over to the desk, where he set it down and lifted the lid with all the ostentatious care of a jeweler exhibiting his merchandise. I was sitting behind the desk and found myself leaning forward as he placed his hands inside and brought them out slowly, as if the thing between them were made of venerable parchment, in danger of disintegrating if exposed too quickly to oxygen.

The finish was sapphire blue, flawless and shining, trimmed in glittering chrome with real glass in the windows. It smelled of fresh paint and new rubber, and when I held it in my hands it felt as heavy as a brick of gold. The door on the driver's side opened at a touch of the handle. Inside, the seats were covered with real upholstery, the dashboard complete down to the clock. I nudged the steering wheel with a finger. The front wheels turned. The miniature license plates on front and back read EDSEL.

"We're going with that name, huh?"

"Hank knew that from the beginning or he wouldn't have let Jack Reith call it the E-car. What do you think? I tell you, any kid would trade all his best marbles for a toy like this. It's entirely to scale. You could buy last year's Cadillac for what it cost to build this model."

The horse-collar grille nudged the front license plate to the side. "I wish we could do something about the front. It looks lopsided."

"Forget the fucking grille." It was the first time he had sworn in my presence. He had on a midnight blue three-piece with a steelpoint stripe, a gray silk tie, and the inevitable black skullcap. His tone too was impeccable. Zed was a man to judge solely by the words he chose. In this he was alone in all my experience. "A good design is one that belongs to a good car. Tell me what you think of it overall."

"I was going to say the grille was growing on me. The lines are nice. Which one's this, the Corsair?"

"Citation. Top of the line. We're using the Mercury body and guts on that and the Corsair, straight Ford for the Pacer and Ranger. Eighteen models. That's more than we've ever issued for any one car. That alone would have killed the old man. At the end he was sending out memos announcing his intention to return to a one-car company, and effectively bring back the Model T." He shook his head. "The model doesn't leave this room, of course. Let GM's spies work for their pay. What's your strategy?"

I turned it over and rolled the wheels with my palm. The driveshaft turned. "Secrecy."

"That's policy, not strategy. I'm talking about advertising."

"So am I. Why spend a fortune on TV and newspaper ads when the press is perfectly willing to promote us for free?"

He hauled up a chair covered in burgundy Naugahyde and sat down, crossing his arms on the desk, the holy man preparing to hear the plea of a supplicant.

"You know as well as I all this cloak-and-dagger crap is hype," I said, holding up a hand when he opened his mouth to respond. "Oh, there's plenty of need for secrecy in the design stages, when an idea can be swiped and rushed into production at GM or Chrysler or Studebaker, but all these car covers on the haulaways and soaped windows at the dealerships are just to make people curious. By the time a new model's on the floor there's no way anyone can push it through the line and out onto the lots in time to steal a march on anyone. All we're doing is building anticipation."

"That's just good business."

"It's a start, but we haven't been doing enough with it. Why not let Joe Nine-to-Five in on our wall safes and guards and blood oaths to silence? Why not take a picture of a carrier loaded with mysterious lumps under canvas pulling out at first light, bound for an authorized Ford dealership near you? Crank them up tight enough wondering what we've got that nobody else has and when we finally unlock those doors they'll spill in like clowns piling out of a midget car at the circus."

"Do you really believe that?"

"Of course not. I'm a pitchman. You can't credit anything I say."

He laughed boomingly, showing perfect molars without a filling in sight. "You've just shown you can obey the first rule of PR: Never fall for your own publicity. Seriously, what can you put on the table? Mr. Ford's beginning to ask questions." His eyes were like pewter despite the laugh lines still in evidence.

"It's plenty rough." I handed him a typewritten sheet I'd folded and put in my inside jacket pocket just that morning. Another thing I'd learned from the ad game was when to have something ready to spring. I'd worked it over enough to memorize the lines and played them back in my head as he read them:

> *Early this week, a group of automotive carriers cleared the yards of____ giant U.S. plants and rolled out into the night.*

"Night?" He looked up.

"Love affairs don't start at high noon."

"I could disprove that statement, but I promised FDR I'd never engage in Washington gossip." He returned his attention to the sheet.

> *. . . into the night.*
> *Balling the jack. Because their steel racks held something they had never held before.*

Maybe you'll see some of these carriers loaded with covered cars on your roads in the next few days.

If you do, you might call to mind what one of their drivers said before he started out. The driver lifted the cover on one of the Edsels in his load and looked it over very carefully. And what he said, plainly and forcibly, was:

"Man, would I like to have one of these."

He let the page refold itself and placed it on the desk. "I won't ask which driver said that, since the only working model is parked there on your blotter. Kind of getting ahead of yourself, aren't you? They won't come out until September of next year."

"Margaret Mitchell wrote the last chapter of *Gone With the Wind* first. I just wanted to show you the direction I'd like to go. I'm thinking of running blank pages in all the magazines worth reading, to start. You know, Watch This Space."

"Been done."

"Show me something in advertising that hasn't. I'm betting when they get around to translating those ten-thousand-year-old pictographs in that cave in New Mexico it comes out 'Look sharp, feel sharp, be sharp.' Anyway, we're not out to shock America. Leave that to this punk Elvis. We just want to give it something to look forward to before Christmas sneaks up on it like the Red Menace."

"Just barely. Your peers in the retail stores hang their wreaths on Thanksgiving now. It's risky, Connie. Suppose you get them all pumped up and then they don't like the car?"

"That part's up to the boys in design. My job is the pumping."

"What *you* think. When Hank crawls this far out on a limb he likes company. It's six plants, by the way. We're bringing in Ypsilanti and Rawsonville." He rose. "I'll take it to him."

"What do *you* think?"

"I like what you've told me. If Mr. Ford doesn't, you didn't hear it here."

"No room for you on that limb, huh."

"Tom Dewey tried to talk me into running for office. Not with him, naturally; there isn't a hook for a yarmulke in the vice president's quarters. He even offered to stump for me. I guess he thought it would help him in New York, where they had enough of him after he got rid of Lucky Luciano. I turned him down. I only gamble with the other guy's money."

"Wise," I said. "Considering the results."

He tugged down the points of his vest. "It's a sound campaign. Simple enough to be brilliant. I never expected less. You ought to stick to advertising and tell Walter Reuther to look somewhere else for his spies. That's what I do." He left me alone with my sharp new pencils.

16

Janet Sherman and I drove to the Tigers' home opener in her Lincoln. I'd had enough of the Skyliner, turned it in, and been told I was third in line for a Mercury Montclair. I'd requested a white-over-red hardtop whose picture in the brochure had reminded me of strawberries and whipped cream. What I could no longer eat I was determined to drive. Janet wore a Tigers cap with her hair in a ponytail, a gray sweatshirt, and red torreadors with high-heeled sandals. Her toenails were painted to match the pants, a gesture toward fashion that made me feel a little less uncomfortable about my navy blazer and white ducks. My generation dressed up for ball games; hers would meet the Queen in pedal pushers. Climbing the stairs behind her to our seats in right field I could see the play of muscles in her thighs.

I craned to see past the green-painted girder in front of me. "The friend who got you these tickets must be in tight with Bucky Harris. Is that Ray Boone on deck or a Dixie cup?"

"I didn't say they were good seats. Anyway, all you're paying for is the hot dogs. If you're planning on being a pain I'll eat a dozen."

"I'm not. Any place you sit at Briggs is a good seat."

It was, too. Everybody seemed to be batting southpaw that day. Harvey Kuenn and the kid, Kaline, both pounded fouls, one of which I lunged for and might have had a chance at if someone invisible hadn't stuck an icepick behind my left shoulder that took the starch out of my joints.

"Are you all right?" Janet watched me mopping my face and neck with my handkerchief.

"Hell no, I'm not all right. I'm fifty-five."

"Fifty-six." She shrugged when I looked at her. "You left the card lying on your desk when I brought you those network rate sheets. That Agnes person has quite a sense of humor, hasn't she?"

It had been one of those jokey over-the-hill birthday cards that pleased me about as well as the stuff that came up from my throat when I rose in the morning. "She's a riot. She laughs so hard at air raids she gives herself a bellyache."

"I guess you care a lot for her."

"We worked together at Slauson and Nichols. Sometimes we see a movie. She doesn't care a lot for Clifton Webb."

"I love Clifton Webb. Did you see *Woman's World*?"

I looked again. I didn't know her well enough to know if she was serious. "You liked it?"

"Well, the executive-intrigue stuff was kind of clumsy. It's more subtle than that and a whole lot more cutthroat. But if I wanted to see real life I'd never leave the office. I went to see Clifton Webb. He was great in *The Dark Corner*. He pushed William Bendix out a window without even knocking off his homburg."

"I thought girls your age liked Marlon Brando."

"Too much mumbling and scratching. I'll choose a nice head of gray hair over a motorcycle jacket any time."

"Provided it wears a homburg." I'd stopped wearing hats because they squashed my face down.

"Lauren Bacall was nicely naughty in *Woman's World*. Is Agnes like that?"

"In some ways. She can be sweet. Anyway we're just friends."

"The Dixie cup's coming to bat."

We stayed to the end and trickled out with the small percentage of spectators who hadn't left before the lopsided home victory. The pain in my shoulder had subsided to an excruciating throb.

"I can't understand people who pay good money for tickets and then won't see a game through," she said.

"You may when we're trying to get out of the parking lot."

"There's no hurry. The Shamrock's close. Do you know it?"

"I'm surprised you do. I used to watch Big Jim Dolan swap mayors for governors from his corner booth—well, a long time ago," I finished shamblingly.

"Before I was born, you were going to say. Does your age bother you?"

"Only every time I get out of a chair or go to the bathroom or think."

"You aren't as old as you seem to want to act. My father's two years older than you and he plays tennis every Saturday."

"I can't breathe fast enough for tennis."

As we came out of the shade of the stands into the bronze late-afternoon light, she curled her good arm inside mine. It didn't mean a damn thing. Women had been doing that since Eve, and Adam was the last man who could be sure she wasn't going home with someone else. Yet I felt a faint stirring in my white ducks that made me forget about my shoulder. That was where the Stegosaurus had it all over the modern American human male; he had a brain below his waist as well as above. Young women who are out to seduce fossils don't begin by telling them they're two years younger than their fathers.

The Shamrock, eternally twilit by the reflected glow off red oak and hand-rubbed brass, was murky with smoke and smelled bitterly of beer and boiled cabbage and phantoms in derbies with gold toothpicks on their watch chains. It was already filled with gamegoers, but Janet spotted a table being vacated, squealed, and disengaged herself from my arm to claim it, caroming off hips and elbows and spilling an ounce of somebody's highball on the way. I trailed her, muttering apologies.

"You take chances." I sat down.

She was already sitting. "I can afford to. I'm told I'm cute."

"I'm told I'm not. I have a punchable face."

"I'm sorry. I forgot." A concerned look claimed her features. When I was released from Henry Ford Hospital I'd found a comic get-well card awaiting me at home with Janet's signature. "That must have been horrible. Did you decide to press charges?"

"I might have, when I was younger and time was cheap. I don't care to take a day off work to let some defense attorney take a crack at me on the witness stand. Anyway, they're juveniles. Even if they got the maximum, which never happens, they'd come out with the same pimples they took in."

"What makes them do it? Rock 'n' roll?"

"Don't mock me, child. My old man said we wouldn't have gangsters if we didn't have the Charleston. A punk's a punk in black leather or a silk suit."

"That sounds like you read it somewhere."

"Wrote it." I tapped my forehead. "In here. It's too long for a dummy sheet."

"I've known a few advertising men, none of them outside the office. I never heard any of them talk about the job the way you do. They were all so . . . " She moved her shoulders, smiling at her inadequacy.

I grinned back. " 'Let's run it up the flagpole and see who salutes'?"

"Did anyone ever actually say that?"

"Someone must have. No business can go a hundred years without one original thought. Go on."

"That's pretty much it. I always had the impression they'd rather sell cigarettes than be President."

"There's a difference?"

She flicked it aside. "How can you be any good at something you have so much contempt for?"

"I don't know if I'm any good at it."

"Mr. Zed says you're a genius."

"Mr. Zed voted for Tom Dewey. I don't know if I'm any good. Fortunately, neither does anyone else." I looked around. "Are you hungry or thirsty or both? It doesn't look like we're going to be waited on before 1960."

She said a vodka tonic would be welcome. I shouldered up to the bar and returned with her preference and a glass of mineral water and bitters for me, with a lemon twist to make it last. I hate lemons.

"Do you really want to hear this rubbish?" I asked. "I'd rather discuss the Tigers' pennant chances."

"The season's young. I'm trying to learn."

"Don't bother taking notes. By the time the numbers come

in on an ad campaign, so many others have come and gone nobody remembers who came up with it except the guy who did, and he's only going to mention it if the numbers are good. If the button-counters ever got around to assigning averages the way they do in baseball, half the fifty-grand-a-year account executives in this country would be on relief."

"Not much incentive."

"Less than none. The vocabulary we draw from contains just forty words. Twenty of them have only four letters and ten of those are 'free.' All the possible combinations were used before the invention of the portable can opener—which by the way is the last absolutely essential item our civilization has produced. Now, there's a campaign I'd have been proud to have participated in. All we've done since is chew our cud."

"Wow."

I held up a finger. "That's one of the words." I sipped from my glass, made a face at the lemon.

She noticed. "Do you miss drinking?"

"Never developed a taste for alcohol. When I was with newspapers it was a diplomatic tool. All the work got done in blind pigs. The most successful reporter I ever knew never left his table at the Anchor Bar."

"Somehow I don't think you could be that kind of reporter."

"I couldn't find the rush in a glass. That was my undoing. My kind of newshawk went out with running boards." I stirred my swizzle. "Bold talk for an old coward."

"Why do you say that?"

Because the only time I ever saw a man murdered I wet my pants. "No reason. It's the mineral water talking. Do you miss Toledo?"

"I miss my parents. I see them every Christmas, though. In a way that's harder than not seeing them at all. I notice how much they've aged from one year to the next. Oh." She put her glass to her lips instead of a hand.

I grinned again to show her I knew how old I was. Give or take a year.

She rotated her glass, making hula hoops with the rings. "What you said about nobody knowing who dreamed up a campaign when the sales figures come in," she said. "It isn't going to be that way this time, is it? I mean, everything's sort of vested in you."

"Your boss is no fool. Our boss. He took the heat when Truman beat his boy, but he's not going to make that mistake in the private sector. He's found a goat."

"Doesn't that scare you?"

"Everything scares me, Janet. Sitting in a wheelchair with my wrists tied to the arms in a state nursing home scares the living hell out of me. Boys one-quarter my age in sideburns and girls with their shirttails out make me cross the street when they come my way. I'm scared of dogs. Not the big ones with deep barks, the little yappy ones that rip at your ankles when you turn your back on them. Failing doesn't scare me the way those things do. I've done it before. I'm good at it."

When she laughed I could see the shallow dents in her incisors where the braces had been removed. "That's quite a pep talk. Do you believe any of it?"

"Enough of it." I emptied my lungs. "Well, it's a great car. The ecomony's booming. It should sell itself with no help from me. I'd be an idiot not to claim credit."

"You're no coward. Courage isn't being unafraid, it's being afraid and going ahead and doing it anyway. Like when I left home. *That* took guts."

"How's it working out?"

"I don't plan to be a secretary my whole life, if that answers your question." She took in a healthy dose of vodka and set the glass down with a bang that turned heads from the packed tables nearby. "You're looking at the future first female division chief in the history of the American automobile industry. Think I stand a chance in hell?"

"You're asking the wrong person. I'm the one who said no woman would last two weeks in an aircraft plant. I thought they'd get their bracelets caught in the punch presses."

"What do you think now?"

We were no longer the object of others' attention. The bartender, a porky butch-cut towhead in a green velvet vest and leatherette bow tie, stood on tiptoe behind the bar, smashing the flat of his hand against the brown Bakelite cabinet of a

Tele King TV set on its high shelf. Wyatt Earp refused to stop doing backflips on the big seventeen-inch screen; the pounding only made him speed up.

"Unless the United States of America declares war on Chrysler," I told Janet, "you've got as much chance at an office with a window and a plant as Duffy there has of getting that picture to look as good as it did in the store."

Her face went smooth.

"Well," she said, "you're honest."

I nodded. "It's a fault."

She covered the hand I had resting on the table with the one on the end of her short arm. It was as soft and pink as a baby's and seemed to have as much strength. The pressure she applied almost wasn't there.

"You're no coward," she repeated.

I had moved from my apartment in the city to a rented house on Puritan Street in Highland Park, a woodsy community hemmed in by Detroit on all four sides like a snag in the current. In younger days, given the brighter turn in my personal finances, I might have popped for something in brick with a trellis in St. Clair Shores, but one thing I had learned about any kind of upswing was that gravity is older and more patient, and real estate is tougher to get rid of than warts when you need cash. It was a comfortable thousand square feet stacked into two stories under a high-peaked roof like the houses Henry the First used to throw up for his employees in Dearborn, and about that old. I had a strip of grass and a flowerbed next to the front stoop with some kind of tough streetwise blossoms poking through the tangled greenery. I shared the driveway with the house next door and the sky was my garage.

Janet pulled into the curb and braked. "Nice place."

"It was the stairs that sold me," I said. "I like to hear my joints in the morning. Thanks for the ride." I pressed down the door handle. "Thanks for a lot of things."

"How are you getting to work tomorrow?"

"There's a DSR stop on the corner."

"I could pick you up."

"It's out of your way."

"I could start from here."

I read her face. She would have to work on that if she planned to become an executive. "You don't want the complication," I said. "Believe me."

"I liked you from the start, Connie. You're one of the few men I've met who haven't told me they were sorry about my arm."

"That's not a reason."

"It's on the list."

"Everybody's got something. I've got a sugar problem and fallen arches to start."

"It's Agnes, isn't it?"

"It's Agnes," I said. "And it isn't Agnes. We're contemporaries. We don't have to fill each other in before we fight. I've got Al Jolson in my record collection, for Christ's sake. I thought James Dean was the head of a college somewhere until somebody set me straight. You and I would just waste six months finding out what we already know: It won't work. You're young enough to squander that much time on a lot of young men who won't be good for you. My time isn't more valuable; I just don't have as much to risk."

She smiled. It was the saddest thing I'd seen that day, and I'd watched three men half my age who made twice as much as I miss pop flies I could have caught with my arms full of groceries. "You know what you sound like? You sound like a man working overtime trying to talk himself out of something."

"You know what? You're right." I leaned over, gripped her shoulders hard, and kissed her. Her lipstick tasted like strawberries. "I'm not so old I've forgotten what I'm passing up." I got out and slammed the door. I went up the walk without turning and got my key out and let myself inside. It was another minute before I heard the Lincoln start up and pulse away. By then I knew I wasn't alone in the house.

17

The Detroit I knew didn't leave its lights on when the house was unoccupied. Back when a quarter was so big you couldn't see around it, the risk of burglary was infinitesimal compared with the certain knowledge that, second by second, your hard-struck pennies were rolling down a cord and out through the meter, and there was nothing to steal anyway. That was changing, but I wasn't. That's why the ellipsis of yellow light poking out of the cramped living room into the little entryway when I closed the door had me reaching back for the handle. Somewhere around age forty-nine I had thrown out my baseball bat, deciding to leave criminal confrontations to the people I fed with my tax dollars.

"Oh, don't leave. I been waiting long enough. You know?"

I knew that sharp pioneer twang, bitter as white dust. I shut the door again and stepped into the living room, where J. W. Pierpont was sitting in the overstuffed chintz chair that had come with the place. He was still rushing the season in his Panama and he had on a brown three-piece knobby-knit suit and yellow shoes with hard round toes like Mickey Mouse wore. My copy of *Kon-Tiki* lay open in his hands under the light from the china lamp I had inherited from my mother, by way of the pawnshop where my father had sold it along with the rest of the parlor furniture for the money to bury her. His thick round glasses were opaque in its light. A water tumbler containing a honey-colored liquid stood on the lamp table beside a dusty green bottle I recognized.

"You don't have no liquor in this dump, you know? This shit is so old it's turned to vinegar."

126

"The landlord threw it in with the stove and refrigerator. You're supposed to use it for cooking." I sidled over to the portable three-speed phonograph I kept on the window seat, my only recent indulgence if you didn't count the Motorola in the corner, and lifted the lid. The little aluminum film canister where I kept my household cash rolled up was still taped inside the cutout that provided access to the tubes. It didn't look as if it had been disturbed. I turned the knob all the way over to REJECT. The long-playing record at the top of the spindle dropped to the turntable and the arm swung over and down. Rosemary Clooney began singing "Come On-a My House." It could have been anything, but it would be that.

"I never cook with liquor. The best part burns off." He let the cover fall shut on the book and refilled his glass. "I don't figure this guy Heyerdahl. Waste months putting together a boat and sailing it all the way from South America to a bunch of birdshit islands in the middle of the Pacific. I don't see no percentage. You know?"

"The book sold two hundred thousand copies last count."

"No kidding, is that a lot?"

"Mine sold twenty-five hundred. They said."

"Mickey Spillane, there's a guy that knows how to clean up in the scribbling racket. He sells millions and I bet he never set foot in no boat. I sure have to thank him, too. Pussy's a lot easier to find since he started writing about Mike Hammer. I just show 'em my license and invite them back to my place to see my big gun." His dry heave of a laugh made bubbles in the glass.

"I'm sure he'd be happy to know he's making a difference."

"Well, you wouldn't know about cleaning up. You got nothing worth having, just an idiot box and a record player with a hunnert and thirty-two bucks hid inside. No wonder you got a lock on the front door I could pick with my dick. Don't worry," he said when I turned back toward the phonograph, "I put it back. The retainer I get from the UAW pays me more'n that in the time it'd take me to put it in my pocket."

"I hope you didn't spend too much of it waiting for me. I identify with labor."

"I sure don't. It sounds just like work. Walter says hello, by the way. Big shot like him, I bet you thought he forgot all about you."

"He didn't get to be a big shot by forgetting people." I excused myself, went into the kitchen, and came out with a small glass, which he filled obligingly from the bottle. It was worth a diabetic episode to me if the wine would blot out the picture of J. W. Pierpont alone in an apartment with a woman. I sat down on the horsehair sofa, a mistake; the weak springs made a hollow that put the glare of the lamp in my eyes. I closed them.

"Walter ain't heard from you," Pierpont said. "He wants to know if the deal took."

"I was supposed to wait for you to get in touch with me."

"He's worried. All you been doing is hanging out with nigger wrasslers and going to ball games with dames half your age. You ought to be ashamed."

"For what, my choice in women or spending time with Negroes?" I'd had a hunch someone had been following me. I was pretty sure who it was, although I hadn't spotted him. I supposed he was good or Reuther wouldn't have hired him to begin with.

"Oh, hell, there ain't nothing like that moist young pussy. You should stay out of them coon neighborhoods, though. I can't watch you and my hubcaps both."

"Pierpont, I don't give a flying fuck about your hubcaps and neither do you. All you had to do was pick up a phone and I'd tell you what I found out."

He held a fist next to his face. "Ring, ring. Hello, Connie? This is Jerry. How you doing? Fine, fine. Oh, I think winter's got its licks in. No, this one wasn't so bad. Well, I got to go. Oh, say, what'd you find out about that plot to ice Walter Reuther?" He lowered the fist.

"Not a damn thing."

"Connie, I'm disappointed. Walter's disappointed."

"I'm watching my step. Israel Zed is on to me. He as much as said he knows all about that meeting with your client. That's a leaky organization you're working for." I had an illuminating idea then, courtesy of the bad sherry. "Or maybe you're walking on both sides of the fence."

He smiled, showing me the wonders of the denture-maker's art. If he wasn't the oldest private detective in Michigan he had a good shot at it. "I tried that. There's no percentage. My partner could give you a second opinion only he's sniffing flowers from the wrong end in Mount Elliott Cemetery. I can't say I'm surprised, though. Them union pimps is too dumb to remember who paid them the biggest bribe and what it was for. So they cross everybody. Now, it *could* be Zed was suspicious from the start and had a tail on you when the boys and me picked you up, but it ain't likely. I ain't the best shadow man around, but I got the best eye for one. Somebody spilt the *frijoles*."

"Anyway, you can see I'm not much good to you."

"I never figured you was. Turning you was Walter's idea. He's got this control thing. I'd of quit him a long time ago, but I can't see going back to traffic court and hanging around waiting for someone to pay me to beat the streets collecting eyewitness affidavits."

"Will you tell him I can't help him?"

"I would, Connie. Honest to Christ I would. But I'm fresh out of leads and Walter's starting to wonder if I'm worth keeping around. You can see why I can't let him do that. So I guess you're going to have to start digging and be quiet about it."

I drained my glass. The sediment in the bottom tasted like soggy pencil shavings, but the glow in the pit of my stomach was welcome even if I did have to deal with what happened later. "You're the detective. Tell me how."

"My old man was a deputy sheriff down in Arkansas when Judge Parker was on the bench. My uncle was an Arizona Ranger. This work's in my blood. I can't tell you how to do it any more'n you can tell me how to tie one word onto the end of the one before. I can tell you *why*. You don't want to spend your sixty-fifth birthday slurping soup cold out of the can in no eight-foot trailer up in Oakland."

"I've been thinking about what Reuther said. He was bluffing."

"Was he now."

"A labor strike is a last resort. It's hell on the union treasury and breeds enemies among the rank-and-file. In the end everyone loses. It's only good as a threat, and he's too smart to consider throwing away such a powerful weapon to bring one reluctant middle-age spy into the fold. The E-car's success means just as much to the union as it does to Ford. If it goes over, the profits will be bigger and so will the payrolls. If it fails there will be cutbacks and layoffs. That attempt on his life is starting to be a long time ago. He's not about to wrap everything he's fought for in an eight-year-old newspaper and throw it down the sewer."

"You're right. A man's got to get up early to put one over on you. Me, I don't sleep. I'm like the Pinkertons that way." He curled a spindly arm over the side of the chair and hoisted a tattered brown leather portfolio into his lap. It was scuffed down to the yellow undergrain at the corners and much of the stitching had come loose. With all the patient care of a dowager determined to preserve the wrapping on a gift for later use, he undid the tie and flayed it open. Out came a mottled-gray cardboard file folder containing a sheaf of stapled sheets and half a dozen glossy eight-by-ten photographs. He held up each of the latter a full ten seconds, facing me, before putting it down and reaching for the next. Somebody who knew a good deal about photography had caught a scale model of the Edsel at all angles.

I felt hollow-headed. My field of vision was closing in. I bent down to set my empty glass on the floor. This put my head between my knees and brought blood to my brain. When I sat back again I felt almost normal.

"I know you're busting to tell me where you got those," I said.

"Well, look at the serial number." He held them out. When I didn't reach for them he got up and laid them gently in my lap.

My vision was still clearing, but I didn't want to bring the pictures close to my face with him watching. I stared until I could make out the row of numbers embossed on the model's detailed undercarriage.

"Maybe you don't recognize it," Pierpont said. "Lots of people don't know their own telephone number or the numbers on their license plate. Maybe you don't know that when Ford strikes off these nifty little toys they record the numbers so they know which one goes to which office. They don't want no extras floating around, you know? So when one of them turns up someplace it don't belong they can look at the serial number and it tells them straight off whose knuckles need knocking. I guess I don't got to tell you whose name is written next to the number you see on the model in them pictures."

"They could've been taken before the model got to my office. Or before I had the chance to change the combination on the safe."

"Could have. I don't think there's room to write all that next to the name and number. Keep the shots. There's negatives."

"What are you going to do with them?"

"Good question. I could sell them to GM or Chrysler or DeSoto and retire, only I wouldn't have time to wet my first hook before Walter's friends caught up to me with blowtorches. Or I could stick a stamp on 'em and send 'em to Hank the Deuce. He'd be grateful. He likes cutting people off at the knees. Ask Harry Bennett."

"Or you could hang on to them until I found out what Reuther wants me to find out."

He moved his thin shoulders. "I got a safe deposit box at NBD. Plus I'm bonded."

That made me laugh despite myself. He surprised me by getting mad.

"You eastern sonsabitches set one hell of a lot of store by what's right. What's right is what you say is right. It's damn funny what you figure you can't live without once you got all the things you really can't live without. I was ten when I found out shoes ain't just for grownups. That was fifty-two years ago and you can still strike a match on the sole of my foot. You try going barefoot in the snow on one plate of fat drippings a day for ten years. Try it for a week. Then come back and tell me what's right. See if it's the same."

I could see his eyes now behind the aquarium glass of his spectacles, swollen out of their lids with the veins showing like bits of broken thread. He was breathing hard, whistling through his nose.

I said, "If you're waiting for an apology, you can stick it up your blackmailing ass."

His breath whistled for another minute. At length it grew even and he felt for the brim of his hat with both hands as if to make sure he was still wearing it. The movement reminded me of a dignified old woman adjusting the pins in her hair. There was something spinsterish about J. W. Pierpont. I wondered if that shoeless childhood had included wearing hand-me-downs from a legion of older sisters. "That the answer you want me to take back to Walter?"

"It sure as hell is," I said. "In the perfect world." I doubled the sheaf of photographs, shredded it, doubled and shredded it again, and went on until my fingers gave out. Then I brushed the bits off my lap. "Check back with me in a week. I've got something working."

"Tear this up too if you want. There's copies." He handed me the folder. I knew what the stapled sheets contained, but I looked anyway. Preliminary specs on the Edsel, from the length of the wheelbase down to the position of the clock in the dashboard.

After he left, I stared at the telephone and willed it to ring. When it did, three days later, I had to climb down from the overhead fixture to answer it.

PART THREE
The Gardens of Barbary

18

Eight miles north of Detroit, the glass and concrete ran out and the primordial world that had existed before the coming of Cadillac reasserted itself with a vengeance. Gravel roads twisted among stands of trees so thick a motorist couldn't see between them, through swamps darkened under clouds of mosquitoes, past lakes whose smoked-glass surfaces had reflected mammoths and mastodons ten thousand years before the first man crossed the land bridge from Siberia onto a continent still damp from the last ice age. Near enough to the Midwest's second largest city to vibrate with the strumming of its traffic, Lone Pine Road ran a mile from one lonely lighted window to the next. The driver who minutes before had rushed to beat a red light on Woodward had now to brake for a line of deer crossing the road behind the eerie green lanterns of their eyes.

I felt the thrum from the Highwayman's Rest through the sole of my foot on the accelerator before I saw anything. The big Mercury, smooth-running and leathery-smelling like the inside of a shoe store, was as tight as an airlock. I couldn't even hear the air rushing past, giving me the impression I was standing still while some unseen grip cranked the scenery past the windows. The car had been delivered that morning and I hadn't yet found out how to dim the dashboard lights; when I glanced up at the rearview mirror I saw a pair of eyes screwed almost shut in a face the color of quicklime. The steering wheel was as big as a hula hoop.

I boated over a hill and there it was, a corrugated barn shaped like an airplane hangar and nearly as large in a clearing solid with automobiles. They were parked three deep and so close together it would take a Houdini to climb in or out of any one of them without nicking his neighbor with the edge of a door; which helped to explain why there was a fist-fight there nearly every night. The Ballistas could have supported a trio of Grosse Pointe debutantes for a year on what they must have been paying the local authorities to remain open nightly.

With the paranoia peculiar to the new-car owner, I parked on the extreme edge of the clearing twenty feet from the nearest abrasion and walked over the bare unpaved earth to the front door. There was no sign identifying the place. Since no such establishment could long exist undetected, with or without the blaring music and heavy traffic, I recognized this as a throwback to the blind pigs of my youth, whose peep-holes and passwords were largely a device to make the casual customer think himself among a privileged shady elite. Melons taste sweeter when they're filched.

No simian doorman impeded my entrance—even the most romantic of post-sunset adventurers had grown too sophisticated for that—and I stepped out of the blowy mid-spring night into a vast room heated almost exclusively by the excitement of its patrons. A pall of smoke clung like cotton candy to the naked rafters twenty feet overhead and a carpet the same thickness and shade of green as the felt on a ping-pong table covered the floor, which would be a poured concrete slab; the place had gone up in three days and the carpenters, generally the most expensive of all the contractors, had finished their work in an afternoon. A Wurlitzer jukebox pulsated pink, green, and blue light to a Jerry Lee Lewis beat, proving that people will happily pay a two-drink minimum to expose themselves to something they would kick their kid out of the house for tuning in on the radio for free. The tables looked like wheels and axles stood on end, with four potato-chip chairs per table, most of them occupied. A four-sided bar formed an island in the middle of the room, because *something* had to block the view of the floor show for those customers who didn't know how to tip. Most of the light came from strings of white Christmas-tree bulbs wound around the rafters and plugged unceremoniously into exposed outlet boxes on the posts supporting the roof, from

the flashing TILT signs on the pinball machines along the
wall next to the door, and from funnel-shaded fixtures suspended over a couple of pool tables and a glistening thirty-
foot shuffleboard already legendary as the "longest in the
Midwest," but the place was bright enough to read a newspaper in the reflected glow of all the glasses, bottles, cufflinks,
and broken blood vessels. It was a hothouse of a sort, supporting all kinds of nocturnal life in its artificially created en-
vironment.

All this covered the electric bill and the local graft. The
wagers made on the pocket shots, free games, and shuffleboard were enough to get the liquor license yanked, but the
Commission inspectors had larger fish to fry, and most of
them in the back room, which would be much smaller with
few frills, and less impressive in inverse proportion to the
size of the profits. There would be craps, blackjack, a wheel,
one-armed bandits, and as many takers as you needed for any
bet you wanted to place on any game from the World Series
to a bicycle race in Bombay. There you would find your
doorman, and he wouldn't be for looks. It was a myth that
the boys with the busted windpipes and the bent-over noses
didn't care where you came from or whether you had collateral. They didn't break legs for fun; that was just a fringe
benefit. They were the most cautious businessmen in the
Free World, and their faith in their country's currency would
be touching if they just spent it on better tailors.

I found an empty stool at the bar just as someone jerked
the plug on the juke, choking off "Hound Dog" in the middle
of the drum lick. An acetylene spotlight mounted near the
roof slammed on, a live combo picked up their instruments
on the corner stage, and a slender baritone in a well-cut
tuxedo began making sly love to a microphone to the tune of
an Italian ballad with a tradition as old as eighty-nine-cent
wine. He was good-looking in a machine-oiled kind of way,
curly-haired and straight-nosed, but he was continually being
upstaged by his partner, who spent most of the song walking
on his ankles among the tables in a busboy's uniform two
sizes too small and spilling drinks from his tray amid frantic
shouted apologies. The mechanics of the routine, the hand-
some organ grinder and his rogue monkey, were obvious,

embarrassingly so, but it made the crowd hysterical. I found myself laughing for no other reason than to be part of the merriment. I got the impression from comments drifting my way that the pair had some fame and had appeared together in a couple of movies; if I had been aware of them at all before this, I must have been distracted. In any case I hadn't gone to see a comedy since Buster Keaton learned to talk. Evidently it was a bright yellow feather in the Ballistas' fedora that the partners had consented to interrupt a long run in Vegas to play a roadhouse unknown to anyone outside the Detroit area. Probably it was payback for a baseball bat swung at the knees of someone who had been giving them grief.

A bulky black cloud blocked out the light. I edged over on the stool to make room for the newcomer at the bar, not realizing who it was until he spoke.

"Guinea sings okay, huh? I wanted to be a singer in the worst way when I was a lot younger. Problem is, that's just how I sung. Billy Eckstine, he was the man."

"Maybe he secretly wanted to be a wrestler." I shook Anthony Battle's enormous hand. Leaning on his elbow with his back to the light, he placed his features in shadow, but his sport coat was bright enough to take up the slack. It was yellow with black checks. The lapels were the widest I'd ever seen. One of them contained enough material to make a pair of sleeves for me. "I'll buy you a drink as soon as I can get the bartender's attention," I said.

He disengaged his hand and thumped a finger on the bar. It sounded like a kettle drum. The barman, olive-skinned with Brilliantine in his hair and a pencil moustache, came over. I asked for a tonic water. Battle ordered gin.

"Mr. Carlo says go back after the show. That door." He pointed. "He says he remembers you."

"What did you tell him I want to talk to him about?"

"The old days. How you get from there to now's up to you."

"Thanks, Anthony. Hear anything more from Leadbeater?"

"That's why I called. He planning a press conference first

of next month. He dropped by the gym yesterday to axe if I
had any names for him."

"What did you say?"

"What else? I say I'm working on it. Mr. Connie, you gots
to help me."

I drank tonic water. It did absolutely nothing for me. My
latest bodily treachery had condemned me to blandness in all
things. The future yawned before me as mild as a filter cigarette. "Where does he hang out?"

"He gots him a office in City Hall."

"Old or new?"

"Old. I don't think anybody done moved into the new one
yet."

"I'll talk to the man."

"What you going to say?"

"Hell, Anthony, I don't know what I'm going to say to
Charlie Balls."

The baritone came to the end of his song. His partner
bounded up on stage to join him as applause splattered
through the room. They bowed and galloped out through the
door Battle had indicated. The spotlight died. I slid off my
stool, smacked the palm of my hand against the wrestler's
upper arm—it was like slapping a telephone pole—and went
off in the performer's path. On the way I passed a large party
gathered around a table twenty times the size of any of the
others with a white linen cloth. It consisted of ten or a dozen
men and women in evening dress, including cummerbunds
and sequins, with bouquets of champagne bottles sprouting
out of silver buckets. They were making enough noise to fill
the room without assistance from the other tables, all except
a thin hollow-cheeked specimen of manhood whose wing
collar was too big for his neck. He sat glumly staring into his
glass amid the fun, standing out the way he probably never
would in any ordinary crowd. He was probably in his twen-
ties but seemed older in his spleen. A pair of crutches with
padded arms leaned against the table next to his chair. I wondered fleetingly if that explained his mood. In any case I forgot his features as soon as they were out of my sight.

The door led not into the gaming room as I had supposed,
but down a short hall with locked doors on either side that I

suspected belonged to dressing rooms and down an open
arch into a storeroom roughly the size of the ground floor of
my house. For that it seemed cramped because of the size of
the room I had just left and because it was stacked nearly to
the ceiling with cardboard cartons. Insulation wrapped in
brown paper lined the walls between exposed studs, shadows
crawling over them from the bare bulbs of four drop cords
slung up over the rafters and dangling down like the decora-
tions at an Old West necktie party. The air dripped sour mash,
rat dung, and that all-pervasive odor of the decade, fresh sawdust.

A Caligari-like aisle twisted crookedly between stacks of
cartons to a work table nearly ten feet square like the ones
garment workers used to trace and cut patterns. Here the
light tunneled down between cartons stenciled *Old Grand
Dad* and *Tele King*. I tried to remember where I'd come
across Tele King before; someplace recent. In any case I
shoved the problem aside to be worked out later. It hadn't
been so long since I'd dealt with the kind of person who was
standing on the other side of the table that I'd forgotten the
wisdom of keeping my mind clear.

It was a type I knew well. You wouldn't have noticed him
on the street, but if he showed up at a party you were giving
and you had security you would place it on red alert. This
one was a small muscular specimen in a shiny black nylon
sport shirt with the tail out over windowpane slacks best described as Halloween orange. Black wiry hair covered his
arms from the backs of his hands to his elbows, making him
appear at first as if he were wearing long sleeves, but his
head was absolutely hairless. His scalp shone like white polished bone, poreless and about as capable of supporting a
healthy follicle as a freshwater pearl. Shadowed under the
downlight, his eyes were a disturbing shade of amber, like a
feral dog's. The rest of him was unimpressive: a thick-
bridged nose that bent up at the end, exposing his nostrils;
gray meaty lips like two slices of headcheese; retreating
chin; a neck that needed washing; and too many years of
cakes and pasta around his middle, eroding a body that at
one time had been all gristle and sinew. His daily regimen of

eye-gouging and kneecapping was getting to be a long time in the past.

For at least a minute after I stopped in front of the table he made no indication that he was aware of me. He stood Napoleon-like with his feet apart, supporting his weight on his hands, but the object he was staring at was no map of Austerlitz. It was a large-scale color photograph of a woman's spread thighs and open glistening vagina with a sheaf of three-by-five calendar pages attached just below her clitoris. But for the true flesh tones—it was clearly the work of a better photographer than its subject usually attracted—I might have mistaken it for a scenic shot of Carlsbad Cavern.

"What do you think?" he said at last, without raising his eyes from the picture. He had a deep voice for a man no larger than I and twenty pounds lighter. Comically deep, in fact. It made me want to look around for the ventriloquist.

I said, "I hope it's larger than life. I don't know of a man with the equipment who can make her happy."

"I do. Or I did. Joey Machine cut it off him in thirty-two and stuck it down his throat for shooting his mouth off to the Treasury Department. I'm talking about the calendar. Think it'll sell?"

"I doubt it."

"Why not? My brother and me sold dirty pictures on the street to keep our mother from getting evicted. After a couple of years we bought her a house."

"Girly magazines were hard to come by then. The Secret Service shut down all the presses and Customs seized foreign material at the borders. Then came Hugh Hefner. Now the customers want their naked women as pink as balloons without moles or scars. No garage man's going to hang a gynecologist's chart on his wall when he can get Marilyn Monroe on red satin."

"You're right. Shit. You can't count on nothing no more." He rolled up the calendar and stood holding it in both hands like a headmaster's baton. "You're Minor, right? I used to hear your name. Never read you, though. Tony and me, we was too busy to read newspapers. Old Frankie kept us hopping. You hear he's coming back?"

I made a noncommittal sound. Every few months since his

deportation, rumors had flown of a deal brewing between Frankie Orr and the United States Attorney General's office that would allow him to return to his adopted country. But the feds never made deals unless you had something they wanted, and when last I'd checked there had been no mad demand on Pennsylvania Avenue for olive trees from Frankie's private grove outside Palermo.

"We won't need this porno shit when the Conductor gets back. It'll be like the old days then, only better. No more of this bumping each other off."

"That's what kept you and Tony hopping," I said. "If memory serves."

He scowled—a man with lips like cold cuts can really do you a scowl—and javelined the tube calendar up and over a heap of cartons. "None of that shit never stuck to neither of us. When they couldn't get Frankie no other way they tried to trump us up with every kill since little Lindbergh to yellow us into talking, but we kept our cake-holes shut and they went away."

"The way I heard it, every time one of you was seen running away from someplace with blood on his shoe, the other one was out clubbing in front of a couple of college deans and a Presbyterian minister. Nobody could tell one twin from his brother under oath."

"It ain't that way now. Tony let himself go all to hell." He sucked in his gut.

"Where is Tony, by the way? The two of you are apart as often as a set of salt and pepper shakers. Or am I your alibi for whatever he's up to?"

"Tony caught cancer. Croakers give him three months."

"Oh." I'd been enjoying so much dealing with him the way I used to with his kind, a way I'd forgotten until I came face to face with one, that the tragedy in that ugly-ordinary face got to me. I was genuinely saddened that mortality should find its way to such a homely and constant part of the landscape as a Ballista. Or maybe it was just another variation on the way I felt whenever a stranger my age showed up in the obituaries.

"Ain't your fault," he said, disregarding the fact that I hadn't said I was sorry. "Life puts you on the spot when nobody else can, and that's the shits. I'm sure as hell going to miss him. He keeps the books."

"Did Anthony Battle tell you why I'm here?"

"I like that boy. I sure hope he beats this pinko rap. I get on with him better than some white men I've known and that's the Lord's truth. He said you had a question." He opened his face, which was what I'd been dreading. When a gangster does that it's like a glimpse into the filthy kitchen of a restaurant you didn't want to eat in to begin with.

I stared right at it and took a bite. "Who put the hit on Walter Reuther?"

19

I'd forgotten how Sicilians worked. Histrionics were their stock in trade; whenever someone close to them died they stopped shaving, barked their knees praying to the Holy Virgin, and pounded the coffin with both fists, wailing at the top of their considerable lungs. But when it came to something that really mattered, business and staying out of jail, they stoned over like the forty thieves' den. I'd said what I said looking for some reaction that would tell me more than his words. I got zero. The yellow eyes were the only things living in a face carved out of Carrara marble.

"I didn't know he *was* hit," Charlie Balls said. "I seen him on TV just this morning."

"This happened in forty-eight. It didn't take."

"I remember. I was getting my kidneys rearranged in the First Precinct basement when it happened. They said I sapped a shylock till his brains showed."

"Where was Tony?"

"Getting a writ, I guess. Ask him."

"Where were you in forty-nine when someone shot Victor Reuther?"

"Shit, I don't know. Probably pissing blood in some other basement. I don't know where Tony was neither. Same place, probably. The feds was coming down on Frankie with both feet by then and the local coppers suddenly found their balls."

"You didn't hear anything?"

"Oh, I heard plenty. Them Reuther boys got plenty of enemies. I heard it was their own union wanted them out. You ought to be talking to the rank-and-file. What's your stake in this, anyhow? I heard you quit scribbling for the papers."

"I need a favor for a favor. You know the song."

"Tell me about it, I could sing it in the dark. I'm stuck with five hundred TV sets that don't work for shit because I need a favor from this Jew bastard in Vegas. You got a TV? I can make you a good price."

As he waved his hand around the inventory in the room I remembered where I'd seen the name Tele King recently. My mind flashed on a beefy bartender pounding the side of a set on the shelf in the Shamrock Bar. "You're in the television business?"

"Oh, Tony and me got the whole territory. That was Vegas' big brainstorm. I get a call. 'Hey, Charlie, you remember how we cleaned up on the jukebox racket? Well, that's day-old bread. TV, that's where the future is. Every schmoe on his way home from the plant stops off for a beer, he wants to watch the fights too, see Jake LaMotta give some nigger a nosebleed. We already got the routes and the procedure's the same. Easiest money we've made since the Eighteenth Amendment.' Only we owned all the distribution rights to the jukes, while anybody with cash in his till can walk into the RCA store and come out with a set and pop it up on the shelf and forget about it. Plus when we owned the juke routes we supplied the records too, and our customers had to keep replacing them at our price. Plus the jukes worked. TV *repair*, that's the racket we should of muscled in on. Meanwhile somebody else buys all the juke routes out from under us, every soda shop between here and Timbukfuckingtu puts one in to play that jungle-bunny rag the kids get all wet over, and I'm stuck with five hundred clothes hampers with windows. The old lady was right. Tony and me should of went to the seminary. You never see no priest in no soup line."

"About Reuther." I must have had one of those faces. Everyone with something to confide sought me out. In the old days I'd thought it was my reportorial savvy.

"Huh? Oh, yeah." He ran a hand over where his hair would have been had anything been able to take root on that bony scalp. "You're barking down the wrong hole here. Frankie come in on the side of labor when everybody else was still bashing heads for the companies. He seen where things was going before they went. Reuther don't play ball the way Brock does over at the Steelhaulers, but he's got most of the checkers in the UAW and hitting him is just plain bad for business. You want to talk to somebody about that, talk to Henry Deuce. He's got a lot more to gain from a world without Walter P. Reuther."

"Why Henry Deuce? Why not GM or Chrysler or DeSoto or Studebaker?"

"Well, to name one. Look, I'm clean out of jawing time. These carpet joints don't run themselves."

But he'd changed the subject too quickly. I leaned forward on my hands. The top of the table was sticky from an old spill. I hoped it was a beverage. "Let's just for the sake of saying something say it was Henry Deuce or one of his people, Jack Bugas or Israel Zed. When they want to make a car they don't go down to Rouge and pick up a welding torch. When they want to kill a man they don't chip their manicures skulking through bushes waiting for a clear shot through a lighted window. They hire it out. Question is, who do they hire?"

"Take your pick. I know some kids'd do their own mothers for a case of Black Label and a new battery for a forty-nine Merc."

"I'm talking about professionals. You don't live in an Airstream when you can afford a house on Lake St. Clair."

"I see what you're getting at. You're still barking down the wrong hole. This idea that Tony and I iced guys, it comes from reading too many comic books. Oh, we roughed some guys around when we was kids and didn't know no better— guys like us, mind; the squares don't have nothing to be afraid of from the Ballistas. It's a long hop from there to the box garden. Swear it on a stack of Bibles."

"The only way I'd believe you didn't make a run at Reuther is if you swore you did. You and your brother would be a lot more than saloonkeepers by now if you knew enough to tell the truth when it counted. You'd lie about your shoe size to screw the clerk out of two extra inches."

His face went liverish. He reached behind his back and swung out a black .45 Army automatic, jacking a shell into the chamber in the same motion. "Brother, you wore it out but good. Go through the door or be blasted through it."

"I was wondering what it would take to make you revert to type." The words tasted like metal. I backed away slowly. When a pile of cartons stopped me I turned and went around it. My skin prickled from the nape of my neck to the base of my testicles. A trickle of cold water wandered down between my buttocks.

"And to think I was going to give you a bargain on a brand new TV."

Anthony Battle was leaning on the same section of bar when I came out into the light. Someone had plugged the jukebox back in: one of those bouncy, hiccoughing tunes sung by some kid from Texas. A few of the younger couples were out on the dance floor, skirts twirling straight out from trim waists like helicopter rotors. Yellow panties seemed to be in fashion that season.

"Talk to the man?" Battle asked.

"Mostly I got talked at." I rested my forearms on the bar next to him. All the stools were taken. The bartender looked a question at me over the glass he was polishing. I shook my head. I only got their attention when I didn't want anything.

"Say anything about me?"

"He said you were a good boy for a Communist."

"That ain't funny."

"Nothing much is these days." A sharp ache had begun to flicker behind my eyes like a loose connection.

"He answer your question?"

"He pulled a gun on me for asking it."

"Mr. Carlo he comes to the point." He drank. Something about the way he lifted his glass, slopping the gin around inside, told me a couple of generations had passed since I'd left him.

"Could be Leadbeater is doing you a favor," I said. "There are better bosses."

"I know. I carried a hod for one for fifty cents a hour. My brother's kid won't carry no hod. That means college and I can't swing that on no fifty cents a hour."

The song slammed to a finish. The next one was all about tutti-frutti. The lyric-writing business was one to consider when I lost too many faculties to continue in advertising. I shifted onto my left elbow, facing the wrestler. His profile had been hacked out of ironstone. "You said you've seen a lot of men come and go in back of this place. Do you know any of them by name?"

"No. They don't talk to me. They don't talk to no one but Mr. Carlo."

"Do they drive here or do they take cabs?"

"Drive I guess. Nobody takes cabs in Detroit."

"Are you any good at memorizing numbers? License numbers?"

He drank. "If I was I wouldn't tell you."

"I guess not." I pushed away from the bar. "Thanks for setting this up. It's not your fault nothing came of it. I don't know what I expected. Information never came that easy, not even when I was young and knew how to get it. I'll talk to Leadbeater."

He made no response. I wasn't sure if he was in a condition to hear what I'd said. I put five dollars on the bar next to him and threaded my way out between flying elbows and whirling feet. The crisp air in the parking lot flash-froze the pain in my skull. The stars were hard points of steel in a sky like black shale. Quick footsteps padded the bare earth behind me as I inserted the key in the door of the Mercury. I spun around, squaring off to defend myself. Anthony Battle's shadowy bulk blocked out the Highwayman's Rest. He was breathing hard, swaying on his big feet.

"One thing I'm good at is numbers," he said. "My old man said if I was white I'd make a good accountant."

I sagged against the car. Ever since the Woolworth's beating, any noise behind me hurled my heart into my throat. "You've done enough. I don't want to get you in trouble."

"You means, worse'n I am now?"

I grinned back.

20

That Saturday night I took Agnes to the Bel-Air Drive-In on Eight Mile Road. There had been the usual discussion of where to go, but when you have a new car whose interior is nicer than your living room you want to spend as much time in it as possible, at least until the novelty wears off. The feature was *Bad Day at Black Rock*. About a third of the way through, Agnes reached across me and dialed down the speaker attached to the window on the driver's side. She had on a green dress with a square neck that showed her collarbone—a part of the female anatomy I had always admired—and a hat that clung to her head like a starfish gripping a stubborn clam.

"What are you grumbling about?" she asked.

"I thought it was a western. It sounded like a western. That's what I was in the mood for."

"It *is* a western."

"The hero wears a fedora and the villain drives a pickup truck."

"There are horses."

"There were neckties in *Earth vs. the Flying Saucers*, but that didn't make it a gangster picture."

"Well, I like it. Spencer Tracy is looking old, though. It's kind of sad."

"We're the same age."

"Ah. *That's* why we're grumpy."

"We're grumpy because there ought to be a law against advertising a movie as a western that isn't a western."

"There is, as a matter of fact. The memo's still on the bulletin board at Slauson and Nichols. I think. There are about eleven months' worth of newspaper cartoons tacked on top of it."

"That's the government for you. Do anything to protect its monopoly on lying."

"Now you're contradicting yourself," she said. "What's wrong, Connie? I wasn't this hard to get along with when I went through menopause."

"Yes, you were."

She shifted on the seat, supporting her chin on her elbow on the back. "Really, what's wrong? Ford getting you down?"

"It's a different world up there. Everyone's writing his autobiography on company time. Whenever the conversation lags during a meeting you can hear ballpoint pens scratching on notepads under the table. They say Henry asked his secretary to hire an exterminator. He thought there were mice in the walls of the boardroom."

"Henry, is it?"

"Kings and emperors go by their first names. He's got a genealogist working around the clock trying to trace the Ford family back to William the Conqueror."

"His grandfather was a nut. I guess some of it was bound to rub off."

"These days it takes a nut to be normal. A couple of weeks ago some joker in Long Island sold a painting for fifty thousand dollars that looked just like my kitchen floor after I finished painting the ceiling. Yesterday I paid a guy in coveralls forty bucks to replace a tube in my TV set and spent the rest of the evening watching a middle-aged comedian parading around in a chiffon dress. And every time Spencer Tracy turns his back I can see the outline of his arm tied behind him to make it look like he has only one. He didn't lose it at all; he just misplaced it. Meanwhile I'm out sixty cents and it's been so long since I've seen a real western I'm about to break out in little red saddles all over my body."

"Crackerjacks."

I looked at her. "Say again?"

"I'm hungry. I want Crackerjacks."

"You ate the biggest pile of spaghetti I've ever seen an hour ago at Dondero's."

"Then I wanted spaghetti. Now I want something sweet and sticky that crunches."

I turned my watch to catch the light from the screen. "Wait ten minutes."

"Why? The concession kid's right there."

"Ernest Borgnine's about to beat the hell out of Tracy. I don't want to miss any of it while I'm waiting for the kid to make change."

"I thought you hated this picture."

"I didn't say that. I said it wasn't a western."

"You'll miss a lot more if you have to go to the stand."

I shushed her and turned up the volume.

Ten minutes later, when the youth with the candy tray had worked his way to the other side of the lot, I got out and laced my way between parked cars to the little building in the center. J. W. Pierpont was leaning on the end of the counter, munching popcorn from a box with Popeye on the front. He had on a tweed sport coat and his Panama. I had never known anyone with so unerring a barometer for bad combinations of dress.

"Esther Williams' playing at the Galaxy," he said. "I wish you'd picked that one. A hundred broads in bathing suits, you know?"

"If you wanted to jerk off you should've stayed home with Betty Page." I paid the girl, put the Crackerjacks in my sweater pocket, and joined him out of the line of traffic.

"I ain't done that since I was a kid. Spillane, you know?" He pried a kernel loose from a molar with his little finger. "What you got for me?"

"I need more time."

"You couldn't ask for that over the phone?"

"I wasn't sure you'd give it to me and I didn't want to have to explain why I needed it. I don't know whose phone is tapped."

"So explain. I'm on the company clock."

"I talked to Charlie Balls last night."

"I didn't figure you went out there to play pinball."

"I asked him flat out who dropped the dime on Reuther. He pulled a gun on me."

"Charlie's getting mellow. In the old days he'd of used it."

"I doubt it. All he had to do was stonewall. I touched a nerve of some kind. It's just a hunch, but I think it has something to do with Frankie Orr wanting to come back from the old country."

He munched popcorn and said nothing. On the surface of his eyeglasses, Spencer Tracy grasped Anne Francis by the wrist. "Hunches come from somewhere."

"Charlie Balls was pretty sure it was happening. Maybe things have changed since I dug up dope for a living, but back then we looked for the thing that was sticking up so we could get our fingernails under it."

"Frankie was still in this country when Reuther got shot."

"He was under indictment even then. He didn't get to be the Conductor waiting for things to happen. That prostitution rap the government hung on him was cobbled up. Everyone knows his power came from the unions. His relationship with Albert Brock and the Steelhaulers put fifty thousand trucks at his disposal for transporting contraband nationwide and his contacts in the UAW and the AFL-CIO gave him access to three million in strike and pension funds. Working capital, impossible to trace as long as you can generate enough cash flow to replace what you've borrowed. And everywhere the mob dips its bucket, it comes back brimming over with currency."

"Walter don't like gangsters. That's a fact."

"His price is more power. Trouble is, so is Frankie's. It's one thing he doesn't spread around. So he gets chummy with someone in the union who wants to be Reuther, but who's a lot more reasonable to deal with on a business basis, and he takes steps to weed out Walter. When that blows up he targets Victor. Object lesson."

Pierpont tilted the popcorn box and slid the last crumbs into his mouth. Then he crushed the box and flipped it in the direction of the overflowing trash can by the corner of the building. It glanced off the pile and started a small avalanche. He ignored it. "That's a lot to get from nothing. You said Charlie Balls wasn't talking."

"It makes more sense than Reuther's theory. Why should the Ballistas do Israel Zed any favors?"

"Joint effort. They all benefit. Wouldn't be the first time Ford went partners with thugs. Ask Walter."

"That was under Harry Bennett. Henry Deuce bounced

Bennett as hard as Bennett's gorillas bounced Reuther off Miller Road. As Charlie Balls would say, you're barking down the wrong hole. There's no conspiracy at Ford."

"You been to an awful lot of trouble. You know? All Walter wanted you to do was poke through a couple of files at the Glass House. Thing like going out to Lone Pine Road, that's my job. I might of cleaned up on the slots while I was at it. You got ambitious."

"It's been a long time since I ran down a lead beyond a tip on a new job," I agreed. "It's been a good deal longer since I spooked for anyone. It's been never. You go with your experience."

"Could just be you want us off your back and you're pointing just any old where."

"Could be. But you're not sure. You must be good at what you do or Reuther wouldn't have hired you. In that case you're too good not to run it down."

"I'll look into it. Like I say, I might get lucky on the slots." He produced a red bandanna from an inside pocket and mopped the butter off his palms. "You don't mind if I hang on to them pictures till I turn something. They're in a safe place. You know?"

Music swelled from a hundred car speakers. The picture was coming to an end. I nodded and went back to the car. When I turned to open the door he was no longer at the concession stand. He moved fast for a man in his sixties.

"What'd I miss?" I pulled the door shut and handed Agnes the box of Crackerjacks.

"Only everything. Who was that you were talking to?"

"Just an Ernest Borgnine fan. We agreed he should have won an Oscar for *From Here to Eternity*. Anyone who would beat Frank Sinatra to death deserves some kind of award."

"He looked like some kind of insect."

"Who, Sinatra?"

"The Ernest Borgnine fan. He looked like some kind of goggle-eyed bug. Not like someone you'd want to talk to."

"My legs were stiff from sitting. It felt good to stand."

She crunched Crackerjacks. "I wish I knew what's happening with you. I'd think it had something to do with that horrible night at Woolworth's, but you were acting strange before that. Ever since you went to work for Ford. I still don't know what you do there."

"I'm selling a car. A new line. Zed liked my work on 'Detroit the Dynamic' at Slauson and decided to put me in charge of promotion for the whole division."

"Fine. Don't tell me."

I let it drift. Around us, engines were starting, headlight beams raking around. "What do you know about Stuart Leadbeater?" I asked.

"Lawyer with the city attorney's office," she said after a moment. "He ran errands for the Kefauver committee when it was in town and got bit by the political bug. Served a term on the school board, then ran for superintendent and lost. Now he's running with the pack for Wayne County Prosecutor."

"What are his chances?"

"I believe the term you gentlemen use is piss-poor. He's a Republican and there hasn't been one of those in local office since Booth shot Lincoln."

"I'm sorry to hear that."

"Why? You told me you voted for FDR."

"Haven't voted since. If Leadbeater were a shoo-in he might be feeling generous. If he's hungry and losing it means he isn't taking prisoners."

"Considering politics, Mr. Minor?"

"Would you vote for me if I were?"

"Not in this world or the next."

"I always said you were a smart woman, Agnes. I owe someone a favor and it means talking to Leadbeater. How much have you got on him down at Slauson?"

"Not a lot. We put together some ads for the Republican slate when he ran for the school board. That means a short bio and professional résumé. A clipping file, of course. I spend all day Tuesday and Friday with scissors."

"Can you send me what you have? I'll get it back to you in good shape."

"I doubt the Admiral will notice it's missing."

"How is the senile old bastard?"

"Getting worse. He plays with that toy ship in his office all the time. If he were in any other business he would be looked on as odd."

"As businesses go it's not so bad. Being a private dick has to be the bottom of the barrel."

She offered me the box of Crackerjacks. When I held up a palm she said, "Sorry. I keep forgetting. Did Henry Junior give you an attractive secretary?"

"Secretaries never are. Neither are nurses. That's a myth. The pretty ones are all on *The Guiding Light*."

"I thought maybe you were dating. That would explain some of your behavior lately."

"I'm dating right now."

"I mean someone young. It would fit the profile. When a woman starts growing old she dyes her hair. When a man starts growing old he goes out with women who are too young to have to."

"Is that what happened to your marriage?"

"Maybe. I never got the chance to ask. I sent him to the market for a loaf of bread and he just kept going. That's when I went back to work and became one of those unattractive secretaries. I had a son at school."

"You must have done a good job. Not many West Point cadets have single mothers."

"It was hard at first. It's still hard, but I don't think he believes any longer that I drove his father away."

"I'm sorry. I didn't want to bring back rotten memories."

She smiled briefly at the politeness. In the light reflecting off the blank movie screen she looked just like Peggy Lee. Most of the other cars had pulled out, leaving us alone in a forest of speaker stands. "Going to church in the morning?" she asked.

"If I were to step through the door of St. Mary's after all these years the roof would fall in."

"Good. I wouldn't want God angry at me if you overslept."

Understanding seeped slowly through my thick Greek skull. I cleared my throat. "When I was a kid I couldn't wait to finish growing up so I could be sure I was reading all the signals right. I'm still waiting. I need to know if you're saying what I sure hope you're saying."

She made a little squeal and pulled something out of the box. "Oh, look, I found the prize."

21

The old Detroit City Hall towered in unassailable if some-what dirty-faced dignity over the block bounded by Woodward, Fort, Griswold, and Michigan, four of the city's oldest and most hallowed thoroughfares, pounded hard as iron long before the invention of asphalt by the booted feet of Cadillac and LaSalle and the softer but no less firm tread of Fathers Richard and Marquette, clerical brigands of a kind of Catholicism unknown to the crumbling faith of Protestant America under Eisenhower. Dominated by a clock tower whose iron bells trummed the hour to the accompaniment of decomposing gingerbread, the building sported tarnished green life-size statues of those four dead giants in corner niches added in 1884 and appeared on postcards and souvenir dishes in middle-class living rooms throughout the world. The ghosts that prowled among the columns in its drafty lobby wore stovepipe hats and side whiskers. The stench of their unwashed coattails saturated the old dirt packed into the fissures in the marble walls, and there were orange stains on the wainscoting that couldn't be explained away entirely by leaks from the rusted pipes in the ceiling. In those days politicians freighted pistols next to their fobs.

The talk, once the building's current occupants had finished carrying their cartons of stationery and family photographs into the new City–County Building down the street, was of demolition. There were those who spoke in favor of maintaining the old structure for historical purposes, but they weren't paying the bills, and anyway the dust from which it rose was a better fate than invasion by men in porkpies and women with plastic purses and unspeakable children. It

156

soared too much for a civilization concerned with spreading out close to the earth as if to foil enemy radar. The glazed obelisk built to replace it represented more worldly ideals. It needed neither God nor gimcrackery, and the best thing that could be said about it was that when its time came the only controversy would be whether to blow it up or swing the ball.

I rode a clanking birdcage elevator to the fourth floor and listened to my footsteps on hardwood in a corridor smelling of tung oil and dry rot. Ceiling fans swooped overhead, typewriter keys snicked behind tilted transoms. I paused before a door with S. F. I. LEADBEATER lettered in gold on the rock-candy glass, then thumbed down the brass latch and went on through. Sunlight, smuggled into the windowless room under the connecting door to the private office beyond, lay on the floor like spilled wheat, stopping at a fruitwood desk behind which a woman in a starched white blouse with pencils in her hair sat clittering the keys of an electric typewriter on a stand. When I approached the desk she swiveled and folded her hands on the blotter. She had made some effort to color her pale face with spots of rouge. The effect was not so much Ann Sheridan as Raggedy Ann. So far my theory about secretaries remained unchallenged.

"Yes." Not a question, but tentative acknowledgment that someone was sharing her oxygen. The nameplate on the desk read MISS HEIMDALL.

"Connie Minor. I called yesterday for an appointment."

She glanced at the clock, a Regulator, on the wall opposite the desk. It and the piece of furniture she was seated behind, hand-rubbed with a beveled top, were the only objects in the room with character, and I was including Miss Heimdall. "Yes. You're right on time. Unfortunately, Mr. Leadbeater is detained. He said for you to go in and wait."

My more devious instincts did a quick roller-coaster loop. I was reporter enough to embrace the time alone in my subject's private office, but familiar enough with politicians to know that if there was anything in there worth looking at it would be under lock and key. I thanked her and let myself through the door. The clittering had started again before I got it closed.

The room wasn't large by contemporary standards—
smaller than my part of the Glass House—but would have
been considered spacious at the time the building went up.
The original ten-foot ceiling had been brought down to contemporary dimensions with suspended panels, and new plas-
terwork had gone in over the wiring to the switches and
fixtures; but someone with taste beyond the purely functional
considerations of the usual bureaucratic remodeling had
taken pains to preserve the atmosphere of late Victorian society set adrift in the swelling torrent of the Industrial Revolution. The shoulder-high tongue-and-groove wainscoting had
been stripped and refinished recently by someone who knew
what he was doing, leaving a surface that gleamed softly
rather than glistened, butterscotch-colored and still smelling
faintly of turpentine. The floor, somewhat darker and made
of two-inch-wide boards fitted so tightly you could have
rolled a piece of buckshot across the room without a bump,
were left exposed for two feet around a deep red Oriental rug
and still showed a couple of charred depressions from an old
fire, lovingly maintained lest-we-forget. The overhead light
was a milk-glass bowl suspended from a five-bladed fan with
a seven-foot sweep and a dangling brass chain ending in a
tassel. Shelves had been erected inside two arched windows,
bricked in during an intervening era when coal was more
precious than light, and supported mustard-spined law books
and unmatched silver pieces of meticulous workmanship
brought together by a collector of some knowledge. The
third, left open, looked north as far as the goldleafed dome of
the Fisher Building.

After all this attention to detail, the furnishings themselves
were a disappointment. From the overcarved ebony of the
Regency desk to the burgundy tufted leather of a sofa that no
one had ever stretched out on or ever would, it was a business cliché of a type not far enough removed from the present to be anything but rancid. The heavy gold frames on the
requisite portraits of Washington, Lincoln, and Eisenhower,
the horsehair pens standing erect in their brass stand on the
desk, and the square cut-glass decanters of coppery whiskey
and oxblood wine gathered cruetlike in their wire rack on a
drum table with lion's-head pulls on the drawers stank of

masculinity in an aggressive and uncompromising way that made me question whether the occupant of the office wouldn't rather be sharing a flouncy four-poster with the boy who emptied the wastebaskets. The very air was layered with a pungent leathery, worksweat, rotting-oak odor, as if Paul Bunyan had paused there to lean on his axe on his way to clear the Pacific Northwest.

"Hideous, isn't it? I made the mistake of hiring an office decorator. She looked up my family tree, found a couple of railroad barons and I suppose no small number of horse thieves, and ordered everything straight from Abercrombie and Fitch. I had to restrain her physically from mounting a boar's head over my Revere ware. I'm Stuart Leadbeater. You needn't introduce yourself, Mr. Minor. When I came out here I made a point to look up the city's recent history. That included a complete run of the *Banner*."

He spoke rapidly—half the inundation had spent itself before I turned from a cast-iron celestial globe on its own stand to face the man in the doorway—but with all his consonants bitten clean through by some kind of eastern-school accent that was to become quite familiar to me, and to America itself, throughout the next political period. He looked younger than the thirty-eight years I knew him to be and a good deal less formal than his background suggested. His skinny tie was knotted crookedly, his three-button coat unfastened to expose a braided-leather belt, and his hair needed combing. It fell in a bunch over one side of his forehead like a strawberry blonde carnation, softening the effect of a lantern jaw and long upper lip that if it weren't smiling might have belonged to a grave cardinal in something painted by Caravaggio. I'd have bet my two weeks' vacation that when he was a few years younger he had flirted with a moustache to cover it up, then decided to live with it shorn after Tom Dewey's defeat.

All very open and casual. But his eyes were tiny and close-set; and although I was no fan of physiognomy, repeated experience had taught me that the condition was caused by the collapse of the skull where the faculties of conscience and mercy were normally located.

"You're a politician, all right." I grasped the hand he presented, well-tended with a practiced grip. My father might have found fault with the lack of calluses, but I had known at least as many black hearts in bib overalls as I had honorable intentions in silk shirts. "For a Republican you have a generous idea of what's recent history and what went out with Alley Oop."

"Surely not. I was in tenth grade when Repeal came. There are young men studying for the bar who never knew another President but FDR until they were old enough to shave. Just the other day my nephew asked me what television programs I watched as a boy. I had to explain radio to him. Yet the leaders of our country, this state, this city, were all born in another century. Time is relative, Mr. Minor. Women mark it with hemlines; men with headlines. Just for now I'll overlook your scurrilous reference to my political affiliation. Truth to tell, I'm not that impressed with some of its more visible representatives. To a man they're bovinely unaware of the cancer spreading through our society. Won't you sit down? That chair's the least uncomfortable of the bunch. I had it reupholstered with foam rubber. Even our hearty ancestors preferred to have a saddle and blanket between themselves and the hair of the horse."

I sat, blasted off my feet by the hurricane of his vocabulary. I'd violated the first rule of survival in the information-gathering business by coming in with a preconceived notion of the sort of man I was dealing with. Now I had lost the first advantage while I sought time to frame a fresh plan of attack.

Stuart Freemantle Ingram Leadbeater had been born in a snowbound hamlet named St. Agatha on a frozen lake in Maine in 1918, taken a degree in contract law from the University of Maine in 1940, passed the bar on the second try, and languished in the legal department at the Kennebec Paper Company in Augusta until Pearl Harbor. He had joined the navy and received a nasty paper cut from a copy of Davis' *Naval Courts and Boards*, for which he was promoted to lieutenant junior grade and stationed in Point Barrow, Alaska, where it may be noted no successful invasion by Imperial Japan took place from the date of his arrival through the end of the war. Having drunk in the sophistication of Prudhoe Bay, he was understandably disenchanted with a future with the pulp paper industry, and after his release from service he assembled a résumé and floated it to prestigious law firms across the country. When the anticipated flood of requests for interviews failed to occur, he downsized his aspirations, eventually consenting to fill the void left in the Detroit city attorney's office by the sudden death of a twenty-three-year-old Michigan Bar hopeful due to congenital heart disease. There he parlayed an ability to spend twelve hours at a stretch tracking down arcane precedents in the stacks of the law library at Wayne State University into a research assignment with the Special Senate Committee to Investigate Organized Crime in Interstate Commerce.

In that capacity, on loan from the city in return for a promise of federal funding for various municipal construction projects, Leadbeater had distinguished himself so far as to prompt a special commendation signed by Senator Kefauver, which went into his jacket at City Hall. Of greater significance were the five seconds of national fame that came his way when he appeared on camera handing a slip of paper containing pertinent facts to Rudolph Halley, the committee's chief counsel. The gesture happened to take place during a dramatic moment in the testimony of Leo Bustamente, bodyguard and sometime leg-breaker in the employ of Frankie Orr, and the footage was repeated during the six and eleven o'clock news broadcasts. I'd noted the presence in the office of a framed blow-up from the *Free Press*'s front-page coverage in which the photographer had captured Leadbeater leaning over the counsel's shoulder. It's not every day you get to study the precise moment when the direction of a man's life changed. Some pursued public office with an earnest desire to improve the world, some for wealth, many for power. The rest just liked to read their names in print.

From this information, delivered to my door by special messenger from Agnes DeFilippo's desk at Slauson & Nichols, and from the pale, slick-haired image in the newspaper photo, I had constructed a repressed, stoop-shouldered fanatic who like so many others before him had turned to politics as an escape from his own mediocrity. The Red-baiting that had drawn him toward the lighted ring of professional wrestling, and into the life of Anthony Battle, was both an opportunity and a deep faith. In the ice-locked reaches of northern Maine it was probably easier to imagine the tread of an invading Soviet Army in Arctic boots and Astrakhan hats than in the comparatively temperate climate of southeastern Michigan, and those long changeless months spent defending a skeleton post on the threshold of Siberia might have skewed anyone's opinions about which group posed the greatest threat to our way of life, the Nazi enemy or our Soviet allies. True to the type, the wife he had acquired after leaving the navy and before the move to Detroit would be a mouse-faced woman in a cloth coat with a monkey collar who volunteered to serve turkey at the Salvation Army mission on Thanksgiving Day; their seven-year-old daughter would wear yellow party dresses and hair bows and dream of serving charity turkey for her future Republican husband.

This was the animal I had come prepared to tame. I had brought nothing with which to handle this sparking wire whose casually unkempt appearance and icon-smashing charm ran counter to everything I had experienced in the greasy half-light of the political arena. It had been too long. I hadn't returned; I had merely been disinterred, and my petrified bones were crumbling in the indifferent atmosphere of an age I was never intended to see.

"Are you a drinking man, Mr. Minor?" He lifted the wire rack and studied the decanters' contents against the light, as if searching for impurities.

"Not any more. I thought members of your party never drank before sundown."

"Yes. I'm somewhat disenchanted with the party of Lincoln. They forget they repudiated Honest Abe in 1864, forcing him to win re-election as an independent. I think sometimes of changing my affiliation, but mugwumps aren't to be trusted. They're like journalists who take it into their heads to run for office. No offense."

I waved it away. I'd known a few, W. R. Hearst included,

and wouldn't have voted for one on a bet. Anyone who spent as much time with politicians as reporters were forced to and wanted to become one was unfit to lead.

Leadbeater poured a stiff jolt into a rock glass from the bottle marked BOURBON. "What brings you to city hall? I was under the impression you were no longer with the Fourth Estate."

"It's the right one. I'm with promotion at Ford." In the absence of ammunition I was moving slowly, seeing how much I could salvage of what I'd brought. "Some of us in the Glass House think you've got a real shot at becoming county prosecutor."

If I was looking for a spark of campaign-contribution avarice, he disappointed me. He leaned a hip against the corner of his desk, swirling the liquid in his glass and frowning down at it. "I can't do much for the auto industry in the prosecutor's office. Surely Mr. Ford knows that."

"Mr. Ford doesn't live in the present. He already considers it the past. Tom Dewey started as a special prosecutor, went on to become Governor of New York State, and nearly stole the presidency out from under Give 'em Hell Harry."

"'Nearly' being the operative word. The great tragedy of politics is you're never remembered for your early successes, only for your most recent failure. What are you proposing, Mr. Minor?"

"You're backing a dead horse in this anti-Communism crusade. It would be a greater tragedy if you were to be sucked down the same hole with Joe McCarthy."

"The nation didn't turn its back on Senator McCarthy because he opposed Communism. It simply decided he wasn't the champion it wanted to carry the banner. His mistake was to take on the United States Army with a former general in the White House."

I couldn't resist. "The prospects of a professional wrestler being elected to high office appear somewhat less likely."

He set his glass on the desk without drinking from it. The small close-set eyes reflected no light. Doll's eyes. "Who told you I had an interest in professional wrestling?"

The temperature in the room had dropped ten degrees, and

with it my opinion of myself. The second rule of survival in the information-gathering business was never to give up more than you got, and I had shattered it. In a moment I had done what Ivan Kohloff, the Beast of Borodino, had been unable to do in ten minutes of brute athletics. Anthony Battle was down for the count.

22

Kick up dust.

"Detroit's a small town for its size," I said. "The ring sports find their most enthusiastic audience here. When someone stirs them up it gets talked about. Actually, I'm surprised you think it's such a secret. Isn't publicity the main reason to go looking for Communists in an unlikely place like the wrestling arena?"

"Hardly unlikely. Wrestling is popular in Russia. They understand it. If they played baseball in Moscow I'd go looking for them at Briggs Stadium. I know exactly whom I've approached on this matter, Mr. Minor. If there's a leak I'll find it. I already have a good idea where to look."

"That's not important. What's important is you've placed your bet on last year's turn of the wheel. This year no one's interested in what the commies are up to."

"John Foster Dulles isn't no one. J. Edgar Hoover isn't. I flatter myself that I am not." He stopped leaning and slid his hands into his coat pockets, leaving the thumbs out. "You're entirely mistaken about my motives. I'm not some political opportunist trying to hitch my wagon to the current popular notion of what counts. Nor am I some tobacco-plug Tennessee ward heeler poking about under people's beds hunting for comical little men in black raincoats with big round bombs in their pockets. I've seen the enemy at close range and found nothing to laugh at."

"You mean when you were stationed in Alaska."

He didn't seem surprised that I was familiar with his service record. "In the spring when the East Siberian seaports opened, I would watch through fieldglasses as their destroy-

ers patrolled the edge of the Three Mile Limit. They were the
best they had, and there were more of them each time. I ask
you, Mr. Minor, why were they so concerned about the wa-
ters separating the Soviet Union from the United States—
their ally—when the enemy lay in the opposite direction?"

"I gave up trying to understand the military mind when
Montgomery destroyed the Netherlands trying to protect
them from the Nazis."

"We could use a few of their minds in our military. While
we were busy fighting that war, they were getting ready for
the next. Are you familiar with Herbert A. Philbrick's *I Led
Three Lives*?"

"I caught a couple of episodes. Richard Carlson's got to be
the dullest leading man this side of Van Johnson."

"I'm talking about the book, not the television program
loosely based upon it. It should be required reading in every
public school. During the nine years he worked as an infor-
mant for the FBI among the ranks of the American Communist Party, Philbrick discovered that its leaders willfully
taught and advocated the overthrow and destruction of the
government of the United States by force. They spread their
Marxist-Leninist filth in schools and colleges and among
groups of well-meaning community-minded citizens who
had no idea that through their innocent contributions they
were helping to finance and foment violent revolution. In
short, Mr. Minor, these gray men and women going about
their everyday business in the drab guise of John and Mary
Public posed, and continue to pose, a greater danger to the
liberties we count sacred than the armed might of Hitler's
Germany and Hirohito's Japan combined."

"And Mussolini's Italy. Don't forget the Italians." I had
him now. Whatever public-relations team had worked the
makeover on him—and I had participated on the edges of
that kind of thing enough times I was appalled not to have
spotted it before this—had thrown me at first, but I had been
right in my prejudice. Fanaticism I could deal with. Conspir-
acists spent so much time doubling back on their own logic
they mistook insanity for brilliance. You could sell them a
refrigerator for the purpose of baking a pie. The only way

they would feel insulted would be if you were to offer an explanation.

"Forgive me, Mr. Leadbeater. You must understand that sincerity was the last thing I expected to encounter in a politician's den."

He didn't appear to have heard me. "For all their devious methods, Communists understand simplicity. They prey upon minds that are unable to grasp an abstract thought. Dick divides his apple equally among four friends. Nikita divides the wheat crop in the Ukraine equally among one hundred eighty million comrades. That's the beauty of wrestling to their plans. There's a good guy and a bad guy. The bad guy is direct and aggressive, the way America has been throughout seven wars. The good guy is sneaky; his way of fighting is complex, his holds difficult to understand and even more difficult to escape. In just that way Russia drew the Nazis deep into its wilderness before closing the trap. And so by compelling the unsuspecting fan to root for the hero's tangled tactics against the brute honesty of his evil opponent, the Communists slowly and subtly win converts to their unholy cause. It doesn't matter to them whether it takes years or generations. They waited four hundred years to overthrow the Czar."

He had begun to frighten me. It wasn't so much his theories as the casually conversational way he laid out this magoozlum of overcooked *angst*, like the neighborhood know-it-all explaining how radiation worked based on his possession of a glow-in-the-dark watch. When you dissected the translated text of an address by Hitler or Stalin it didn't go back together, and indeed fell apart at the touch of a reasonably sharp scalpel. What made it work was the delivery; that, and the speaker's unshakeable conviction that he was saying things that everyone knew were true but lacked the courage and the ability to put them into words everyone could understand. Fifty years ago, even forty, this kind of spellbinder could have seen the limits of his influence from the podium he stood behind, the egg crate he used to lift himself a few inches above the level of the pavement where his listeners stood. Radio and now the cathode ray had swollen those limits beyond even the speaker's imagination. But the pitiless glare of the television arc light would have done no service to the bug-eyed demagoguery of a Hitler, the foam-flecked doomsaying of a Stalin or a Huey Long, magnifying as it did the ugly distortion of a shouting face. It would have embraced the chiseled chin, rumpled hair, and cool mannerly sociability of this eastern-bred young Turk. His poison would glide down the coaxial cable and spill out into a thousand living rooms like notes from Liberace's piano, gently, insidiously, challenging you not to hum the tune all the following day. This was a new creature for a new jungle, incalculably dangerous.

I said, "I can see you've given this a great deal of thought."

"Not nearly as much as the people on the other side, nor for nearly as long. Why are you here really, Minor, and who do you represent? I don't know Henry Ford personally, but from what I've heard he wouldn't send a PR man to discuss politics." Although he placed no emphasis on the change, there was significance in his having jettisoned "mister." With it went the gloves.

"He would if he didn't want to attract attention. It's a delicate business whenever the public and private sector make contact."

He stretched an arm across the overcarved desk and snapped the switch on the intercom. "Miss Heimdall, please see if you can get Henry Ford on the line. Try the new Administration Center in Dearborn." He straightened. "I have no doubt you'll pardon my suspicion once we have this settled. These days it's difficult to follow the rules of baseball. Even baseball. Yalta changed everything."

Not to mention Mickey Mantle. "Cancel that call," I said.

"Belay that, Miss Heimdall." He flipped off the intercom and leaned back against the desk, folding his hands in front of him.

"I'm a friend of Anthony Battle's," I said. "He hasn't told anyone else about the conversations you've had. He just wanted to ask my advice."

"I thought as much. That it was Battle, I mean. He's the

only man I've approached on this matter who seemed reluctant to cooperate."

"It isn't that. He doesn't know the first thing about Communists or Communism. He thinks Karl Marx is the brother Groucho never talks about."

"That's just where the Party finds the best hunting. Among those who haven't yet made up their minds."

"He's a wrestler, not an idealogue. All he wants is to be left alone."

"He's an unwitting dupe. I saw that from the first. It doesn't make him any less dangerous; quite the contrary. The Reds thrive on ignorance. Understand, it's not Battle I want. If I'm to find the source of the corruption in his profession, I'll need names. His unwillingness to provide them can only lead me to one conclusion."

"Most of the people he associates with don't even have names. They call themselves Bobo and Leaping Larry and the Sheik. Their conversation runs to better holds and improved brands of jockstraps. You tell me how that's going to save America from the godless horde from the East."

Leadbeater's long upper lip skinned back from a pair of abnormally long and sharp canines. No doubt a trip to the orthodontist was in the offing before the November elections. "I offered him a way out. It's plain he doesn't want it. Your presence here is evidence enough of that. I've yet to hear one good reason why I shouldn't just go ahead and pull the plug on Mr. Battle."

"I can give you something better than Reds behind the wainscoting."

"A clever phrase. I'll have to remember it. Be more specific."

"I can lay in your lap the names of people involved in the biggest criminal conspiracy to hit this area since the Ferguson-O'Hara grand jury investigation of 1939."

His lip came down. Maybe his gums were just drying out. "You were part of that investigation, if I recall my reading. Names, you said?"

"Walter Reuther. Victor Reuther, his brother. The Ballista brothers, Tony and Carlo. And Frankie Orr."

"Orr's in Sicily."

"Detroit Metropolitan Airport takes jets now. Flight time from Palermo to here is less than twelve hours."

"Federal agents would be waiting when he set down. They'd bundle him aboard the next flight out."

"Not if he buys his way out of the original deportation."

"Impossible. That would take millions."

"I said it was big."

"Anyone can reel off a list of names, Mr. Minor. And draw up a plot to connect them. You're a writer, after all." But the "mister" was back.

"The Reuther brothers have no love for organized crime, particularly when it's organized by Frankie Orr. The no-necks who roughed him around during the Battle of the Overpass were Frankie's, on loan to Harry Bennett. That was before Orr found out how much untraceable cash is lying around your typical union strike fund. There are dissenters in the UAW who are only too ready to pipe that cash into Frankie's pocket in return for a leg up in the union. In 1948 he tried to give them that leg up by shooting Walter. When he survived, an attempt was made on Victor to help him see the light. The only thing that kept Orr from finishing the job was the federal indictment that eventually got him booted out of the country. Now he wants back in. I'll give you three guesses where he hopes to dig up the working capital."

"You mentioned the Ballistas. I recommended against subpoenaing them to appear before the Kefauver committee. They're mouth-breathers, nothing more. They push slots and jukeboxes."

"These days they're in the entertainment business. And they're Frankie's only link to his old territory."

"Except for his son Pasquale. Don't forget Patsy."

"Why not? Everyone else has. He's a weakling and cripple, getting along on his father's name and the Ballista's muscle." I caught a flash then of the big party at the Highwayman's Rest and the sallow youth in evening wear with his crutches leaning against the table next to him. I hadn't made the connection before. But then the last time I had seen him he was less than seventy-two hours old, fighting for life in an incubator at Detroit Receiving Hospital.

Leadbeater was chewing on some mental picture all his own. "I'm interested in your source."

"Call Anthony Battle and tell him he's off the hook."

He chewed some more. "Where can you be reached?"

I gave him my home number. It was finding its way into some interesting address books of late.

23

"Thanks don't cut it, Mr. Connie. I already seen Ginny and me in the canned-meat line at the government warehouse. Little Charlie don't finish school and winds up carrying a hod for fifty cents a hour, just like me and my old man. You done saved the Battles, Mr. Connie. Saying thanks just ain't near good enough."

"When you're out of the woods you can send me a couple of tickets to your next championship bout. Leadbeater hasn't forgotten about you yet."

"He sounded like it when he called. He couldn't wait to get off the phone with me so's he could stick it in some other sorry son of a bitch."

Neither could I, but not for the same reason. I can accept gratitude as well as the next man, and better than most, but I hadn't earned it from the wrestler until I could place evidence in Stuart Leadbeater's lap to prove that all of southeastern Michigan was in cahoots to put an over-the-hill expatriate mobster back in business. I thanked Battle for calling and cradled the receiver.

Agnes turned over in bed and slid an imperfectly shaved thigh across my groin. The tiny bristles awakened a semblance of life in my aging member, so recently exhausted. She smelled faintly of Chanel, more strongly of me. "That didn't sound like auto business," she said sleepily.

"It was, though. Kind of. I keep backing up for a longer head start. I'm so far away now I can't see what I'm running at."

"What's Leadbeater got to do with it?"

"Nothing. Everything. A couple of years ago I read a sci-

172

ence fiction story about a group of time travelers who were warned not to step off the path while they were hunting dinosaurs, because if they altered something no one could tell how it might affect history. Someone stepped off anyway and killed a butterfly. When they got back, everything had changed. This would just be another selling job if someone in the Navy Department had assigned Leadbeater to the Philippines instead of Point Barrow."

"He doesn't stand a chance of being elected. If that means anything."

I grinned at the religious picture on the wall opposite the bed, once the property of an acquaintance, long dead. He'd have enjoyed my situation. Not thinking things through had gotten him killed, but it had kept him out of the sort of trouble I spent my life in. "That's the hell of it," I said. "Getting him off my back may just clinch the election for him."

She propped her head up on her elbow. She looked younger with her hair loose around her bare shoulders, and she never looked her age. "You know what your problem is? You spend too much time figuring the angles. I bet if you just went ahead and did your job the way it was described to you when you were hired, you'd come out just as well as if you chased down all the loose cannons. And you'd have a lot fewer gray hairs."

"It's a theory."

"But you won't try it."

"Maybe I will. After I've chased down one more cannon. I need your brain one more time."

"Shit." She turned over, giving me a view of her back all the way down to her right hip, fished a pack of Chesterfields and a Ronson lighter out of her purse on the nightstand on her side of the bed, and sat up to light it. "I'd hoped you wanted me for my body. Okay, shoot."

"Who knows where all the bodies are buried in Detroit?"

"Narrow it down."

"I mean in the labor racket. Don't say Walter Reuther. I can't go there."

"Albert Brock."

"Next suggestion."

"Sorry. Brock's your man. His hands aren't as clean as

Reuther's, but his people are better off because Brock knows enough to put his cufflinks in his pocket before he shakes hands with the mob. He speaks their language."

"I interviewed him for the *Banner* when he was just a grunt. My editor twisted the story all around to make him look like an anarchist. He'd as soon run me over with a Kenworth as talk to me."

"My brother-in-law's a twenty-year man with the Steelhaulers. He's crazy about me. I should have married him instead of his brother. He can get you an interview."

"Am I lying on his side of the mattress?"

She blew smoke at me. "I don't ask you about your little friend at Ford. She smashes your views on good-looking secretaries all to pieces."

"If one more person starts following me I'm going to have to put in for a parade permit. What do the kids say? I didn't know we were going steady."

"It's a small town. Someone I know saw you with her at a ball game. Israel Zed's secretary has a withered arm. You don't have to be Rocky Lane to put it together."

"Does it bother you?"

"Does my brother-in-law bother you?"

"I asked first."

"Jesus Christ. Any woman who doesn't have to wear a bra to keep her tits out of her soup bothers the hell out of me. Does it bother me that you're dating one? I'm not sure. My opinion of men is already tarnished, so I don't expect much. Not that it's any of your business—unless you say it is—but my brother-in-law is a dispatcher at McLouth and he has pictures of his wife and four daughters all over his desk. He'd sell secrets to Khrushchev before he'd betray them."

"Not that it's any of your business," I said, "unless you say it is. Janet Sherman's a nice girl I've gone out with a couple of times and talked shop talk. She left the definite impression last time she wouldn't mind if it went further. I left the definite impression I would."

"Is it her arm?"

"No, goddamn it. It's the twenty-five years I spent finding out the world smells like bad meat before she was born. I can barely keep up with you. She'd kill me."

"That again. Everybody gets old, Connie. You're no pioneer."

"Let's just say I've got enough on my plate right now without going back to the young love table for seconds."

"I'll say. Politicians and union thugs. For someone who thinks he's Bernard Baruch, you sure act like Dick Danger. Speaking of Dick." She squashed out her cigarette in the saucer on the nightstand and reached under the covers. Her aim was remarkable.

When she left I was ravenous. I found a frozen steak in the ice compartment of the Kelvinator, left it to thaw under the hot water faucet in the sink while I pulled on a pair of pajama pants under my robe, and had a skillet heating on the stove—*I changed my plans for the evening when he told me he cooked with gas*; one of my most successful print campaigns at Slauson—when the telephone rang for the second time that night. The kitchen extension, a luxury I was just beginning to take for granted after a lifetime of apartments decorated around the single unit in the living room, had a long enough cord to allow me to introduce meat to hot metal while I spoke.

"This must be serious. You're the first woman who ever called to tell me she got home all right."

"Mr. Connie?"

"Oh, hello, Anthony. Get another championship shot so soon?"

"No, that don't come up for another six months. I got so buzzed over what you done for me I forgot I owed you. I took down some license numbers like you said."

"License numbers?"

"You know, from folks' cars that come to the Rest just to see Mr. Carlo."

"Hell, I forgot. Second." I found a fat ballpoint with the name and number of a garage printed on it and scribbled on the clean side of the butcher wrap the steak had come in until the ink started. "Okay, spill 'em."

He had seven. Two belonged to Cadillac Sedan deVilles. There was a Buick Roadmaster, two Lincolns, an Olds

Starfire convertible, and a Henry J. For a man who drove a six-year-old Chevy he knew his cars.

"What's a Kaiser doing in that crowd?" I asked.

"Oh, I knows that one. He run numbers down on Hastings. He don't spend money on nothing. I hear he gots pretty near a million stuffed in his mattress."

"There's always someone people say that about. When some rock 'n' roll punk finally gets around to slitting his throat he'll come up with a double handful of cotton batting and the dock bill on a hundred-foot yacht in Lauderdale. What about the others?"

"They mostly comes and goes in the dark. The Starfire's a lady. I think she's a McGuire sister."

"Thanks, Anthony. I may not need this stuff after all, but I'm happy you remembered."

"Anything you wants, you call. I mean that, Mr. Connie." He hung up.

I tore off the section with the numbers on it and stuck it in a drawer under the knives and forks. I'd been distracted by my cooking and hadn't paid much attention to what I was writing. A week went by before I looked at them again; by which time it was almost too late.

24

Summer came to Detroit as it always did, with the suffocating suddenness of two hundred pounds of wet canvas hitting a concrete slab. Buildings squirmed in the waves ribboning up from the asphalt, mattresses hung like seasick passengers over the railings of fire escapes, cars lolloped beside the curbs with their doors open while their owners stood around smoking cigarettes and waiting for the oven air inside to find its way out. The river lay as flat as hammered iron under a baked white sky.

But in the Glass House, twelve stories closer to heaven than the streets of Dearborn, the air remained a comfortable seventy degrees, filtered and chilled and circulated by a silent central system that wrung out the perspiration and let it drip discreetly into the cutout where the dumpsters rusted. You only knew it was July when you scribbled an appointment on your desk calendar or rode the elevator down and stepped out into the deadhammer heat and sick-sweet stench of automobile exhaust. That leaden reek was enough to make anyone nostalgic for the moist fresh stink of horse manure during childhood summers when the Industrial Revolution was just a dull hum in the East and motor transport remained a hobby for the rich, along with croquet and kept women.

I found Israel Zed not at his desk but seated on the tapestry sofa where he conducted most of his business, paging through a sheaf of papers stapled in one corner. Rare event, he was in his shirtsleeves, and his big rounded shoulders holding up a pair of black suspenders and his bowed head with its ubiquitous yarmulke looked at home among the Hebrew bric-a-brac that seemed to breed and multiply in the space, swallowing

177

room and light and whatever dreams the architect might have
entertained about the next century of corporate style. Though
he had been in residence only a couple of months, the place
smelled of rotted bindings, melted wax, and the shabby doom
of the cloistered existence. Zed was anything but monkish,
and so the effect was an illusion, created at no small cost to
the Ford executive expense account. I could only guess at the
clerks' reaction in Payable when the bill came in on the
seventeenth-century Talmud flaking away on the glass-and-
chrome coffee table in front of the sofa.

"Hello, Connie. Find a seat."

I found one—a stodgy old spinster aunt of an armchair
with bowed legs and crushed-velvet cushions faded the color
of rose petals imprisoned between the pages of Emily Post—
but didn't sit down on it, preferring to perch on one of its
bony arms. It smelled like old newspapers. "How bad's the
diagnosis?"

"Bad as it gets. By which I mean I have no idea what it
signifies. An acquaintance on Grand sent me these figures
this morning at my request. They represent General Motors'
second-quarter profit picture as they would have their stock-
holders believe to be gospel. I don't need to tell you this is
top-secret stuff. It doesn't go public until Monday."

"Has Harley Earl designed a grille funnier-looking than
ours?"

"No," he said; and the fact he didn't respond to the ex-
ploratory needle suggested he was concentrating in another
direction. "You know Hank's pledged to match them model
for model. That's why he threw out his grandfather's demand to return to the one-model company of prehistoric
days and established a five-model hierarchy to compete with
Buick, Cadillac, Chevy, Olds, and Pontiac."

"I didn't know. I guess it makes sense." Why not? The
whole of the present was traveling on borrowed gas. I hadn't
seen a fresh idea since belt loops.

"According to these figures the medium-price segment
among automobile consumers is in remission. The steam
from V-J Day is playing out, the Russkies are monkeying
around in outer space, Uncle Miltie's losing in the ratings;
call it what you will, but the number of buyers looking for

something in the middle range between the Bel-Air and the Eldorado has shrunk seven percent. Even allowing for poor-mouthing to avoid hefty taxes and salary hikes for employees, we're looking at a diminishing market with a year still to go before the Edsel hits the showroom."

Someone dropped an icicle down inside my shirt collar. Discontinued models don't carry bonuses or early retirement. "H. P. Curtice could be wrong. He's throwing a bundle down that rathole of a tech center in Warren. That would give anyone cold feet."

"He's never been wrong yet. The Corvette was a bigger gamble than the tech center and it paid off. You can call Hank a copycat if you like, but he didn't turn this company around in eight short years by betting on the wrong player."

"The market will probably bounce back. You said yourself we're a year away."

He smoothed down the top sheet. "I'm advising Mr. Ford to cut back production on the Edsel thirty percent. Maybe more. We can't risk dumping a hundred thousand units of an untested model into an unstable economy."

"That's no good, boss. We've got the dealers fired up to sell a hundred thousand. You can't fill them full of smoke, then kick them in the belly and expect them to blow out only thirty percent. It's all or nothing when it comes to incentive."

"I know a bit about incentive. John Maynard Keynes and I spent some time discussing it when we were helping FDR pull the world out of the Great Depression. It doesn't do much for incentive to have shiny new cars piling up at the dealerships and no takers."

"If you won't gamble you can't win."

"This is Detroit, not Las Vegas. I'm making the recommendation." He slid the papers into the portable safe he used for a briefcase. "You needn't worry, Connie. We're not gutting the American Dream. Just modifying it. We've already trimmed the car down from a high-end super-Mercury to something the Man in the Gray Flannel Suit can expect to finish paying for in five years. We took some of the power out of the engine but redirected it toward the windows and seat adjustments. We're keeping the Teletouch transmission and adding a rotating drum speedometer. It still spells class."

"Junking it up doesn't make it a better car."

He smiled his square perfect *goyim* smile. "We aren't in the business of making better cars, just more expensive ones with new features to make last year's model look like a pair of high-top shoes and make people ashamed to take it out of the garage. The first car we ever made was the best. It climbed mountains and crossed deserts on a teaspoonful of gas and any kid with a pair of pliers could fix anything that went wrong with it. It's all been downhill since the Model T. We just add lights and horns and whistles so people won't notice."

"What makes you so sure they won't?"

"The record speaks for itself. *White Christmas* is just *Holiday Inn*, with Technicolor and an inferior cast to boot. They didn't even bother to change the score. Even so it made a lot more money than the original. See, we're smarter than the Chinese. When some old Mandarin whom everyone trusted declared that everything that could be invented had been, they stopped inventing. That was a thousand years ago. Now we've got the bomb, Moscow has the bomb, and Mao Tse-Tung rides a bicycle to the office."

"Would he get there any quicker if he had a bomb?"

His grin set in concrete. "Anything new from layout and design?"

"I'm asking the Rembrandts downstairs to concentrate on the front of the car and leave the back out of the ads."

"Change of heart?"

"Choice of evils. As weird as it looks up front, those boomerang taillights look like a pair of inflamed ingrown toenails. People can only take so much that's new and revolutionary at a time."

"Why don't we just hide the whole thing behind a bush and save us all a lot of trouble?" His smile was still in place. I think he'd forgotten he was wearing it.

"I didn't say it was bad. People get scared when you throw something at them from left field; that's why those bullet-shaped concept cars never go into production. They make jokes. We don't want them laughing so hard they can't sign the finance papers."

"It's your campaign. I just hope your sour attitude toward the car isn't going to affect your promotion."

"I don't know how I feel about the car. I didn't know how I felt about blue mouthwash, but the manufacturer sold out its warehouse in a month and re-upped with Slauson, asking for me specifically. All I did was stick a green parrot in the ad. It didn't have anything to do with mouthwash, but it distracted people so they didn't think they'd be gargling Windex. No salesman worth the name thinks of himself as one. When I draw up a campaign I'm a customer. Maybe they sense that. Maybe you did too and that's why I'm selling cars instead of mouthwash."

"Okay, no ingrown toenails in the advertising. Anything else you want me to suggest to the boys in design? Maybe drill some holes in the front fenders?" He sat back, relaxing his mouth. I knew then why Roosevelt had selected him from among all the young geniuses in his stable to represent American interests in Palestine. He had the same control over his moods that a contortionist has over his body. I disliked him thoroughly.

Later, in my worst humors, I would blame everything that happened with the Edsel on *Reader's Digest*.

In its issue for July 1954, the magazine, which was too small to hide behind at the dentist's office but too large to carry in one's pocket, ran an article under the byline of an M.D. warning of the health hazards attendant upon smoking cigarettes, including the possibility of contracting lung cancer. Readers who believed that sort of thing either quit cold or switched their allegiance to Winston, which had hit the market recently with a dandy little gimmick involving a built-in plug filled with shredded fibers designed to "filter" the impurities out of the tobacco lest they defile unsullied tastebuds. The effect, some smokers told me, was similar to sucking the stuff through a bedsheet, but this was the market that turned cartwheels over Ivory Soap because the careless way it was milled caused it to float in the bathtub, and the feature caught on with some who didn't want to give up the weed entirely. Pall Mall, Lucky Strike, and Chesterfield reacted to the slump in their sales by coming out with their own filtered variety. Philip Morris, ever the rebel, canceled its long-time sponsorship of *I Love Lucy*.

Roger Greene, the cigarette company's advertising director, had clucked his tongue over the faltering sales figures, decided that the television comedy's viewers were laughing too hard to take advantage of the corporation's product, and severed the association with a polite statement to the press extolling the program's virtues but declining to give reasons for bugging out.

This was the show America stayed home to watch, the one whose episode surrounding the birth of Little Ricky knocked Eisenhower's inauguration clean off the Nielsen charts; the show whose producers squared off with Senator McCarthy and came out on top in the popularity contest when Lucille Ball stepped forward to confess a youthful membership in the Communist Party. If Tailgunner Joe couldn't shoot down the zany redhead, how to justify her sponsor's decision to toss the program into the groping hands of the gang of merchandisers who went to sleep nights dreaming of hearing their products' names spoken by those pontoon-shaped lips?

Explanations didn't matter in the end. Although the show remained at the top of every list until it was torn literally in two by its divorcing stars, the mania toned down after the departure of its original underwriter. Call it perplexity or doubt or fear of being caught laughing after everyone else had stopped, but the funny lines and situations never again reached the heights of audience hysteria they had found in the past, and in time rang as tinny as the canned track that accompanied them.

Philip Morris left in March 1955. That same year Winston Churchill resigned and Ike suffered his first heart attack. That confidence born of victory in Europe and Asia, which had survived the tragicomedy of Korea and the first successful atomic blast by Russia, stumbled. Housing starts fell off for the first time since Hiroshima, the birth rate slowed. Couples still shopped for new cars, but walked right past the medium beauties in the showroom, heading for the economy line at the back of the lot. Not fear, not quite that; but caution, which when spoken aloud amounted to the same thing to the biggest bull market of our century.

If Lucy wasn't invincible, who was?

PART FOUR
The Sixteenth Hour

25

When I called on Carlo Ballista I had been merely reluctant to rebuild my old burned bridges to the Underworld. The prospect of a second meeting with Albert Brock after all these years inspired something closer to terror.

Tempting as it was, I couldn't delude myself that the lead I'd given J. W. Pierpont had banished that wizened little bloodhound from my life forever. If I didn't have something solid for him when he came snuffling back my way, he'd leak the confidential material he'd swiped from my office and pull the plug on my future at Ford. Then there was the bone I'd promised Stuart Leadbeater to get his teeth out of Anthony Battle's throat. Knowing all this, I still let forty-eight hours pass between the time Frank DeFilippo called me at my house offering to set up an interview with Brock and the time I called back to tell him to go ahead.

A quarter of a century had elapsed since the day I interviewed a young striking laborer for the *Banner*. At the time he was bleeding from impromptu negotiations with Dearborn police and rented hoodlums involving brass knuckles and blackjacks. None of these details survived editing, and when the article appeared it had been chopped and twisted in favor of management. Brock had spent the intervening years bulling his way up from the iron seat of a Mack truck into first the local, then the national leadership of the American Steelhaulers. Under his direction the union had expanded far beyond its origins among a handful of trucking companies to embrace such unconnected occupations as airport baggage handlers, migrant farmworkers, pipefitters, Linotypists, and garment cutters. From his third-floor office among the Pewabic tiles and fussy Dutch Modern architecture of the Guardian Building, he controlled two and a half million votes, and the story was widely circulated that he had placed the country in the hands of the Republicans in 1952 after Adlai Stevenson snubbed him at a Democratic fundraiser in the Book-Cadillac Hotel.

All this had taken twenty-five years, of which the time we had spent in each other's company came to less than a two-hundred-thousandth part; yet I had no doubt he'd recognize and remember me as one of the last of his fellow creatures in whom he'd placed his trust and had that trust betrayed. He'd held smaller grudges as long. The local joke ran—and few laughed when it was told—that through Brock's contacts in the Brotherhood of the Broken Windpipe, North America's postwar freeway system was stronger for the number of these disappointments who lay buried in concrete from Portland to Poughkeepsie.

He lived modestly in one of the older homes in St. Clair Shores, a tall narrow saltbox that would need repainting in another year, and which predated the community's founding. This was no effort by French pioneers in bateaux, but by Jewish and Italian visionaries in long black Lincolns with Tommy guns in the trunks, seeking a safe place to raise their children away from the street wars they had fought since the Eighteenth Amendment passed. The house stood on a quarter-acre lot on one of the less fashionable streets, two blocks removed from the lake, and was a source of surprise for those few journalists who were granted an interview there and came expecting to find the nation's number-one labor chief bronzing himself beside the pool of a marble villa guarded by blue-chinned lower primates in black suits with gun harnesses. Actually the guards sat around in their undershirts watching television in the four other houses that comprised the block. Brock owned them as well. Frank DeFilippo~had told me that the old signal system had recently been replaced and that all that was required to seal off the block was a call to the radiophones installed in the big Chryslers parked at both ends. Vehicular roadblocks were more effective than a drawbridge and attracted less attention.

This was a legacy of the attempts on the lives of the Reuther brothers. To date no one had challenged Brock for the Steelhaulers presidency. The rank-and-file would have voted for him three days after he was dead, counting on the rock to move.

Having supplied Agnes' brother-in-law with my license plate number and a description of my car, I entered the block unaccosted and parked against the curb directly in front of the house. On the lawn, a small dark-haired boy dressed like Dennis the Menace, in overalls and a striped shirt, looked up from the toy truck he was playing with as I started up the sidewalk to the front door. "Papa's in back."

I thanked him and followed a path that had been worn in the grass around the side of the house. I had read somewhere that Brock's eldest son by his first marriage had a daughter older than this four-year-old uncle. The union leader had been widowed a year or so before marrying a young lady landscape architect from Melvindale.

At the end of the path stood a building of much more recent vintage than the house and one-fourth as large. I took it to be a garage because of the wide flayed-open doors, and it was that, but from the built-in bench that lined all three solid walls and the number and variety of tools glittering on their pegs I concluded that it was also a workshop, extremely well equipped. The rest of the space was taken up by a midnight-blue 1938 Packard convertible, as long as a pier with a tan canvas top and wire wheels. Cars had gotten smaller since the reign of its kind; I doubted the shop's doors could have been shut with it inside. This posed no problem, as no auto thief with brains enough to cross two ignition wires would have dared to try to make off with it.

The hood was folded up on the right side and a short blocky figure in a greasy sweatshirt and green work pants was bent over that fender, racheting a socket wrench at an awkward angle beneath a manifold I could have eaten off of and cursing in the breathless voice that came with that constricted position. Approaching, I noted that Albert Brock had gained weight since our first encounter, most of it through the middle and across the seat. Well, so had I, and my suit didn't hide the fact as well as the ones he wore when he appeared on TV.

I stopped on the concrete pad in front of the building, not sure whether I should move any closer or say anything. I felt suddenly as if I'd stumbled upon a bear in the middle of its feed, and I remembered a piece of advice Frank Buck had once given me, about making a lot of noise when walking through bear country because the animal didn't take being startled with any sort of grace. Right about then my throat began to tickle. I swallowed and tried to think moist thoughts. Finally I thought, *To hell with it*, and coughed discreetly into my fist.

"Hand me the pliers, will you?" Brock said then. "They're on the bench by the headgasket."

Fortunately the time I had spent on the floor at River Rouge enabled me to distinguish between the headgasket and a smutty carburetor lying among its entrails a little farther down. He seized the pliers from my grasp without looking and delivered eight or ten ringing raps to something inside the engine with the heavy head. Not feeling sure enough of my ground to ask why he hadn't just asked for one of the dozen or so hammers that hung on the walls, I said nothing. The shop smelled of old grease and new steel. Betty Grable grinned at me over a creamy shoulder from a calendar nailed above a collection of fan belts. It was a 1942 calendar, foxed and spotted with rust stains. The backs of Betty's million-dollar legs looked ulcerated. She'd been hanging there so long I doubted that Brock was even aware of her. For the first time in my life I felt I had something in common with Betty Grable.

The man under the hood barked a final triumphant oath, wriggled a little to place the toes of his sneakers in contact with the concrete floor, and straightened. The difference in our heights was infinitesimal. I'd forgotten how small he was, how compact the package that had grasped the flickering candle of the American labor movement and made of it a blazing torch, illuminating the dehumanizing conditions of the working man and burning away the veneer that protected his exploiters from the public. If you didn't know any of that you'd think he was just a man of fifty, shorter than average, muscular but running to fat with graying crewcut hair and a face that hadn't seen a razor in twenty-four hours. You might have taken him for a retired truck driver, and you'd have been right; but if you thought he was nothing more you'd have been as wrong as those broken enemies whose pieces lay strewn on Capital Hill and along the interstate. As for me, I saw little of the bruised idealist I'd spent an hour with over bootleg beer in the spring of 1931. But then I suppose he saw even less of the underfed and headline-hungry journalist he'd been with during that hour. The main difference between us was he'd invested the time between then and now propelling the world through its revolutions and rotations like a log-roller, while I'd spent it trying to hang on. It was a fearsome difference.

"My first new car was a thirty-eight Packard." He wiped off the socket wrench and pliers with a streaked chamois and hung them on the pegboard. "It was a black hardtop. I couldn't afford a convertible. This one's going to be a graduation present for my daughter. I'm putting a governor on the throttle. It's too much car for a girl otherwise."

"I had a Packard. It got out and scratched."

He wiped his hands with the cloth, watching me. He had long since lost the baby fat that had rounded his face in youth, making it the only thing about him that wasn't square. The corners of his mouth turned down harshly and his eyes glittered like nail heads in splintered wood. "Drink before noon?"

"Depends on the drink." I thought it best not to mention the diabetes. I didn't know why.

"Beer's all I keep out here. If you want anything stronger we'll have to go inside."

"Beer's fine."

He laid the chamois on the bench, pulled open the door of a ten-year-old Westinghouse refrigerator with coils on top, took out two bottles of Schlitz, and levered off their tops with a Coca-Cola opener screwed to the bench. He handed a bottle to me. "If you want a glass, I got one here with screws and shit in it. I can empty it out."

"From the bottle's okay." I thanked him and tipped it up. The beer tasted like stewed barbed wire. It had been a long

time since my last one and I'd never liked the stuff to begin
with. I watched him drink and flick foam off his upper lip
with a grease-stained knuckle. "About that piece in the *Banner*."

"Your editor fucked around with it. I figured that. Not
right away, though. I didn't know much about the press then.
Later I learned a lot. What happened to you?"

"Not much, unfortunately."

He waited for more. His silence and motionless eyes were
hard to ignore but I didn't elaborate. Effective though it was
across a bargaining table, as a journalist I recognized the tactic and withstood it. Finally he took another slug from the
bottle. "Frank DeFilippo said you had something important
to ask. This is the first personal day I've taken in months, so
I guess we might as well get with it."

I appreciated the way he phrased the command. "Thanks
for seeing me, Mr. Brock. It's about Walter Reuther."

"Did he send you?"

"No, but he's the—"

"Because if he did you can go back and tell him—don't
tell him nothing. He's a pissant publicity hound. When
things don't fall his way at headquarters he runs to the press
and bawls his eyes out. You'd think he was the only one ever
got stepped on by strikebreakers, just because he had his pet
photographers on hand at Miller Road. I was in Detroit General for six weeks after Wally Chrysler's gorillas hauled me
out from behind the wheel when we blockaded Dodge Main
and bounced me up and down Joseph Campau, but nobody
took my picture. Now they've named a freeway after that
cocksucker Chrysler, and I got a subpoena to testify in front
of the fucking McClellan Committee on labor racketeering."

"There weren't any photographers around when Reuther
got shot." I hoped I sounded more bold than I felt. His casual
dismissal of the ancient wrong that had given me nightmares
about approaching him had surprised and relieved me, leaving me unprepared for the outburst. His face had darkened
two shades and the corners of his mouth had bent down farther, pulling deep creases all the way to his nostrils. In the
timbre of his voice I heard something of the haranguing tone
he must have used to reach the last cauliflower ear at the ex-

treme edge of a crowd of frostbitten and disheartened strikers when the union was young. When we were all young. The blood had been black between Reuther and Brock since that time, when the publicity-savvy UAW firebrand had aced out his meat-and-potatoes rival for the top spot in the organizing committee, deciding Brock to follow his star into the even more primitive domain of the long-haul trucker. Those who had been around long enough to remember that old feud claimed it was that same rancor that had driven Brock to the top, and his union to the national contract that remained the envy of every labor organization in the country. The implicit accusation, that there would be no Albert Brock if there were no Walter Reuther, was the fire that burned eternally without consuming.

Calming himself, Brock ran his fingers through his hair without displacing a strand of the stiff bristly fiber. "Even so I wouldn't put it past the fucker to forget to stand out of the way when his own man put a bullet through his window."

"Do you really think he arranged it?"

He didn't reply. I hoped it wasn't what he thought, or the whole trip was a waste.

"As I started to say, Reuther didn't send me, but he's the reason I'm here," I said. "He's got a hard-on to trace that shotgun blast to the man who ordered it."

"Asshole."

"I'm sorry?"

"Reuther. He spouts all this pinko shit about the good of the many, but when it comes down to it, his own skin is all that counts. That's getting to be ten years ago. What good's it to the union if he finds out who ordered it? Comes to that, what good's it to you?"

"I can't answer for him or the union. Only myself."

He took another swig, stood his bottle on the counter, and leaned back against it, folding his arms. He had thick forearms like Alley Oop; the tendons stood out under his jersey sleeves.

I told him then, all of it except the part about Anthony Battle and Stuart Leadbeater. It told as well without that and I didn't want to get off on a tangent. He was the first one I'd told. I wasn't sure why I chose him. Maybe I'd gotten just too full of it to hold it any more and he was just handy. While I was talking a cobbled-up Model A with the hood removed to expose a lot of chromed engine chortled around the corner trailing Connie Francis out its windows. The boy and girl in the coupe were as unaware of the world I lived in as they were of life on Pluto. Their biggest problem was whether the change in the boy's jeans would buy enough gas to get the girl home in time for curfew.

Brock listened without expression or comment. When I finished he felt his bottle, found it too warm for his taste, and hooked another out of the refrigerator, raising his eyebrows at me in good-host fashion. I shook my head. It had begun to feel hollow from the amount I'd drunk already.

"You're in too deep to walk away." He opened the bottle and thrust it out from his body when foam welled up and over the lip, letting it splatter to the floor. "You should've laughed in Reuther's face when he threatened you. He isn't going to pull a strike or a slowdown just to get your goat. Nobody's that pig-headed."

"He gave me the impression he was. Anyway Pierpont nailed it down with those pictures of the car model." I spoke slowly. My consonants were starting to slur.

"Why come to me?"

"You're the court of last resort, the only man I know in Detroit who knows who's wearing what this season, bullet-proof vests or cement overcoats. People owe you favors. As I recall, one of the items the McClellan Committee wants to ask you about is a two-million-dollar loan you arranged for Frankie Orr from the Steelhauler's strike fund."

His face darkened once again. "I'm telling them what I'm telling you. That was a business deal. His people put up two casinos in Las Vegas for collateral. They're legitimate enterprises with a profit margin as big as Boulder Dam. Even if they defaulted on the loan, our interest in the casinos would more than double the investment. I'm only telling you that because you'll be reading about it in a couple of days, after I testify. I don't owe you an answer and I sure as hell don't owe you any favors. The way out of here's the same way you came in."

His words rang inside my empty skull, distorted by feedback. I'd never been much of a drinker, but a few sips of beer weren't enough to make me drunk. I decided I needed air, and turned to go. That was a mistake. The room swung around and hit me in the back of the head. My field of vision collapsed, first from the sides, then from the top and botttom, just like a broken picture tube. My knees folded.

26

I never lost consciousness.

I was aware that I didn't make it to the floor, that someone caught me from behind and half-dragged, half-carried me to a soft seat, but my brain was in a kind of brownout, capable of sensation but not thought. When the power came back on I was sitting on springs with my head tilted back, looking at an impressive display of cobwebs in a cross-hatching of rafters. I made a noise of some kind. Albert Brock's face shimmered in from the edge of my vision. He still looked angry. "I'm sorry, I didn't understand you. What did you say?" He didn't sound angry.

"Something sweet." My tongue grated against the inside of my mouth. "If you have candy or orange juice." I was having trouble finishing sentences.

"Grapefruit juice okay?"

I nodded.

"I got some in the house."

While he was gone I got a hand under me and pulled my pelvis against the back of the seat. I felt as weak as an infant. I was in the rear seat of the Packard. He'd lowered the top for clearance. The interior of the car smelled of dust and dry wood. There was nothing left of the atmosphere that had greeted its first owner, that combination of hope and self-approbation that went hand in hand with the purchase of a new automobile. No amount of restoration could bring it back.

Brock returned carrying a pitcher of pale yellow liquid and a small glass with orange flowers printed on it. He filled the glass and brought it toward my lips, but I intercepted his hand, taking it from him. I hated grapefruit juice. I drank it dry. The tart-sweet liquid stung the hinges of my jaws and slicked my throat like thin oil. I handed back the glass, waggling my palm at him when he started to refill it. He set it and the pitcher on the floor. The dizziness had begun to pass, and behind it the weakness. I thanked him.

"I didn't know you were diabetic."

"I didn't expect it to come up. Sorry for the trouble. All I need is a few minutes' rest and then I'll be out of your hair."

"I got gout," he said. "I can't eat liver."

I managed to grin. "Do you like liver?"

"Can't stand it. What's that got to do with anything?"

"Not a damn thing."

He stooped to pick up the pitcher and glass and put them on the workbench. When he leaned back and crossed his arms his belly poked over his waistband. There was no suet in it, just gravity. A fist would have bounded off it as off a tire. "How much water you draw at Ford?"

"Some."

"I know a little about the E-car. That kind of secret don't keep."

I said nothing. I hadn't referred to the Edsel even by its experimental designation.

"When something big like a new division starts up," he said, "the company-owned trucks aren't enough to ship all the cars out to all the dealers. They got to farm it out."

"Usually."

"Ever hear of Musselman Trucking?"

"Ann Arbor firm, right?" The name had appeared on a list that had crossed my desk only a few days before.

"They run a fleet of car haulaways out of Ann Arbor and Jackson. They always get a bid in whenever there's a push. I want them to get the E-car contract."

"Why?"

"They didn't throw in when we signed on with the nationals. They're scab, but they're too small to hurt. If they get the Ford contract and we shut 'em down, then they'll hurt."

"Let me see if I understand you." I put one foot on the Packard's running board. "The Steelhaulers want to put the screws to a non-union shop and you're asking Henry Ford to help."

"It wouldn't hurt him. They bid low. They got no overhead. Not yet."

I hoped the acceleration in my heart rate had nothing to do with my blood sugar. "I'd sure like a peek at your hand."

"Tony Balls. Carlo's brother. We used to be pretty tight back when the Steelhaulers did most of its negotiating with axe handles. Reuther was too good for all that. Getting his teeth kicked out was the way he did business. A note from me would get you in to see Tony."

"Fat lot of good that would do me. I've been bounced by one Ballista already."

"Tony couldn't bounce a ping-pong ball. He's in the oncology unit at St. John's, dying of cancer. He's got no reason to clam up or lie. Not any more."

"I heard that." I put my other foot next to the first. "I could lie and say I had something to do with the decision of which trucking company to use. You'd give me the password or whatever to talk to Tony and I could always claim Mr. Ford spiked Musselman at the last minute. I won't do that in your car in your garage with your grapefruit juice in my system."

He took that in, nodded. Then he unfolded his arms and straightened. "Are you strong enough to walk?"

I slid off the seat. The floor stayed put under my feet. "Thanks again, Mr. Brock. Sorry I interrupted your day off." I walked.

"Minor."

I was standing on the concrete pad where it had started. When I turned he was holding the socket wrench, slapping it softly against his other palm. I imagined he had manipulated an axe handle just that same way. "Any say on what time the cars are shipped?"

"You mean a date?"

"Did I say anything about dates? I mean day or night."

"Why?"

"Old Man Musselman crowds the highway laws. That's how he turns a profit. At six P.M. all the truck scales on all the interstates and U.S. highways shut down. That's when his trucks roll. He routinely overloads by three or four tons."

My heart rate went up a notch. "So if I say night . . ."

"No snake alive can crawl under a Musselman bid on a shipment after dark."

"I'm not saying I can swing it," I said. "But if I can, and you shut down our carrier, I'm up shit creek."

"Musselman's bonded. He's pledged to ship or pay to ship it with another firm. Nobody loses. Except Musselman." He shifted the wrench to his left hand and held out his right.

I didn't take it. "I might not be this honest if I didn't feel responsible for that newspaper piece. I've already persuaded Israel Zed to ship the cars at night. The press is better."

He moved a shoulder. "It wouldn't be the first time I got the short end of a bargain." He didn't withdraw the hand.

I took it. His grip was brutal. A generation had passed since he'd last slapped around a heavy vehicle without benefit of power steering, but when after days of haggling a handshake is the only contract you have until the papers are drawn up, you learn to make it last.

"One more thing," he said, hanging on. The nailheads glittered. "For the rest of your life, you and I never had this talk."

I agreed. He let go then. The ends of my fingers had just begun to tingle when I curled them around the wheel of the Mercury.

It was Saturday and no office. St. John's Hospital would be admitting visitors, but the way I felt just then I couldn't be certain they'd let me out when I was through visiting, so I went home to stretch out. At twilight I woke up feeling better than I had in days. I showered and shaved, just as if it were morning, put on clean clothes, and went downstairs to see about supper.

I had surrendered another yard of ground to the march of time and laid in a stock of frozen TV dinners, which had fused together in the freezing compartment as solidly as a course of bricks. While rummaging through the silverware drawer for the ice pick I hoped I hadn't thrown out with the Blue Network radio directory and my old spats, I came across the scrap of butcher wrap on which I'd written the license plate numbers Anthony Battle had given me. They belonged to the automobiles whose owners had gone to and from Carlo Ballista's office behind the Highwaymen's Rest without stopping to play the slots or take in the floor show. I'd had some recollection of looking for the list a while back, not remembering where I'd put it, and giving up the search as unimportant. I suppose it was only in consideration of the time I'd wasted that day that I didn't throw it away without looking at it first.

I noticed nothing familiar right off about the second number from the top. The only reason my eyes rested on it at all had to do with its symmetry, three letters followed by three numerical digits. Michigan plates ran two letters and four digits. I thought at first it must have belonged to an Ohio plate, not unusual with the border only thirty minutes south of the Detroit city line. Then I looked at the letters, and thereupon spread a decent layer of sod over the coffin containing what remained of my reportorial instinct.

FMC.

Ford Motor Company.

Company cars driven by the senior staff all displayed the prefix on their plates, with the numbers that followed ascending in reverse ratio to the order of importance of the executives whose automobiles bore them. Henry Ford II's, of course, was FMC-001; company chief Robert McNamara's was 002; Jack Bugas', 003; and so on. Mine was 009, after which the conceit was abandoned to the rabble that gathered around the water cooler to discuss the president's health.

The number on the list was FMC-004.

Just to be sure I dialed a number out of the State Government section of the telephone book.

"Michigan Secretary of State's office. Can I help you?" She sounded sincere, a break.

"I hope so," I said. "I was coming out of the downtown Hudson's this afternoon and happened to see a well-dressed lady put her handbag on top of her car to get out a dollar to give the valet who drove it up. Then she got in and drove away, only she forgot to take her purse off the roof."

"Gracious."

"That's exactly what I said. Anyway I ran after her and picked it up when it fell, but she didn't see me waving. I'd like to return it to her, except there wasn't any identification in the purse. All I have is her license number." I read it off.

"Yes, sir. You can turn the purse over to the police. She'll probably go to them anyway when she misses it."

I made an embarrassed little cough. "Uh, I thought of that, but there's quite a large sum of money in the purse. If I return it in person there might be a reward."

"I see." The voice chilled a degree.

"It's not what you think," I hurried on. "At least, I hope not. I've been out of work for six weeks, and I can't collect unemployment because my last job was part-time. If I miss another payment on my car the bank will take it. You know the chances of landing a job in Detroit without your own transportation. Frankly, I was tempted to just keep the money, but that wouldn't be honest."

"Yes, sir." There had been a thaw. "It's against policy, but I'll put a trace on the number. It will take a little while, so if you'll tell me where you can be reached?"

I gave her my name and number. She didn't know me from Garry Moore, but then her parents might have used my last column to line her cradle.

While I was waiting I heated up an order of Morton's salmon croquettes with rice and peas and ate them on a folding tray in front of *Highway Patrol* and John Cameron Swayze. The telephone rang in the middle of a story about Grace Kelly's wedding. I got up and turned off the sound.

"The license plate belongs to a green 1956 Lincoln Continental registered to the Ford Motor Company," reported the woman in the Secretary of State's office.

"Do you have a principal driver?"

"Yes. You may want a pencil. This one needs spelling."

I didn't bother to get one. I saw the name practically every day.

27

Evening visiting hours at a hospital are the worst. The quiet is preternatural, pointed up by the occasional squeak of rubber gurney wheels on buffed linoleum and the dry slither of a paperback book page being turned over by the nurse at the desk. Without the ungodly racket of the daytime bustle there is nothing to distract the visitor from the smell of carbolic or the sight of restless figures stirring under green sponge-rubber blankets in the half-lit rooms with their doors standing open. I wondered why the architects bothered with doors at all.

The nurse in charge of Oncology, thirty and plump, with powdered cheeks and the red lacquered lips of a geisha, informed me politely that Mr. Ballista was in Intensive Care and that only members of his immediate family were allowed to see him. When I mentioned that Mr. Brock had suggested an exception might be made in my case, she didn't blink but gave me directions to ICU. On the way I passed a metal plaque listing the names of the hospital's founding board of directors. Albert Brock's was fourth from the top.

Nobody accosted me as I pushed through the swinging doors into Intensive Care. The carbolic odor was strongest here, covering the stench of human corruption, and the suck and wheeze of life-support paraphernalia created the impression that the room itself was breathing. There was, in fact, an organic quality about the whole place, from the carefully maintained temperature approximating human body heat to the click-bleep-click pulse of the electronic monitors. I felt as if I had entered a living artery.

Screens hung with gauze separated the beds. I asked a

young resident or something in a white coat and sneakers with pimples on his neck for the whereabouts of Anthony Ballista. He finished reading the page on the clipboard he was holding, looked up at the ceiling as if committing something to memory, and hooked a hulking blonde nurse on her way past carrying a tray heaped with bloodstained cotton. "Ballista?"

"Second from the end." She passed on.

The resident or whatever had an afterthought. "Are you a relative?"

I said, "I'm his Uncle Guido."

It satisfied him as much as it had to. Nurses run hospitals. Doctors come and go like disposable gloves.

Tony Balls lay cranked into a semi-sitting position, entirely devoid of movement. The tubes running from his wrists to the IV bottle strapped to the stand next to the bed, and from his nose and penis to the draining apparatus underneath, might have been thick cobwebs. Picturing him as the identical twin of his hyperkinetic brother was like trying to match a stripped hulk rusting in the weeds of a neglected field to a well-preserved antique speeding down the highway. The naked polished-ivory scalp that was their most prominent feature had in Tony's case puckered and gone yellow and resembled nothing so much as a squash forgotten on the vine. The meaty lips had thinned and withdrawn to his gums, exposing teeth that seemed to have outgrown his mouth. Only the vulpine eyes the brothers shared had remained; bright, swollen, and yellow—those, and the uptilted nostrils, now dehydrated by the drain tube, cavities in a dry gourd. His one visible arm was just veneered bone. The thick calcium of an old break, improperly set, stood out on the wrist like a shackle.

"Tony?" I was whispering, God alone knew why. The big room was full of noise, human and mechanical. I wasn't disturbing anyone.

The eyes grated my way. Into them came that glad hand expression that people who work with people turn on everyone, regardless of whether they recognize him. "That's me. The good-looking one, I used to say." He laughed carefully. His voice sounded like a snow shovel scraping a sidewalk.

"I'm Connie Minor. We never met, but you might remember the name. I wrote for the *Banner*."

"Sure. I remember." It was clear he didn't. "Fetch me a drink of that water, will you, son? I think I got a jute mill stuck in my throat."

I handed him a half-filled glass with a jointed straw from the table by the bed, not flinching when his dry puckered fingers brushed my palm. The weight of the glass bent his wrist. His lips closed around the straw and he sucked until there was nothing but air. The dry gurgle set my teeth on edge. I accepted the glass and put it back.

"I got a hose hooked up to my phizz," he said, looking down at the Y where the sheet had sunken into his crotch. The water didn't seem to have lubricated his vocal cords any. "Fine-looking nurse picked it up in her hand and hooked it up. Time was when just the thought of it'd give me a honey of a hard-on, but it stayed limp as linguini. Guess it's time to dig a hole." He laughed again, even more carefully than the first time. In the days before the Ballistas had latched on to the simple tactic of separating to confound eyewitnesses, Tony had been the charmer, the brother who distracted the marked ones with jokes while the other came up behind and slipped the wire around their throats.

"Albert Brock got me in to see you," I said.

"How is Al? I ain't seen him since—well, water over the dam. I sent a nice present when his boy got married, one of them console TVs, and not a Tele King, neither. I never got a thanks."

"Maybe it got lost in the mail."

"Maybe. Them Brocks never did think much of Charlie and me. Too bad. They had a lot of nice nookie handing out coffee and sandwiches on them picket lines."

"What about Walter and Victor Reuther? Get along with them?"

"You better fetch back that glass, son. I don't want to spit on this here floor. They mop it regular." He made a ghastly grin. "Al Brock treated Charlie and me like rich uncles compared to them Reuthers. They run us off with truncheons during that Kelsey-Hayes strike. Frankie only sent us to help out."

"What did Frankie say?"

"Oh, Frankie didn't talk much except to tell us where to go and what to do when we got there. But he was pissed, I can tell you. I think that was the start."

"What was the finish?" My hand ached. I was gripping the tube frame of the gauze screen.

He started to cough, a rolling convulsion that started with little explosions in his chest and wound up shaking the bed to its frame. I thought at first he was faking, stalling for time to think after having said too much, but then jets of pink appeared in the clear tubes stuck in his nostrils. A slender nurse with a flushed face materialized, studied the green blips on the heart monitor, fiddled with the IV bottle, and placed a hand on Tony's chest. The fit had subsided and he lay sucking air with the whites of his eyes showing.

She straightened, looking at me. "You won't stay long." It wasn't a question.

"I just want to ask him something and then I'll be going."

Her eyes said a great deal of what she knew or had guessed about her patient. Then she was gone as abruptly as she'd come. It was all so brisk and without waste that I wasn't sure afterward if she'd been there at all. Hospitals breed hallucinations. It's the medicated air.

Tony's amber gaze was fixed on me. "Who the fuck are you?"

I told him again, although I was sure he hadn't forgotten. It meant nothing to him. I said again I was there on Albert Brock's ticket. That didn't seem to mean anything either. If I'd hoped he'd be out of his head and susceptible I was disappointed.

I had run out of time for euphemisms and diplomacy, not that they had ever been my long suit. "I always heard you were the smart brother," I said. "Smart enough anyway to know you won't leave this place through the front door. Frankie's in Sicily, and you and I know he isn't coming back, whatever Charlie thinks. Nobody has much to lose if you tell me who put up the bounty on the Reuthers back in forty-eight. You least of all."

"Charlie always was a dreamer. He kept saying Prohibition was on its way back right up until the Japs hit Hawaii."

I waited for him to take that somewhere, but he seemed to have finished. I tried another door. "You know Anthony Battle? Your brother's backing his wrestling career."

"Sure I know that boy. Us Tonys got to stick together, even if he don't look Italian." He laughed, not carefully enough. It brought on another coughing fit, but it was over quickly. No hemorrhages this time.

"Anthony's in trouble. He's got a politician on his back calling him a Communist."

He grinned the ghastly grin that made me wish he were coughing instead. "Shit, that boy ain't red. He's blacker'n a cast-iron skillet."

"Even so he's going to be thrown to the wolves if I don't give the man something better. I need the name of the man who pulled the string on Walter and Victor Reuther."

"What's your angle? Everybody's got a angle."

"I've got people on my back too. It isn't every day you get to climb out from under and drag someone else out with you."

"Yeah, I figured it was something like that. So what's my angle? You gonna fix me up with a new pair of lungs?"

"No. And if I could I wouldn't. You earned this a long time ago. You're as bad as they come, Tony."

"I ain't sorry for a thing I done. Charlie ain't neither. Our old man sold shoes to fat ladies to live. You know what they done to him at the store when his knuckles got too stiff and swoll up to pry size sevens onto size ten clodbusters? Stuck a mop in his hands and cut his pay by half. I guess he's in heaven now. He should be, it's all he ever talked about. I'm telling you what I told that stick-shaking priest come to see me the other day to hear my confession: If that's what I got to do to make the cut, I'd just as soon shovel coal for Old Nick. At least I'd get to see all my friends."

"You don't have any friends. None that wouldn't roll over on you for a plea to a lesser charge."

He reached up and curled his fingers around the IV stand. The gray flesh under his arm hung like a washcloth. "If I push this thing over, half the floor will come running. You won't wait for it if you want to leave on your own two feet."

"I'll leave as soon as you take a look at this." I shook

loose a fold of butcher paper from my jacket pocket and held it in front of his face.

He didn't look at it right away. After thirty seconds or so he took his eyes away from mine and focused on the sheet. He let go of the metal stand, took the paper from me. "What's this? Letters and numbers."

"Any of them familiar?"

"I know the alphabet. I can do my sums. Charlie and me got through third grade."

"They're license plate numbers. The second one from the top's the one I want you to look at. It belongs to a green Lincoln Continental. This year's model."

I caught the glint, although he covered it quickly. I might not have, in the full bloom of his health. Weasels are sly survivors. "I don't look at cars much. Charlie, he likes 'em big with plenty of flash. He had an Auburn once but he wrapped it around an Edison pole. I just drove whatever got me from here to there."

"This one belongs to the Ford Motor Company. Israel Zed drives it."

"If you knew that, why ask me?" He held out the scrap of paper, but I didn't take it. He let it drift from his fingers. A current of air took it and spun it to the floor.

"That list was made from cars parked at the Highwayman's Rest on Lone Pine Road. The people who drove them all had business with your brother not connected to the customer's side of the roadhouse. What's Zed got going with the Ballistas?"

"Nothing. Now."

His eyes were closed. He was so near to a skeleton I got panicky, but the monitor continued to beep rhythmically. I moved closer.

A hand touched my shoulder. I jumped six inches and looked into the flushed face of the slender nurse. She moved on a cushion of air and struck like a fuse blowing.

"You're going now," she said.

"Five minutes."

"You've had twenty. I don't care whom you represent, you have to go."

"I like the company."

The nurse looked at him. His eyes were open. Their feral amber color was always a shock.

"Five minutes." She vanished again.

I rested my hands on the bed rail. "Okay, that's now. What about then?"

"When?"

"You're not that far gone, Tony."

"Okay. I don't owe the son of a bitch nothing. Getting him to stop around and pay his respects is like pulling teeth with your toes. I told Frankie he'd live to regret throwing in with a Jew."

"Zed knew Frankie?" I leaned in. We were breathing the same air now. I thought I could smell the medication through his skin, the morphine or whatever that was dripping into him to curb the pain.

He made that death's-head grin. "What's the matter, you never hear of the Frankie Orr College Scholarship Fund?"

I absorbed that. Before I could frame another question he went on.

"Old Izzy, I guess he didn't neither, but he had a good excuse. Him being the first."

For the time remaining to us I listened to him talk against the mechanized eternity of that floodlit room.

28

John Bugas—Jack to his friends, of whom from certain knowledge I could identify but one, he whose name graced the company we both worked for—sat at his large neat gray desk listening to me without once looking away, as if I were a radio set airing his favorite program. His long frame in its simple blue suit remained motionless in the wingback, and his polite eyes canting back from his icebreaker nose never blinked. His shoulders were precisely parallel to the desk. He seemed of a piece with the matching desk set that occupied its top, as regulated as the framed portraits of the Ford Trinity tombstoning the walnut panels behind him. Substitute Washington, Lincoln, and Eisenhower for the two Henrys and Edsel, and the office would check in every particular with recommendations from FBI headquarters in Washington, his late employer. There was even a tasseled American flag on a stand in the corner.

When I finished, the silence crackled. His was the quietest office on the executive floor, cork-lined, with a rubber pad under the carpet and a jacket of silicone on every caster and bearing in his chair. I figured all those qualifying sessions with earphones on the Bureau target range made his ears abnormally sensitive.

"I wish you'd come to me at the start." His pioneer inflections were gentle. Company scuttlebutt said he was embarrassed by stories about his obstreperous past and had taken steps to eradicate the frontier influence from his manner, including speech lessons.

"I was new to the neighborhood then. I didn't know who

my friends were." I didn't add that I still didn't. What I had learned was just too big for me to contain.

I'd wrestled with it all day Sunday, and was still undecided when I went to bed Sunday night. Monday morning I'd awakened with the determination to lay the whole thing in Bugas' lap. His background in law enforcement might give him a different perspective from the standard executive flank defense. In any case I wasn't Atlas; the weight of the world was raising hell with my bursitis.

"There isn't a chance this man Ballista is lying."

"I doubt it."

"His type can be convincing. Their testimony is an amalgam of inside gossip, personal fantasy, and straight dope. Even they don't know the difference in some cases. Lie detectors are useless."

"I know these people, sir. I'm a pretty good judge."

"I know them too. I've interrogated my share."

"Excuse me, sir, but you only know them from a cop's point of view. I always got on with them because they thought of me as a neutral party. I was their ear to the straight world. They all had stories they were busting to tell, but I was their only safe audience. If the heat turned up they could always claim I invented it."

"Did you invent it?"

I nodded. "That's a fair question. I could just be spreading lies about my immediate superior because I want his job. I don't. I'm an ad flack, that's all I'll ever be. You heard me tell Mr. Ford I wanted to turn whatever success I made of the Edsel into a position in the field of journalism. I know now that will never happen, but I don't intend to slink away from advertising with my tail between my legs. I still want the chance to show you what a first-class snake-oil salesman can do when he has something worth selling. I can't do that from Israel Zed's office."

"Would you be willing to sign a paper stating that you would not accept his position if it were offered to you?"

"Only if you insisted."

A barely discernible crease appeared in his forehead. "If you're sincere about not wanting his job, why should I insist?"

"I've thrown away enough paper in my time to build a city of frame houses. I don't value it much. I'd rather shake hands on the deal."

The crease vanished. "That's a good answer. Harry Bennett had a paper signed by Hank's grandfather promising him complete control of the company after old Mr. Ford's death. It didn't do him much good when push came to shove."

I wanted to ask him if it was true he and Bennett had once pulled guns on each other. I didn't. It would have been like asking a rising starlet about her old nose. In the bland, burnished, climate-controlled atmosphere of the Glass House, such behavior was as out of place as pen wipers and open inkwells.

"I'm still not clear on what any of this has to do with the assaults on Walter and Victor Reuther," he went on. "What did Zed have to gain?"

"Frankie Orr's good will. Zed was a poor boy from the Jewish ghetto with a first-class mind. Frankie always had one eye on the future and saw the advantages of having a good lawyer whose loyalty he could count on, so he ponied up the cash for Zed's education at the University of Michigan School of Law. Trouble was, when Frankie most needed him, Zed was up to his eyes in Washington politics. FDR's brain scouts plucked him out of Detroit when the ink was still wet on his bar exam and put him to work on the Great Depression. Then came the ambassadorship to British Palestine. By then I guess he thought he was out of Frankie's reach, and had probably talked himself into forgetting just how much he owed an old bootlegger. Frankie waited until he came back into the private sector to work for Ford, then paid him a call."

"He threatened to expose him."

"He had a lot less to lose than Zed if it came out whose money had taken him so far from his old man's pushcart in the downtown corridor. That federal indictment for violation of the Mann Act wasn't going away. Fixing the feds is expensive. He needed the money in the UAW pension fund, but the Reuthers were standing in front of it. But taking them out was only half the battle. He needed flashy legal help to take the stink off what amounted to the single largest bribe in the history of organized crime. Israel Zed had to come back into the fold. Coercing him with the threat of exposure wasn't enough, not for the Conductor. He had to be reminded just how deep his debt went."

I stopped. All this talking was making me lightheaded. I slipped the Hershey bar I had lately taken to carrying from my shirt pocket, peeled down the paper and foil, and helped myself to a row of chocolate squares. Candy didn't taste nearly as good as it had in the days before it became medicine. Bugas said nothing, waiting for me to continue.

"The pimping charge was a frame." I replaced the wrapper and returned the bar to my pocket. "The reason the feds couldn't get anything more on him is Frankie never gave the order to kill someone to the person he expected to carry it out. He always used buffers. That way, if one of his button men bungled and got arrested he couldn't bargain his way out by pointing a finger at Frankie. The buffers he used are anyone's guess, probably junior execs, Frankie wanna-bes. Except in this one case. In this one case he made Zed carry the message to Tony and Charlie Balls."

"Diabolical."

"An Orr trademark. If he behaved like the silkshirt thugs you see in Syndicate movies, he'd have gone to the chair twenty years ago. As soon as Tony told me I believed it. It had his thumbprint all over it."

"But why should he confide in you? Doesn't he believe in the Code of the Underworld?"

"Another Hollywood invention, sir. Though I expect you ran into your share of hoods who imitated what they saw in the pictures," I added quickly, knowing full well his job at the Bureau had mainly involved shifting documents from the In box to the Out box. "They love to gossip, as I said. So much the better if there's something in it for them. In his case he had nothing to lose and time to kill. Terminal patients don't draw many visitors."

He rose for the first time since I had entered the office and strode to the window. His glossy patent-leathers, his sole affectation and likely a source of friction with erstwhile boss J. Edgar Hoover, doyen of tidy invisibility, made no sound at all on the steel-gray carpet. For a time he stood with his back to me and his arms hanging at his sides. There wasn't much to see beyond the late-summer glare, except the new construction creeping across the pastures beyond the city limits. Like a spike driven into the trunk of a moribund oak, the Ford towers had sparked a sudden blossoming in Dearborn's industrialization, dormant for decades. New housing projects would follow; long-barreled, low-roofed homes with attached garages and basketball hoops crowding out barns and plowed fields. Where did all the old farmers go after they sold out? You never saw them on park benches.

"I wish you'd come to me sooner," he said again without turning. "A large part of me wishes you hadn't come at all. The last thing we need on the eve of launching our first major new division since we acquired Lincoln is a scandal."

I said nothing. After another minute he turned. His features were invisible against the bright glass. "This is my fault. I'm supposed to be an expert on security. That's why Hank hired me, to shield him from Harry Bennett's snoops while he worked out his plan to rescue the company from his grandfather. That an independent operator should waltz right in here, crack a safe under my protection, take pictures and documents, and walk out without anyone seeing him is a disgrace. In my place a Japanese officer would fall on his sword."

He fell silent again. For all I could see of his eyes he might have been looking around for some sharp object in the room that would suffice. I said, "If it's any consolation, sir, all Pierpont did was force me to gather information you needed to know."

"I'd rather not know. Not for another year, anyway. Until the Edsel's off the proving ground. Which brings me to the favor I have to ask."

The lightheadedness returned, but I didn't reach for the candy bar. I had a feeling it wouldn't help this time.

"Israel Zed is harmless where he is," he said. "He isn't about to start telling people he's Frankie Orr's man, and at this point only you and I and a dying small-time racketeer know it. Orr too, of course, but he's in exile and even if he weren't he has no reason to expose Zed now, especially if there's anything to this pipe dream of Carlo Ballista's and he has hopes of coming back; if that comes to pass he'll need Zed more than ever. So does Ford. He's a promotional genius."

I was gripping the arms of my chair hard enough to hurt. The lightness was spreading. I felt that if I didn't hold on I would float away.

"I think you know what I'm asking," he said.

"I think so. I just want to hear you ask it."

He came away from the window, returning definition to his bold nose and mild, slightly melancholy eyes. "Don't say anything to anyone about what you've told me. No one, not even Mr. Ford. I'll handle that when the time comes. Until then, this is just between us."

"And just when will the time come? When the Edsel's on the road?"

"About then, yes. Believe me, it's as difficult for me as it is for you. Conspiring to harbor a criminal goes against all my training."

"What about Pierpont? I put him on the track I just left. He's bound to come to the same conclusion."

"Perhaps not. For you, getting in to see Anthony Ballista was a special privilege owing to a chance contact with Albert Brock. You said yourself he hasn't much time left. Chances are he won't last long enough to tell Pierpont anything."

"In which case Pierpont will come back and put the screws to me."

"You've stalled him this long. If he's foolish enough to throw away his hole card and leak that information he took from your safe, I'll know the source. We already know Reuther's threat of a strike or a slowdown is just posturing. If Pierpont becomes a pest, tell me. I've dealt with the type before."

"What about Stuart Leadbeater?" I'd told him only as much about the lawyer-candidate as he needed to know, omitting Anthony Battle's name. Something about the ex–G-man's manner made me hold back certain things. "I can't stall him for a year. The election's in November."

"Leave him to me. I know a bit about politicians." He took his place behind the desk but remained standing. "I realize what I'm asking. The nature of your work requires you to keep close contact with a man you find repugnant. You'll have to behave as if you suspect nothing. I wouldn't request it of anyone else I work with. Mead Bricker always says what's on his mind, especially when he's drinking, which is most of the time. Jack Davis wears his conscience on his sleeve. Even Hank is apt to down one too many and blurt something out just for the shock effect. Your background is entirely different. You couldn't have survived in the newspaper business as long as you did without the ability to dissemble."

I no longer feared floating away. I wasn't sure if I could conquer gravity long enough to get up out of the chair. "You're saying I'm the only man dishonest enough for the job."

"Disingenuous, I think, is a better term. It will profit you in the end. Not that much time has passed since Hank himself had to play the diplomacy game that he's forgotten what it costs. You will be reimbursed. Say, a twenty-five percent pay hike and an upgraded expense account to equal your annual gross salary?"

I did the arithmetic in my head.

I said, "I'd like that in writing."

"I thought you had little regard for the value of paper."

"Consistency being the hobgoblin of little minds, Mr. Bugas," I said, "I'm not as stupid as I look."

A faint smile grazed his lip. It was the kind undertakers jack up onto dead faces. "I'll have my personal attorney draw something up. There's no sense bothering the company firm with this."

I stood and shook his hand. His grip was solid, the way they rehearsed it in Washington. I snicked the door shut behind me on the way out, making no more noise than wolfbait.

By the elevators I ran square into Israel Zed and Janet Sherman. Zed had on gray gabardine. Janet wore a long-sleeved leaf-print silk blouse and a green skirt and carried her handbag slung from the crook of her short arm.

"Hello, Connie," Zed said. "Business with Dick Tracy?"

"He was just asking me how things were going. Hello, Janet."

"Connie." She had been cool to me since the night I had sent her home from my door.

"How are they? We haven't talked in a while."

"Not bad. I'll have some new dummies on your desk before five."

"Good, good. Plans for lunch? Janet and I thought we'd hop to Greektown." The expression on his big face said a positive response to the invitation would be poor office etiquette.

"Thanks, I had my fill of moussaka and saganaki by the time I was twelve."

The elevator doors sloughed open. "Suit yourself. Don't work the day away. Life's too short."

I watched the doors close. My stomach sank with the car. Secretaries shouldn't date their married bosses. Especially that secretary, and that boss.

29

Davy Crockett's coonskin cap was everywhere in 1956.

Fess Parker wore it first, for Walt Disney.

Jackie Gleason wore it on *The Honeymooners* in his capacity as member in good standing of the Loyal Order of Raccoons, Bensonhurst Chapter.

So many little kids wore them to a Saturday Felix the Cat matinee at the Roxy that the theater's insurance company declared the practice a fire hazard and threatened to cancel its policy.

Estes Kefauver, like Crockett a Tennessee native, wore it to celebrate his Democratic nomination for vice president under Adlai Stevenson. It didn't help.

Agnes and I watched the election returns on her spanking new color console Admiral in the living room of her duplex in Madison Heights. It had a round picture tube, a speaker covered with orange cloth shot with glittering gold threads behind diamond-shaped wooden slats, and sliding doors with recessed handles that concealed the screen when the set wasn't in use. Too common now to be a status symbol, the domestic oracle seemed to have entered a new stage of delicacy, pretending to be a credenza.

In the cheesy cloakroom studio set-up with numbers clacking into place on the wall behind the talking heads, the blues looked gray, the reds were beige, and even Edward R. Murrow's bourbon-flushed basset hound features might have been cast in dirty plaster of paris. I didn't see much color at all until a commercial came on for *Sergeant Preston of the Yukon* in blazing primaries, after which the ghost of Preston's scarlet tunic continued to haunt the screen like an incarnadined Marley until the Nevada ballots were counted. Until that night I'd been monkeying with the notion of diverting some of my improved finances toward a color set of my own. Now I gave some thought to replacing the old gas four-burner in the kitchen with a Hotpoint electric range.

California was just reporting in when Agnes sprang up off the sofa and snapped the knob. The picture imploded into a pinpoint and took its time fading. "Four more years of that grinning skinhead. It's enough to make you want to move to Canada."

"Stevenson doesn't have that much more hair. At least when Ike smiles he doesn't look like someone's pulling out his toenails with a pair of pliers." I helped myself to a handful of potato chips from a bag with a woman's silhouette in red on a field of yellow.

She put her hands on her hips, facing me with the TV at her back. She had on Capri pants and a fuzzy pink sweater that flattered her clean figure. Some people just aren't intended from the start to submit to gravity and changing metabolism. "Is that what we've come to? Choosing our leaders on the basis of their bridgework? Why don't we stop kidding ourselves and elect Errol Flynn?"

"Can't. Foreign-born. I'd run Randolph Scott. A cowboy actor would know how to deal with the Russians."

"We're the Russians."

I crunched chips and waited. She could never leave a line or a TV dinner alone.

"I mean it," she said. "Khruschchev doesn't have to bury us. We're already doing a good job of digging ourselves under a pile of atomic waste and red-baiters and plastic radios that cost more to fix than they do to throw away and replace with a cheaper model that lasts half as long. We're the enemy, not the Communists."

"I knew if I hung around long enough you'd give up on Kerouac and start quoting Pogo."

"Why not? I'd sooner vote for a comic-strip character than anyone who'd run with a thug like Nixon. Did you know that when he was in charge of rubber rationing during the war his best friend was in the tire business?"

"I expect Ike will keep him in line."

"Until his next heart attack."

"Do yourself a favor and stop chewing on the state of the nation. Whoever wins, we lose. I don't know why something that happens every four years should come as such a surprise to so many people."

"If you think that way I'm surprised you decided to vote."

"I was only interested in one of the races. Which reminds me." I got up and walked around her to turn the set back on. A girl singer with capped teeth was wondering where the yellow went. I tried channels 4 and 7, but Huntley and Brinkley and John Daly were still wading through the national returns. The smaller stations were all showing movies and every third one seemed to be *Stella Dallas*. I came back to 7 just as the local feed was starting. Sander Vanocur, seated in a set even more cramped with a painted plywood background, was reading figures from sheets passed to him by a hand belonging to someone beyond the camera. A number of small communities had changed mayors; Wall Street was losing momentum for the first time since Truman canned MacArthur and people were beginning to worry about their Christmas bonuses.

Five minutes of vaguely familiar names and ambiguous numbers crawled past before the grave anchorman turned to the results in Wayne County. In the race for prosecutor, Stuart Leadbeater finished six thousand votes behind his Democratic opponent. "A dark horse early in the campaign," Vanocur intoned, "Leadbeater appeared to be closing the gap in September with a media barrage allegedly fueled by rumors of heavy financial support from an undisclosed source, then dropped back when the rumors proved to be without basis and his war chest rang empty. Despite a last-ditch effort to attract attention with a bizarre claim concerning subversive activities in the field of professional wrestling, of all places, Leadbeater failed to recapture his late-inning momentum."

"That should restore some of your faith," Agnes said.

"I'd have to have had some first." I turned off the set. *Leave it to me. Bugas. I know a bit about politicians.* Enough anyway to know what it meant to lead one to the edge of the trough, then kick it over. The picture made my back prickle.

Agnes stuck a Chesterfield between her lips and fired it up off a table lighter shaped like a palomino. "I wish you'd tell me about Leadbeater. Frank's getting you in to see Albert Brock; it had something to do with this, didn't it? Is Brock the one who pulled the rug out from under his campaign?"

"No. Even Brock isn't that big. No one man is. I'm not being mysterious, just tired. Sometime I'll tell you the works. You'll think it's a fish story. Maybe I will, too, by then."

"You get tired a lot, chiefly when I want you to tell me something."

I had no answer. I'd been prepared for a pleasant evening of television watching and poking fun at each other's politics. It was turning into something else and I hadn't the energy for it.

"You don't *talk*, Connie. *We* don't talk. I'd get more company out of a parakeet."

"We talk all the time. What do you call what we're doing now?"

"We're forming words and stringing them into sentences. It's all very civilized and about as enlightening as stuffing envelopes. I don't know, maybe it's not your fault. Maybe it's your background. Maybe Greeks don't talk, or maybe it's the fact that you were a reporter and spent most of your time asking questions and listening to the answers. In my family we yelled and screamed and shook our fists. It sounded like World War Three, but we all knew what everyone else was about."

"That's Italians for you. I stopped going to their weddings when I lost my hard hat."

"See, that's my point. The most I ever get out of you is some cynical comment that says we'd all be better off if we took cyanide. We've worked together and slept together, but I didn't even know what your job was at Ford until you'd been there almost two years. Would you have told me if we were married?"

"Is that what this is about? What I do at Ford?"

"Hell, no, it's not what this is about." She dragged deeply on the cigarette. The tip glowed as fiercely as her eyes. Leaking smoke out several orifices, she stabbed it out in a heavy glass ashtry. "I'm going to change something I said, about you asking questions and listening to the answers when you were in the newspaper business. You never listened to anyone in your life. You had all the answers written in your head before you asked the questions. It's no wonder the profession deserted you. You stunk at it."

"Agnes, it isn't my fault Stevenson lost. A lot of other people voted Republican."

I ducked just in time. The ashtray whistled past my ear, struck something that rustled, and thumped the carpet without breaking; pre-war goods. She made claws of her fingers, curled them into fists, and squeezed her eyes shut hard enough to cause a headache. I'd seen her angry, but not like this. I was suddenly afraid she was having a stroke. But when she opened her eyes she was breathing normally.

"Don't you think I know you're in trouble?" She laid the words out carefully, like cards in a game of solitaire. "That you've been in trouble for a long time? At first I thought it was a woman, and when I found out you were running around with one half your age it seemed to explain a lot. Then I wasn't so sure, and when you asked about Leadbeater I knew it was much more serious. Well, I thought, this is good, now he'll open up; he needs me after all. But you never did. You don't need me. You don't need anybody. You're as self-damn-sufficient as a goddamn diesel locomotive. So why am I wasting my time on you?"

"My problems are mine. Who am I to dump them in someone else's lap?"

"That's one of the reasons for having a lap. For my having one." Her eyes were brimming.

"I've been alone my whole life, Agnes. You can't expect me to just go ahead and do something I have no preparation for."

"I'm asking you to do just that. Is it that hard?"

The big television set was still cooling off. The tubes ticked and crackled.

"There's no point to it now," I said. "It's working itself out."

She let out a chestful of air, picked up the pack of Chesterfields, and shook another one out. "Go home, Connie."

"We took your car, remember? I was sleeping here tonight."

"I'll call you a cab. I'm sorry. I just can't handle any more of you tonight." She lifted the receiver off her pink Princess, pressing down on the standard with her other hand out of habit to keep it from following.

"I'm sorry too."

I wasn't, though, then. I was hollow. The break was ragged; we went out a couple of times after that night, but we didn't sleep together. I called her the last time around Christmas. The silences on the line were hard on my thickening eardrums. Years later I heard she was seeing a Kennedy delegate, but by then I was having trouble picturing what she looked like. It's only recently I've begun again to see her clearly, and her dead five years.

30

At 6:03 on a Monday morning late in September 1957, with an hour and a half to sleep before I had to get ready for work, a virgin set of tires squished to a stop in my driveway and a pair of horns tuned deliberately off-key, B-sharp and E-flat, tore me out of some damn dream in which I was running in slow motion toward an appointment I was late for with someone I didn't know in some location I'd forgotten. I'd had the dream the first time shortly after I started at Ford, and it had recurred just enough since for me to recognize it and have some control over it, which was why the interruption annoyed me. I made a face at the alarm clock, untangled myself from the sheets and blanket, and lurched to the window overlooking the corner of the porch roof. It was Indian summer and the sunlight lay in a brazen trapezoidal patch on the grass and asphalt in front of the house.

It was emerald-green with a white top and elliptical white cutouts along the rear fenders. The tires were whitewalled, and the chrome plate on the divided front bumper and around the tandem sealed-beam headlights and all over the fish-mouth grille glowed with silver fire in the damp morning light. It was the top-of-the-line Citation, and its 124-inch Mercury chassis filled the driveway almost to the curb. While I was looking at it from the window, Israel Zed, who was standing next to it on the driver's side, leaned in through the open window and whomped the horn a second time. In spite of my grogginess that was the thing I most liked about the car at that moment, that virile horn. It was a clarion, an audio erection that managed to capture the youth and audacity of a Klaxon while filtering out the schleppy comedy and pushing its essence through the brass section of the New York Philharmonic. It was the end product of 10,000 years of evolution, conception, invention, revolution, and celebration, but its provenance was as old as the first full-throated bellow of a tree-dwelling half-ape over the body of his vanquished foe.

I hurried into some clothes and went down unshaven and -showered to accept Zed's meaty hand, a gesture that had lost all significance for me more than a year since my private meeting with John Bugas. In the same movement he transferred the keys to my possession. They were shiny steel and attached to a plastic tag bearing the Ford logo.

"Registration's in the glove compartment," he said. "We can transfer the plates after we get back."

"Back?"

"Well, let's take it for a spin. Make sure you like it. I'll drive the Merc back to Dearborn. We can't have our number-one Edsel salesman driving a two-year-old wreck all over town." He laughed his booming laugh. "Didn't that sound familiar? Seems to me I said something just like it at the end of our first conversation at the Glass House. Of course, it wasn't the Glass House then. Hard to look at the old barn now and picture it as empty girders. A lot's happened in three years. Incidentally, Hank's considering a name change. No more Ford Administration Center. He wants to call it Ford World Headquarters. We're planning plants in Germany and Japan, show 'em how to make cars instead of plastic hula girls."

"A lot's happened," I agreed.

I had to kick tires and things. The trunk was big enough for the spare and a small piano. There was an acre of engine—410 cubic inches, actually, with an air cleaner the size of a charcoal grill—under a hood that opened in reverse, tilting forward from the windshield with the hinges up front. It was a design feature predicated on the theory that a faulty latch could cause the slipstream to lift a conventionally mounted hood at high speed, obstructing the driver's vision and causing an accident. I had never heard of a thing like that happening, but mechanical duffer that I was I saw a hundred potential headaches for the garageman in the arrangement, most of the things that required regular maintenance being located near the front, where the clearance was zero. Every new model has its bugs.

The green-and-white interior smelled like chewing gum. The Teletouch transmission buttons mounted in the steering-wheel hub, which cleverly didn't rotate, took some getting used to—I kept reaching for a phantom shifting-cane—and the self-adjusting brakes seemed to have been adjusted with some other self in mind, snatching at the pavement before I was ready and catapulting both of us toward the dashboard at the first several red lights we came to, but the suspension was woven from clouds; I took deliberate aim at a pothole that had broken one of the Montclair's shock-absorbers back in February and we might have run over a rubber hose for all the effect it had on us in the front seat.

A row of chromed, pedal-shaped switches operated all four power windows from the driver's side. After a bit of comedy I got the sequence figured out and hummed down the glass beside me to let in fresh air and compromise that Spearmint odor. I missed the aroma of virgin leather and oiled wood that accompanied the new cars of my youth. I located the speedometer and gas gauge and the radio controls, which included push-buttons for calibrating my favorite stations and knobs for shunting the sound around the recessed speakers at each end of the dash and inside the rear window ledge. The pull-out light switch was on the left where it belonged, the stomp-button that operated the dimmer on the floor beside the brake. The windshield wipers worked, the washers squirted blue-green liquid at the glass without apparent prostate trouble, the cigar lighter popped out fifteen seconds after I punched it in and sizzled at the touch of a wettened finger. That had always been important to me, although I had never smoked. I could figure out the rest of the buttons and gauges later. Much later, as it turned out; the purpose of a tachometer still eludes me, yet I've never felt diminished by my ignorance.

The big V-8 was almost silent when the car was rolling, a tribute to both its exhaust system and the soundproof insulation inside the hood and firewall. When the car was stopped I could feel the vibration of its three-hundred forty-five horses through the steering wheel, like the deep somnolent rumbling of a lion at rest. I'd driven more powerful vehicles, but none so modest about it.

"Well, what's the verdict?" asked Zed after we'd been cruising for ten minutes. I hadn't been through some of those neighborhoods in years and hardly recognized them for the new construction. Here and there the tall peak of a 1920s clapboard or the complicated roofline of a turn-of-the-century Queen Anne poked above the ground-hugging tract miracles like a blue-veined nose at a sock hop.

"It rides nice and smooth."

I left it at that. There were times since the talk with Bugas when I could carry on a normal conversation with the man who hired me, but it required more concentration than I could manage when I was driving. Afterward I always felt even guiltier than I knew he was. It was one thing to be a party to an attempted murder, another to behave in the presence of that party as if nothing were wrong. Somehow the extra remove from the crime in question had cast me in deeper shadow.

"You should've ordered the convertible," he said. "If any day was made to ride around with the top down, this is it."

"Ragtops are for kids." In fact I'd been planning to ask for one almost until the time I placed the order. All my life, the open car had represented a world of hand-rolled cigars, easily rolled women, winters in Miami, and hundred-dollar tips. Tom Mix had driven a white Auburn with curved horns on the radiator and the top down to make room for his ten-gallon hat, Clark Gable and Carole Lombard had roared off to their honeymoon in a red Bentley convertible, and James Dean had hurtled a black Porsche bareheaded off a desert road into the Milky Way of immortality, two years dead now and still climbing. It was something that, offered the opportunity, you didn't even have to think about. But approaching my fifty-seventh birthday I was starting to have trouble keeping my head warm, even in summer. The choice was clear: Either drive everywhere with the top down and hat on, a visual oxymoron, or keep inventing answers for the same old question about leaving the roof up on a beautiful day. I put in for the hardtop; and sold yet another share in my own mortality.

I was afraid the silence was turning moody. "How are the figures?" I asked.

"A little slow, but I'm not worried about it. Some of the older dealers have been with us since the Tin Lizzie. The new paperwork was bound to bollix them up at first. Also it's this damn recession. Things will pick up by Christmas."

"The new Fairlane's doing well, I heard."

"Hank shouldn't have let McNamara beef it up. I told him it would draw attention from the new division. It's bad enough GM goosed up Pontiac, Olds, and Buick to meet us head on, but anyone could have foreseen that. More competition from the other side of our own building we didn't need. So what does McNamara do when I call him on it? Slap a two-hundred-dollar price hike across the board, starting with Edsel. You're driving a thirty-six-hundred-dollar automobile."

"Jesus."

"I think the son of a bitch is out to sink us, Connie. He told me himself we can't expect to outsell his Ford. *His* Ford! But we'll show him."

"Someone told me Drew Pearson's going to write up the Edsel in his column," I said hopefully.

"Write it down, you mean. He told Winchell we ought to call it the Ethel, on account of the grille looking like the, uh, female sexual organ."

He blushed, saying it; and for some reason I thought of Janet Sherman. Despite his size and bluff appearance there was an almost womanish reticence about Zed that made him seem out of place in the men's locker-room atmosphere of the Glass House. In fact the anatomical possibilities of the car's front-end design had already made the rounds of the Ford Engineering Department, and it had been suggested that if the phallic taillights of the 1957 Cadillac were to back into

an Edsel, the result in nine months would be the 1,400-pound
Crosley.

I'd thought of Janet Sherman when Zed brought up the
reference because an office complex, even one as hermeti-
cally sealed as Ford's, was a breeding ground for gossip, and
it had been known there for some time that the two were pursuing a relationship beyond the professional. When the story
reached me I had thought of warning her about him, but in
the end I'd decided it would be a violation of John Bugas's
confidence, which I saw in animated form as a tiny version
of its owner with the same disconcertingly mild and all-
seeing eyes. It was a good excuse for not approaching Janet.
I congratulated myself on it whenever I felt like being smug.
I had several more excuses just as good, going back to the
one I had used to run away from her and hide in my safe
empty bachelor's house.

I refrained from reminding Zed about my early reservations concerning the Edsel's grille. I had not, in truth, mentioned them in more than a year. It had begun to grow on me.
I only hoped the car's more obvious merits would capture
and hold the consumers' fickle affections long enough for it
to grow on them as well.

Something else had been absent for more than a year. As
suddenly as the scrawny spectre of J. W. Pierpont had appeared in my life, it had just as suddenly left. I had neither
seen nor heard from him since that night at the Bel-Air
Drive-In when I had sicced him on Carlo Ballista in full
view of God and Spencer Tracy. For months after that I had
expected him to pop up any time. I was certain he'd come
around after Anthony's obituary ran in all three Detroit papers—SYNDICATE KINGPIN DIES WITH HIS BOOTS
OFF, blared Hearst's *Times*, characteristically mixing its
gangster and cowboy metaphors while promoting the little
street-level hood far above his station—and wondered from
which corner he'd spring this time, giving me pause to contemplate the ingenuity of an aging private snooper in never
using the same approach twice. But Tony Balls's embalmed
remains had been taking up space in the family plot at Sacred Heart Cemetery for six months and my days remained

sans Pierpont. I had begun to ponder whether Bugas had outbid the UAW for his retainer, in spite of his insistence that I deal with the detective as I saw fit. In any case I'd never ask him about it. Quite apart from the fact that the old FBI bureau chief was not the kind of man who answered questions put to him by simpler cells in the corporate culture, the thought of raising the Devil by speaking his name kept me silent. I didn't care to tempt fate.

Zed looked at his big gold watch, bringing me up from the depths with the movement. "I guess we'd better get back. Hank is expecting us in his office at nine."

"Us?"

"It's fairly unprecedented. He doesn't call many informal meetings at the store. It probably has something to do with Jack Reith."

Jack Reith, head of the Mercury Division and the man who had come back from Europe with his head full of daring new designs that would eventually come together in the E-car—the father, if ever there was one, of the Edsel—had resigned from Ford at the end of August, the loser in a three-year struggle with president Robert McNamara, the mildest-looking of the pale tigers Henry II had brought in during the Harry Bennett years, all of whom struck without snarling. Reith's departure on the eve of his brainchild's birth seemed to have caused no ripples at all in the company lagoon, a circumstance that chilled me to my shoes. Where do the peasants stand when the gods begin to fall?

I wasn't thinking of Reith just then, though. He wasn't the reason for the meeting or I wouldn't have been invited. *I'd rather not know*, Bugas had said, a little over a year ago. *Not for another year, anyway. Until the Edsel's off the proving ground.* Why I had thought I would be spared the final act was one for Mr. Wizard.

I remember nothing of the drive home to pick up the Mercury. I only came out of my thoughts when I stopped in the driveway, leaving the room for Zed to wheel the other car around the Edsel, and went inside to get the keys and clean up. My neighbor next door, a retired bus driver with a hear-

ing aid, stopped raking leaves and cupped one hand around
his mouth.

"Hey, Meaner! Tell your car to cover up when it yawns.
It's spreading germs."

31

Not counting chance encounters at the elevators, I hadn't seen God—for there is no sense in not stating it plainly, he held us all in his great enveloping paw—since August 27, when I'd persuaded brothers Henry, Benson, and William Clay to lay aside their family and business differences long enough to pose atop the front seat of a Citation convertible one week before the car was unveiled in showrooms. There was even less of a family resemblance among the siblings than there had been between Henry and his grandfather, and the three came off looking like young executives employed by the same company in positions that seldom had anything to do with one another.

On Edsel Day, as part of the costliest christening since the Spanish Armada, one of the Indians in Israel Zed's PR tribe took advantage of friendly negotiations to establish Ford plants in Japan and launched five thousand bottle rockets of Tokyo manufacture into the Michigan sky, which upon explosion rained down parachutes supporting inflated rubber Edsels nearly as large as the original. The stunt carried a price tag of forty-five thousand dollars and marked the debut of the Japanese-made car.

In an unexpected departure from his imperial style, Henry met us at the door of his vast office, all whiskey fumes and aftershave and stultifying body heat, shook our hands in order of rank, and strode ahead of us to take charge of the bar, out from behind its demure panels for the occasion and stocked as well as any liquor store I had ever seen, which in Detroit was saying something. With three hours to go before noon, Zed accepted a double vodka and I took Scotch and soda as a prop. (Never plead problems of health to the man who holds your professional future in the file drawer of his desk.) Until Ford waved us toward the grouping of modern chrome-and-black-leather chairs that occupied the corner opposite the windows, I don't think either of us was aware of the presence of John Bugas, seated with his legs crossed and a glass in one hand containing a clear liquid that might have been pure grain alcohol or plain water. He wore unadorned gray flannel to his master's blue and his customary expression of quizzical good humor. I suppressed a faint shudder of fears confirmed and sat down.

"John." Zed took a seat. He seemed only mildly surprised to see him, an achievement. Bugas almost never took part in conferences, poking his bowsprit beak outside the circle of home, private office, and liquid luncheons only in times of crisis. It was generally assumed that whatever repercussions Reith's leaving might have had were settled.

Ford didn't sit but leaned a forearm against the back of the chair left vacant for him and sipped from his glass; bourbon, if my nose could still be trusted. His big face was flushed. The effect was that of a debauched minister supporting himself on the pulpit. "Mead tells me you rounded up Crosby and Sinatra for *The Edsel Show*," he told Zed. "Congratulations."

"Congratulate Connie. It was his idea." Zed seemed relieved. So it was to be a butt-patting session after all.

"We're pre-empting Ed Sullivan October thirteenth," I said, when the Chief looked at me. "Ed Krafve okayed the expenditure." Krafve headed the Edsel division and had assumed some of Reith's duties at Mercury.

"Ed's a good man. If the Edsel flies at all it will be his doing. And yours, of course," Ford added, taking us both in with a pontifical swing of his basketball-size head.

That *if* banged around the office for a long time, like a ricocheting bullet. Since I had joined the firm it had not been a word in the local lexicon. Zed noticed it too, flinching a little as if grazed. Ice cubes collided in his glass as he helped himself to a drink.

Ford was still talking. "Jack, what was that break-even figure for the first year?"

"Two hundred thousand units." Bugas was watching Zed.

"What about it, Izzy? Are we going to make it?"

"No doubt about it, Hank," Zed piped up. "Let me tell you what we've—"

"Please don't call me Hank. I've always hated it." Ford spoke gently.

"Oh—sure." Confusion. "Connie and I are negotiating with NBC to buy a cowboy show, lock, stock, and gunbarrel, an old-fashioned sponsorship like on radio, every ad a spot for the Edsel. Chevrolet wants it too, but I've got an inside track with the producer. It's a *color* western, imagine that, about this rancher and his three grown sons, good family stuff, only with plenty of shoot-ups for the action fan. It will be the best example of product identification since *Lux Radio Theater*."

I worked on keeping my jaw from dropping during this spurt. He was starting to sound like a huckster. It was Ford who brought it out, Ford and his habit of leaving silences into which people around him felt compelled to pour words. The quiet years in Henry I's shadow had been excellent training ground. Zed, whose education during the same period had been filled with campaign rhetoric and the language of diplomacy, words embroidered around meanings, was completely unprepared for so passive an assault. He was literally burying himself with his mouth.

Ford drank but didn't speak until his cubes stopped clanking. "Well, you can leave all that with Connie. I'm sure he knows what to do."

"I—" Belatedly, Zed seemed to have recognized the peril in talking without thinking. He shut his mouth, leaned down to set his glass on the carpet, and straightened, resting his palms on his knees. "I don't think I understand your meaning, Hank. Chief."

"I think you do. You're not dense. If I thought you were I wouldn't have hired you out from under the Dewey campaign in the first place. I have an aversion to deadwood, as Jack here can tell you. By the time that program airs, with or without Ford sponsorship, you won't be here to see it. You'll be home watching it in your living room. You're out, Izzie."

"Fired?" The political arena had trained him well. You

had to have been watching him closely to spot the greenish cast behind his face, which remained immobile.

"No one fires anyone these days, you know that. They accept their resignations with regret. I've saved you the trouble of typing one up. It's there on the desk. All you have to do is sign it."

Zed went fishing. "If this is about the push-button transmission on the fifty-seven Dodge, that leak wasn't in my department. You should be asking the boys in Design."

"Jack?"

Bugas smiled shyly at the man opposite him. "How long did you think you could get away with it? Were you in politics so long you thought this institution would harbor a corrupt simply because he was good at his job?"

"What did you call me?"

"Shit." Ford drained his glass, pushed off from the back of the chair, and trampled back to the bar for a refill. "I didn't bounce that felon Bennett to put another one in his place. I've got better reasons than you or anyone else to hate Walter Reuther's guts. That doesn't mean I want to see them splattered all over the floor of the kitchen in his own house. His own house!" He bellowed the last three words. Bottles rang.

The lull that followed was a vacuum. After two beats, certainly not as many as three, Zed turned his face on me. I knew at that moment that those same spies who had told him I had been to see Reuther had been keeping tabs on me ever since. He knew what I knew at the time I knew it. I wondered then, and I wonder now, why it should have come as so much of a surprise to have it flung in his face there on Olympus. Maybe Bugas was right; maybe the year's delay between the time I had dumped all I had learned at Bugas' feet and the time Ford kicked it back at Zed had confirmed his belief that the company would swallow any pill, no matter how large or bitter, rather than acknowledge the corruption in its bowels.

I, in my turn, looked at John Bugas. Obviously he had told his friend and superior a highly simplified version of the story, editing out Frankie Orr in favor of Walter Reuther's original suspicion, that someone high up in the Ford organization had authorized the attempts on his life and his brother's in order to promote a union official whose interests coincided with Ford's. And in that moment my general disapproval of J. Edgar Hoover lightened a shade. Small wonder that organized crime should have uncoiled its tentacles into every corner of American life, with the attention of the nation's top cop distracted by reports filed by subordinates who chose not to take up the director's time with details.

In answer to my look, Bugas went on smiling his shy smile and looking harmless. It wasn't a pose; or if it was, he had held it so long he was no longer aware of doing so.

"This is absurd," Zed broke in. "Who told you this? Minor? He's been after my job from the beginning. This ridiculous story only proves the lengths he'll go to in order to get it."

Ford, at the bar, raised his eyes in my direction from the stick he was swizzling. "What about it, Connie? Do you want Izzie's job? It pays sixty thousand."

I hated him then almost as much as Zed. I had never at any time considered that the position would be offered me, so I had no answer ready. Ford, obviously thinking otherwise, had tossed it at me at that moment, confident I'd turn it down in the face of Zed's accusation. And I knew then that attempted murder meant nothing twelve floors above Dearborn, beyond a bargaining chip. In a malicious flash I thought of accepting, just to see his expression change. But it was too late to start playing his game by his rules, and besides, I didn't want the job. I wouldn't have lasted a week in that tank of piranhas.

"No, thanks," I said. "I'll stick with the ulcers I have."

Ford smiled at Zed, who stood.

"I have a contract, *Hank*; and by God I'll make you stick to it if it means five years in court."

"I don't think so. I'd just have to state my reasons."

"A charge like that requires evidence."

"Well, if you force me to defend myself in court I'll just have to come up with some. Meanwhile you'll be branded a murderer in every paper and broadcast in town, and probably the country. Of course, you might have enough socked away not to have to worry about working ever again. That will leave you plenty of time to worry about the union hotheads who might not be as civilized as us when it comes to dealing with past mistakes. A lot of them are pretty Old Testament."

Without moving, Zed smoothed himself. Big and broad-shouldered in his tan double-breasted, he had looked for a moment as if he might take a swing at his tormentor. Now he seemed almost amused. "These aren't the thirties, and you aren't the man who built a company on a piece of machinery he put together in his backyard. Who are you to show me the door?"

Ford drank, savoring the taste of the bourbon. He was one alcoholic who truly seemed to enjoy his vice. "When you're outside the building, which you will be in five minutes under someone else's power if not yours, you might take a look at the sign out front. That's my name. Those four letters say I can do anything I want."

"It's because I'm Jewish, isn't it? You're just as anti-Semitic as your grandfather."

"That's where you're wrong. I'm the opposite of my grandfather in everything that counts. I fought a war to end that shit you're talking about. A lot of the guys I fought it with were Jews. Some of them weren't very good Jews, as a rabbi might see it; they sneaked a ham sandwich now and then, and I doubt many of them had spent more than ten minutes with the Talmud since their bar mitzvahs. But they were better Jews than you, for all your *tchotchkes* and that black beanie. I know damn well they were better men. Don't forget to sign that letter on your way out."

"What if I refuse?"

"Then you won't have to sue me to start the ball rolling."

Zed wrestled with it. Then he went over to the desk, read the letter of resignation, and snatched a silver-barreled pen from the set. "This is under duress." He signed his name.

"It always is, Izzie."

So far as I know, those were the last words that passed between them. Israel Zed left without another word. Three or four years later I heard he took a post as currency advisor to the military junta that deposed Juan Perón in Argentina, and died in a hotel fire in Buenos Aires. The North American obituaries were respectful.

After the door closed, Ford winked at Bugas, who nodded

back. "How are things in promotion, Connie?" the Chief asked then. "Need anything?"

I hesitated. "No, sir."

"Good. Keep us posted on this horse opera thing, will you? I'm nuts about westerns since I was a kid."

It was a dismissal, and I took it out. From then until the day I left his employ he never referred to Zed or that meeting in my presence, and he was always politely interested in how I was getting on. Now as then my thoughts on Hank the Deuce are all mixed up with varying parts apprehension and admiration. I guess I'm not alone.

32

On December 27, 1957, acting on a discovery by a shaken ice fisherman named Dierdorf from Highland Park, police in St. Clair Shores dragged a body out from under four inches of lake ice at the foot of Liberty Street. The corpse was so badly decomposed that no immediate identification could be made, even from fingerprints, after which the laborious process began of checking the teeth against the dental records of persons reported missing within the last six months. At the end of three weeks, the remains were identified positively as those of Jerome Winstead Pierpont, a licensed private investigator with an office in Detroit and an Inkster resident whose landlady had reported his disappearance in June. Despite a flurry of press speculation when it was revealed that at the time of his demise he had been investigating the 1948 shotgun assault on Walter Reuther, nothing on the body indicated foul play, and for lack of evidence to the contrary the cause of death was listed as accidental. Pierpont was known as a man of nebulous habits who kept no notes and took off on mysterious leads without telling anyone where he was going or why. Neither his files nor his safe deposit box in the downtown office of the National Bank of Detroit contained anything vaguely sensational.

It could have been an accident. He was an old man by just about anyone's standard—the newspapers couldn't agree whether he was born in 1894 or 1895—and he might have had a stroke or a heart attack while walking along one of the canals and fallen in, snagging in the weeds or under a dock until the currents tore him free. His wallet was never found, so it might have been a simple mugging. But for a long time I wondered what became of the photos and documents pertaining to the Edsel that he had dangled under my nose like a piece of meat on a stick. And that opened a string of possibilities from Reuther to Carlo Ballista to John Bugas that I didn't care to contemplate.

I couldn't think of a good thing to say about the man, except perhaps that once he was paid to do something he never let go until either it was finished or he was. You know?

On April Fool's Day 1958 I was jamming the last of a dozen cartons into the Citation's capacious trunk when a car pulled into the curb behind me. It was a loading zone belonging to the furniture store down the block from the house I had been renting for two years, so I assumed the driver was a customer and didn't bother to look.

"Taking it on the lam, eh, Minor?"

The female voice was familiar. I turned. Janet Sherman was sitting behind the wheel of a five-year-old Nash sedan, the turtleback Ambassador, built like a tank with a chromed front like the baleen of a killer whale. There were piles of rusty snow on the sidewalk, but she had the window down on the driver's side and her short arm resting on the ledge. Wearing a red cloth coat with black tabs on the lapels and with her black hair tied back, she made me think of a figure in a hunting print.

"How do you like it?" She inclined her head toward the long hood. "It's the first car I've actually owned. Paid cash for it."

"It needs its own area code. The least Ford could have done when they laid you off was let you use the company car for a while."

"I didn't ask. Anyway, I wasn't laid off. I quit. You can't keep 'em down in the secretarial pool after they've seen the twelfth floor. I'm on my way back to Toledo. I've got an interview for a job next week. The pay's no good, but it includes classes in engineering."

"Congratulations." I meant it. Awkwardly: "I'm sorry about Zed."

She closed her eyes wistfully. Her cheeks reddened a little, but there was a stiff breeze. "He should've known better than to get so close to Jack Reith. You can't make friends at that level." That was the company line. She seemed to have decided to accept it. "What about you?"

"I put away enough to keep me for a couple of years, provided I move out of this place and into an apartment. After that, I don't know. An old friend of mine owns a gardening supply store in Troy. Maybe he can use a first-class salesman."

"I'm sorry, Connie."

I moved a shoulder. "The severance pay was good. The hard part will be living down the fact that I had the Edsel account. I don't think it will go on my résumé."

"I'm sorry about that, too, but I meant Agnes. I heard she left."

I wondered from whom. It was a small town for its size. "She wanted someone who could give her signposts along the way. I can't blame her for that."

While we were talking, a red Corsair driven by a man my age in a corduroy coat and a season-rushing cocoa straw hat with a yellow band boated around the corner and blasted its horns at sight of the Citation. He waved derisively. Someone had jammed a white plastic toilet seat onto the red car's horse-collar grille.

There wasn't much more to say. Janet and I wished each other good luck, promised to write while the post office was still forwarding our mail, and she put the big car in gear and swung into the street and away on a cushion of bubbling exhaust. Of course I never heard from her again.

There isn't much more to say here, either, except it was a tragedy what happened to the Edsel. Sales picked up briskly in October 1957, then began to lose steam just when everyone thought the car was in the clear. In December Henry Ford II came on closed-circuit television to pep-talk wavering dealers. Shortly thereafter, Ford began jettisoning personnel to lighten the burden, changed advertising agencies, and replaced the entire division promotional staff. My successor was a business-school graduate exactly half my age who had worked on the "Be Happy, Go Lucky" cigarette campaign. Ford shook my hand warmly and told me to go on driving the Citation until I found a replacement. "We can use the advertising."

The top-of-the-line Citation and the second-from-the-bottom Pacer disappeared with the 1959 model year. The grille was made less noticeable and a number of mechanical improvements were engineered to satisfy *Consumer Reports*, who sniffed at all the gadgetry and complained about the steering and suspension. But by July 1, 1959, only 84,000 units had been sold, a significant number of which were raffled off at church bazaars and school carnivals, causing people to ask of new Edsel owners: "Where did you win yours?" The joke went into the bin with all the rest, including variations on the comment that the car looked like an Oldsmobile sucking on a lemon.

But it might have survived the jokes; and in fact the 1960 Edsel Ranger, minus the hilarious grille and unpopular push-button gearshift and with a more manageable wheelbase, won the admiration of most critics, for both its performance and its realistic price. But by then Ford was just selling out its inventory. The Edsel died, aged twenty-six months.

The fifties died about the same time. Dwight D. Eisenhower was on his way out, having lost his characteristic mongoloid grin and most of his sense of humor in a blow-up with Nikita Khrushchev that promised to prolong the Cold War another generation at least. The Democratic Party, dormant for eight years, was talking of running the bootlegger Joe Kennedy's son for President, the United Nations was pressing Washington for a show of solidarity in Indochina, preferably with men and material, and Vice-President Nixon was preening himself for a run at the Oval Office. Batista was out in Cuba, Fidel Castro was in. On a more local level, the Senate Select Committee on Improper Activities in the Labor or Management Field, chaired by Senator John McClellan of Arkansas, had turned up sufficient heat under the American Steelhaulers Union to bring national president Albert Brock to the serious attention of the Justice Department. Chief counsel to the committee was a young Washington attorney named Robert Kennedy, another son of the bootlegger. Assisting him in Detroit was Stuart Leadbeater, in private practice after having resigned from the city attorney's office to run unsuccessfully for county prosecutor, and reborn as a Democrat. Both men would continue to be festering thorns in Brock's side throughout the rest of his tenure. It seemed I could bring that man nothing but grief, even when I wasn't trying to help him.

The new era was already assuming a shape completely foreign to the ten years that preceded it. What the next generation would think about those years would be based entirely upon the evidence of warped gray Kinescopes, overripe theatrical epics, a stack of 45-rpm records, and a handful of books. But the whole added up to so much more than just the sum of its parts. It was braggadocio and hope, fear and comfort, bad taste and good intentions, innocence and cynicism—Little Richard and Eleanor Roosevelt, tucked as securely as a lace valentine between the glossy four-color pages of a magazine. It was the most improtant time of our century.

On Labor Day 1959 I was standing in a crowd gathered in Grand Circus Park when Walter Reuther swept through behind a flying wedge of bodyguards on his way to the podium. He had on a light topcoat against the gray mist and a black felt hat with the brim pulled low on his forehead. Our eyes met when he came past, but only for an instant, and there was no recognition on his side. As I'd predicted he had continued to put on weight, and there was more of the bulldog in his heavy-jowled face than the terrier who had nipped at the heels of Big Auto until it was forced to acknowledge him, first with fists, then with contracts. I have no memory of what he talked about that day. I was distracted by the realization that there are men who can in a moment subvert your life to their own agenda, and in the next forget you ever existed. To this day, whenever I hear a news report of a hit and run, I picture Walter Reuther at the wheel.

The Ford Motor Company lost three hundred fifty million dollars on the Edsel. Its stock fell twenty dollars per share from an all-time high recorded during the first years of Henry II's leadership. Why the venture toppled depended on where you were standing when it began to teeter. Some said it was a bad car, but they were only repeating the opinions of others who never drove one or even sat in one. The recession, our first since the uncertain days immediately following the end of the Second World War, is an easy target; or if your preference runs to the obvious you can blame the strange grille. Most likely it was the human factor that brought it down, the petulant backbiting at the senior executive level that inspired company president Robert McNamara, six days before the Edsel was unveiled, to confide to a companion: "I've got plans for phasing it out."

What difference does it make why? It was a good car, and they killed it. They being us. But like the Oscar Wilde hero, when we plunged the dagger through the physical embodiment of our collective soul, we pierced our own collective heart as well. The first failure is always entertaining. After that they become commonplace, even expected. Success becomes the diversion.

And so the whole damn dizzy decade was an Edsel.

of it. Turning and leaving the meeting room immediately following
the end of the Second World War. It appears... began with
our increases. Turn to the directors you can of the the
future guide. Most likely it would be human factor that
brought it about... the Behind backfiring, if the scientists were
involved that required congress president Robert M. La...
men... exodus before the ideas was anxious... to combine to a
companion. "I've got them for missing it out."

When Dr. Lawrence poss... knew what it was a good idea, and
other takeoffs. They being us for the the boom will... been
when we shipped the danger through the physical section
men of our collective soul, the just for and each sufficient
but it is well. The this future is always one of many. After
that there become comprehensive, overseparated. Success becomes the directive.

And so the whole damn dizzy dance was at an End...